# WIDE COURSES

## JAMES BRENDAN CONNOLLY

# Wide Courses

## James Brendan Connolly

© 1st World Library, 2008
PO Box 2211
Fairfield, IA 52556
www.1stworldlibrary.com
First Edition

LCCN: 2007935395

Softcover ISBN: 978-1-4218-9348-8
Hardcover ISBN: 978-1-4218-9448-5
eBook ISBN: 978-1-4218-9248-1

Purchase *"Wide Courses"*
as a traditional bound book at:
www.1stWorldLibrary.com/purchase.asp?ISBN=978-1-4218-9348-8

1st World Library is a literary, educational organization
dedicated to:

- Creating a free internet library of downloadable ebooks

- Hosting writing competitions and offering book publishing
scholarships.

Interested in more 1st World Library books? contact:
literacy@1stworldlibrary.com
Check us out at: www.1stworldlibrary.com

# 1$^{st}$ World Library Literary Society

## Giving Back to the World

"If you want to work on the core problem, it's early school literacy."

**- James Barksdale, former CEO of Netscape**

"No skill is more crucial to the future of a child, or to a democratic and prosperous society, than literacy."

**- Los Angeles Times**

"Literacy... means far more than learning how to read and write... The aim is to transmit... knowledge and promote social participation."

**- UNESCO**

"Literacy is not a luxury, it is a right and a responsibility. If our world is to meet the challenges of the twenty-first century we must harness the energy and creativity of all our citizens."

**- President Bill Clinton**

"Parents should be encouraged to read to their children, and teachers should be equipped with all available techniques for teaching literacy, so the varying needs and capacities of individual kids can be taken into account."

**- Hugh Mackay**

# CONTENTS

# THE WRECKER

Sometimes the notion comes to me while I'm talkin' to people that maybe I don't make myself clear, and it's been so for some time now—the things I see in my mind fadin' away from me at times, like ships in a fog. And that's strange enough, too, if what people tell me so often is true—that it used to be so one time that the office clerks would correct their account-books by what I told 'em out of my head. But sometimes—not often—things come back to me, like to-day—maybe because 'tis a winter day and a gale o' wind drivin' the sea afore it in the bay below there. Things come to me then—like pictures—wind and sea and fog and the wrecks on a lee shore.

In my business—but of course you know—runnin' after wrecks, from Newfoundland to Cuba, I had to be days and maybe weeks away from home—which was no harm when I had no more home than a room in a sailor's boardin'-house, and no harm later with Sarah. Even if anything happened to me, I used to feel that Sarah—that's my first wife—Sarah'd still have the two lads to hearten her and keep her busy; but 'twas different with—but there, my mind's off again....

Maybe some things—comforts, refinements—I might 'a' practised myself in, got used to 'em like, but could I see in those early days that I'd ever have a grand home—me who'd been cast away at fourteen—even if I'd had time? It was to be able to do without comforts—to make a pleasure out o' hardship—that meant success almost as much as knowin' the business. And I did know my business in those days—or people lied a lot. And it always meant more to me—the name of bein' the great wrecker—than all the money I made, and in those last few years I made plenty of it—I did that. Me who once slaved for six dollars a month as boy in a Bangor coaster. And I mind how I used to look back and say—or was it somebody tellin' me?—that 'twas a great day for me and mine when the old lumber schooner wrecked herself on Peaked Hill Bar—because when she was hove down I was hove into a bigger world. Once in my pride I used to cherish praise like that—but sometimes now I'm not so sure.

And this man, an upstandin' handsome man—no one that knew him but spoke well of him, to me anyway, for I would not allow aught else after I come to know him. Since that last wreck it seems to me I've listened to other talk of him, but that's not so clear to me ... my brain, as I say, clouds up like on things that happened since.

No one ever met Her—my second wife, that is—but said she was beautiful and good—said so to me, anyway. It is true— but that came afterward, like the other talk, and it's not too clear in my mind what they did say. But he came to me and I liked him. And he liked me, too ... I think he did. He'd heard of me, he said, and would I examine his yacht—the *Rameses* that was—to see if any damage had been done—she'd grounded comin' in by Romer Shoal the day before. There'd be too much delay to put her in dry dock, and he wanted to sail soon's could be—if she was sound—on her regular winter West India cruise. 'Twas in January, a fine clear day, and I said, all right, I'd send my oldest boy down and look at her. My oldest boy—but you know him? Aye, a grand lad.

Both grand lads. Modelled off their mother, the pair of them. If I'd only a daughter like her ... the woman she was! A wife for a seafarin' man. "Watch and watch I've stood wi' ye," she said, goin'—"watch and watch, but I'm no good to see the lights nor to grip the wheel longer. The sight's gone and the strength, Matt. Watchmate, bunkmate, and shipmate I've been to ye, but ye're in smooth water now ... and no longer ye'll need me." A daughter to stand by you she'd be. All my money I'd give for one such.

And while he was in the office She came in. "Ah-h!" he said—and then, "Your daughter, captain?" I said, "No—my wife," maybe o'er-proudly. I was not ashamed of my years, for it's not years but age—leastwise so I'd always held—that sets a man back. Those lads of twenty-five or thirty, I could wear them down like chalk whetstones. Maybe she heard—I don't know; but she didn't let on she did. My proud days those were—my office in the big building by the Battery. You remember? Aye, a grand place—the name in fine letters on the door, and on the window the picture of my big wreckin'-tug, the best-geared afloat and cost the most—a sailor's fortune just in her—yes—and I'd named it for Her. And 'twas to that same office I used often to come straight from my rough seawork. She used to come there to take me to drive. Me, who'd been a castaway sailor-boy—but I could afford all these things then. I could afford anything She wanted. And She wanted the fine office, and so it was fitted up with fine desks and clerks, though it wasn't what the clerks put in their account-books that kept my business goin'. There were those who said that I'd pay the price some day for tryin' to carry so many things in my head, but small heed I paid to them—and 'twasn't in those days my memory dimmed.

There was but little damage to the yacht's bottom—a small matter to find that out—though the skipper he carried was no master of craft. So many of them like that, too. To face the sea like men is not what they're after, not to take winter or summer as it comes, rough or smooth—no—but always the smooth water and soft winds. But he did not sail for the West Indies that day, nor that week, nor winter—something'd gone wrong with the machinery. No concern of mine that. There were those who said later—but that was when my head begun to trouble me—as it does now sometimes, as I said. There was a time, when Sarah was alive, before we had even the old ship's cabin on the end of the old dock by way of an office, when I carried my business in a wallet in my breast pocket—that is, what we didn't carry in our heads—but the mother of those two lads, she was with me then. That's long ago.

A most interestin' man he was. As I say, he made no West India cruise that winter—the machinery kept gettin' out of order—but he made a few trips with me—wreckin' trips—for I still looked after the big jobs myself. There were those who used to say that if I'd only learned to stand by and look on long enough to train a good man to take my place in the deep divin', that I'd be goin' yet. Maybe so, but maybe, too, they didn't know it all. I'd yet to meet a man who would do my work half as well as I could myself—never but one, and she was a woman and could do her part better—Sarah, my first wife, and her kind aren't livin' now.

He was not so soft, this yacht man, as I used to think. He stood the rough winter trips with me well. I learned to like him—rarely. I could talk to him about the work, and he'd try to understand—as so few of his kind would. He understood better after he'd been some trips with me, and I came to love him—almost. When I was away on those trips, my wife would be at home—until the time her aunt took sick. I recollect her speakin' of her aunt—or did I? No matter. She lived out West somewhere, and didn't want her to marry

James Brendan Connolly

me—or so I made out. I didn't go too deep into it. When she hinted that she hadn't told me of her aunt before for fear of hurtin' my feelin's, it was enough. Women feel things more than men, and no use to rake 'em over. I knew I was a rough man, not the kind many women folks might take to—I never quite got over Her likin' me—nor did a whole lot of people—and 'twas natural a woman of the kind her aunt must be, didn't like her marryin' a man like me. But no matter; her aunt was bein' reconciled, she used to write me, and when your wife is makin' up to her only livin' relative, and she dyin', it's no time to be exactin'. So she stayed on in the West. I've forgotten where—Chicago maybe?—too far, anyway, for me to go to her, because I had to stand ready in my business to leave at a minute's notice. A gale c'd rise in an hour, the coast be cluttered with wrecks in one day. And there were so many big people, steamboat people and big shippin' firms, who counted on me, would 'a' been disappointed, you see, if I wasn't on deck when needed. It's something, after all, to be honest in your work all your life, not leave it to careless helpers.

He lost his interest in the wreckin' after a while, and natural, too. He hadn't to build up his family's name or provide a livin' for anybody by it. And her aunt still lingered, she wrote. And then I wrote that I would give up the business if she said so, and go out there. I could begin again—there was great shippin' on the lakes—better sell out a hundred wreckin' plants than be so much apart, for it's terrible to be comin' from the sea and never find the woman afore ye. But she telegraphed to wait, she would be home soon, and she wanted to see me, too, about something partic'lar. That was the night before the Portland breeze—in the year o' the war with Spain—yes, '98 that would be, the year the *Portland* went down on Middle Bank with all on board. A foolish loss that, and nobody ever went to jail for it; but it's mostly that way, nobody sufferin' for it—but the families o' the lost ones—when passenger ships go down at sea.

There was half a dozen steamboat firms telegraphin' and telephonin' the morning after that storm, and I had to leave without waitin' till she got home. There was a wreck off Cape Cod, and that kept me away a week, and I was hurryin' back by way of Boston. And I saw him—me hurryin' up Atlantic Avenue to take the train and him headed for the docks. I hailed him. There was a rumor—'twas in the papers—that I'd gone down with the wreck I'd been workin' on off Cape Cod—Chatham way—but of course no one who knew me well believed it. But he must've believed it, for—"What, you!" he says—not even puttin' in the "Captain" that he never before forgot. I missed that little word from him—and he didn't look at me the same—him that had always such a friendly way with me. He seemed to be in a great hurry, and so I left him without more talk. He did not even tell me that the *Rameses* was in the harbor and he leavin' on her, but the thought of that came later.

I had to stop off at Newport, to get things started for another wreck there, and that took me the rest of that day and the next, and then I was all ready to take the night boat for New York, but my oldest boy came hurryin' down the dock to me, and an old lady—no—not so old, but lookin' old—with him. And they told me how the *Rameses*, that had left Boston the morning before, 'd been wrecked off Gay Head durin' the night and sunk; and this was his mother, and she wanted me to go to the wreck right away and see if I could find and bring up his body.

I wanted to go home—a week of days and nights—and I was tired, too, and not easy to tire me in those days, but I thought of him and the trust he had in the skipper that didn't know his business, and I looks at my boy and at his mother, and Sarah's face came to me; and who's to gainsay a woman whose son lies drowned? So my boy and me we put out that night and was there next morning in our big wreckin'-tug.

'Twas a cold day, but clear, only there was a big sea runnin', makin' it dangerous, everybody said, to be lyin' alongside her. And, I suppose because o' that, my boy wanted to do the divin', but 'twas me that went down and fastened the chains so she wouldn't slip off into the deep water; and then I came up to rest, and it was while I was up restin' that the chains slipped and she slid off and on to a ledge twenty fathoms down. Twenty fathoms is deep water for divin'—but one or two 'd been that deep before, and what one man has done another can do—and I'd promised the mother to bring her son home to her.

I went down and made fast the chains again, and then I went inside her to make one job of it, though I'd told the lad I'd come up after I'd made fast the chains. I needed no pilot—I'd been on her often enough—though I did find use for the patent electric hand-light I'd carried. Down the big staircase I went, through the big saloon, and toward his quarters I felt my way—through the fine cabin and the marble bath-room and his own room—all as rich and comfortable as in his own home ashore.

It was deep down, as I said—maybe too deep to be stayin' so long—but I'd never known what it was to give up on a job, and I kept on.

I found him ... and he wasn't alone.

And hard enough it was on me, for never a hint had I of it. 'Twas my boy hauled me up that day. No signal o' mine, but I was gone so long he feared I'd come to harm below.

When I found myself better I made ready to go down again,

for once you've promised to do a thing there's nothin' but to do it. But just as they were about to slip my helmet on, me with my foot on the ladder, the chain that was holding her slipped again, and into two hundred fathoms she went—too deep for any diver in this world ever to raise her.

I thought of his mother and I grieved for her, and it was the first job, too, that ever I'd messed.

"Never mind," says my son. "Twas me, not you. Nobody that knows you, father, will blame you." A great lad that, and his brother, too—off their mother's model—both of 'em. Sarah said I'd never have to worry about them, and I haven't, but I wish she'd lived to have the joy of them.

I don't remember much more of that, but when I got back to the office there was a letter from her. But I never read it. Nothing it could tell me then that I hadn't already guessed.

'Isn't often now it comes so to me, things being' generally dim in my mind, as I say, slipping away and drawing nigh, like ships in a lifting fog-but to-day—like that day—a winter's day and sunny and cold—with the seas running like white-maned ponies before the gale in the bay below there—as it is now—always on a day like this it comes clearer to me.

James Brendan Connolly

# LAYING THE HOSE-PIPE GHOST

Sometimes, for one reason or another, or perhaps without reason at all, it just happens. So, say a handful of gossiping yeomen find themselves together, and when that comes about, from some member (if the session stretches to any length at all) is sure to come a story of particular interest to the guild; and perhaps it ought to be explained that a yeoman's story is never mistaken in the Navy for a stoker's, a gunner's, a quartermaster's; never for anybody's but a yeoman's.

One night, a pleasant-enough night topside, but an even pleasanter night below, at least in our part of the ship below. A few of us were gathered in the flag office, where Dalton, the flag yeoman, sometimes allowed us to call when his admiral was ashore. Getting on toward middle-age was Dalton, with a head of gray-flecked hair and an old-time school-master's face. A great fellow for books.

In the flag office store-room, which to get into he had only to lift a hatch in the deck under his revolving chair and let himself drop, he had a young library, which after-hours he, used to delve into for anybody's or everybody's benefit. He was particularly strong on folk-lore, and could dig up a few fat volumes any time on the folk-lore of any nation we had ever heard of. He liked to lie flat on the coffer-dam to read, with a row of tin letter-files under his head for a rest, the electric bulb and its shade so adjusted as to throw all the light on the page of his book. He had done a lot of reading and writing in his time, and his eyes were getting a little watery. If he had had his way he would have been an author. In the hours of many a night-watch he had tried his hand at little sketches; but somehow or other he could not catch on, he said. Perhaps if he had tried to write as he talked, tell the things just as they popped into his mind, he would have been luckier; but that wasn't literature, he said, and so most of his written things read like one of Daniel Webster's speeches. We could listen to him talking all night long; but when he brought out one of his manuscripts, it was good-night and hammocks for all hands.

Taps had gone this night, and so it should have been lights out and everybody below turned in; but this, as I said, was the admiral's office, and only separated from the admiral's cabin by a bulkhead; and even the busiest of Jimmy-Legs don't come prowling into the cabin country of a flagship after taps. And the flag lieutenant and the flag secretary were pretty savvy officers who never by any accident came bumping in on Dalton's parties at the wrong time.

There came a knock at the door, and following the knock came the captain's yeoman. Nothing wrong with the captain's yeoman, except that his bow name was Reginald and he was rather fat for a sailor. Also he had ambitions, which was all right too, only we knew that privately he looked on the rest of us as a lot of loafers who would never rise to our opportunities. He'd been wearing his first-class rating badge a month now, and before his enlistment was out he intended to be a chief petty officer; which was why he was working after-hours. But the captain's yeoman, this particular captain's yeoman, has nothing to do with the story, except that his errand set Dalton off on a new tack.

The captain's yeoman had come for a little advice. He always was after advice—or information. A department document had come into the office that day with seventeen endorsements on it, and it had him bluffed. We all laughed at the face he drew. "But," said Dalton, turning on us, "so would most of you be bluffed if one of those winged-out documents came at you for the first time. But you're foolish, son Reginald, to be worrying over any little thing like that. Seventeen endorsements! What's seventeen endorsements? I wonder what you'd think if you'd—Sit down there and listen to me, and perhaps it'll be time well spent. If you don't learn enough from it to get that C.P.O. you're after, then—Well, I won't call you any names here now. Listen."

Now this story of Dalton's is a classic among yeoman, and only a yeoman should tell it; but not even a yeoman, no matter how gifted he may be with letter file or typewriter, has a rating to tell a story—no, no more than anybody else aboard ship. Some of us had heard the story before, and it had always been mangled in the telling, through the teller not knowing all the facts, or having perhaps never met any of the principal characters in it. But Dalton not only knew the tale from beginning to end; he was, though he would never admit it in a crowd, himself concerned in it. And now when he began to relate the history of the famous length of hose-pipe, we knew that he would have it right.

"I was in—well, call her the cruiser *Savannah*—this time—"

"Were you a yeoman, Dallie?"

"Yes, a yeoman, bright Reggie boy; what else d' y' think I'd be—a signal-girl? A good old ship, the *Savannah*, and were tied up to the dock at the Navy Yard."

"Boston yard, was it, Dallie?"

"Never mind what yard it was, son. And I'll name no names, either, and then by no accident will there be a general court-martial coming to me some day. There were three of four other ships fitting out at the same time, and after a while these other three ships got their stores aboard and proceeded to sea, leaving a lot of old gear behind them on the dock.

"We were making ready to pipe water into our ship, when Mr. Kiley, our boson, always a forehanded chap, thought it all a pity to have to use our bran-new hose for that kind of work. You all know how hose gets lying chafing around with people stepping on it, carts and wagons running over it, coal-dust grinding into it, and so on. A pity, our boson thought, to subject our nice new hose to that kind of abuse, when in the condemned heap on the dock there was a length of hose that would do the work, and he put it up to Mr. Renner, the officer of the deck at the time.

"Now Mr. Renner was a new-made ensign, and we all of us here been long enough in the service to know how it is about a middy that's just got his commission. We all know how it is with ourselves when we first get our C.P.O.—except you, Reggie, and you'll get yours some day. Am I right? Sure I am. If there's one thing on earth we're going to do then, it's to live up to regulations.

"No, we'll never again remember so much about rules and regulations as we do then. No catching us in anything irregular; no sir. And so with Mr. Renner, the new-made ensign. He brings out the blue-book and shows the boson. 'Look,' he says. 'Paragraph fourteen thousand four hundred and forty-two,' or whatever it was. 'Hose,' he goes on to read, 'is expendible property, to be surveyed and wiped off the property-books by condemning to the scrap-heap and sold in the open market to the highest bidder. There,' says our new-made ensign to our boson, 'what it says. And according to

James Brendan Connolly

that, the admiral himself couldn't take that hose from that scrap-heap without authority. No, not if it was no more than an old shoe-lace, he couldn't.'"

"'But that won't fill our water-tanks, and I'd like to use that hose, sir,' says the boson."

"'M-m!' says Mr. Renner. 'M-m! now if Mr. Shinn was aboard—' Mr. Shinn was our executive. 'But Mr. Shinn is ashore. However, I'll tell you what; I will speak to the captain about it,' and he steps inside the bulkhead and writes a message to the skipper."

"Now our skipper was a good old soul, and thought a lot of his boson, and wanted to do everything he could to help him out, but also, like a good many other good old captains in the service, he'd forgotten a lot of this stuff about regulations. Ordinarily—say, if 'twas anything to be done out to sea—he'd have said, 'Why, of course, Kiley; go ahead and do it,' But this was in a navy yard, ashore, and when he gets a note with something about regulations in it, he begins to haul to.

"And many a good sea-going old skipper is bluffed the same way about anything that spells regulations, you betcher. So now our good old skipper begins to tumble his hair and pull his moustache and look again at Mr. Renner's note. At last he tells the messenger to say to Mr. Renner that he will look into it and let him know.

"Another hour of studying, and the captain calls in his new yeoman that—"

"Was that you, Dallie?"

"Never mind—and cut out the personal questions, Reggie son. And remember you don't rate any more questions than anybody else here. I'm telling you the story, and I'll tell all that's good for you and just the way it happened.

"Now if this yeoman had been better acquainted with his skipper, he'd have been of some use just then. He might have suggested, in a way any of us can at times without interfering, or jarring an officer, even as topsided as a captain, how the thing could be fixed up without any correspondence game. But this new yeoman hadn't yet learned what his captain's steaming radius was. And the captain, having regulations on his brain and not getting the hint at the psychological time, he dictates a regulation communication to the commandant of the yard, which the new yeoman frames up just as he was told. It was a letter inquiring of the commandant the status of the condemned hose in question, and could it not be loaned for temporary use, to be returned in due season—say, next day? and so forth.

"Now the commandant was a good old soul, too, and nothing would have pleased him better than to accommodate his old friend and classmate, the captain of the *Savannah*; but seeing this thing come to him in such formal style, and himself being just off a three-years' cruise, and always a little doubtful about these port regulations, anyway, and wanting to do things up in a seaman-like way, he turns to his chief clerk and says, 'What do we do about this?'"

"Now what the commandant meant and what he would have said, if he'd put it in more words, was: 'I want the *Savannah* to have the use of that condemned hose, but I suppose there are certain formalities to be observed, and your business is to know what these formalities are. Here, you attend to these formalities, but see that the *Savannah* gets the use of the hose.' That's about how he would have put it aboard ship, but he hadn't quite savvied this shore-going chief clerk at his elbow. Toward him he didn't have that same sea-going feeling that he'd have toward one of his old ship's crew.

"And the chief clerk wasn't the kind that lost sleep trying to make trouble for anybody; but he was the combination of being twenty-five years on one job and having a manager of a wife—an upstanding, marine-sergeant sort of a woman, with the beam and bows of a battleship, and an eye—oh, an eye!—and the chief clerk and his missus, they'd just finished paying for their house over in the city, and they'd had to scrimp and scrape for the Lord knows how many years to get it paid for, and there was a marriageable daughter to provide for, and his wife never let him forget that he mustn't risk their real estate or jeopardize his job or the marrying prospects of the daughter, who was just getting to where she was making a lot of desirable acquaintances. There was a young staff officer, a passed assistant surgeon, within easy range, and there was a young paymaster above the horizon, and no telling but they might yet capture one of the line, and that was all the old lady needed to be happy. But if papa was shifted to another city, they'd have to sell the house at a sacrifice and start making friends, all over again. They say that the chief clerk used to get his instructions every morning like it was the uniform of the day. Above all things he must never do anything that the department or any superior officer could ever censure him for.

"He was a little man, the chief clerk, with an upturned moustache he was always flattening fan-wise. 'Heels' they used to call him at the yard, because he was so sensitive about his height that he wore regular female opera-singer's heels on his shoes. Some said his wife made him wear them. Even then he only came up to the top of her ear. Well, Heels considers things now, and recollecting that this would come under the jurisdiction of the captain of the yard, and that the captain of the yard had his little spells, he says to the commandant, 'I think, sir, we'll have to refer it.'"

"'Refer it? To who?'"

"'To the captain of the yard, sir.'"

"'Captain of the—D'y' mean the *Savannah* can't use that bit of rotten old hose without authority?'"

"'Well, sir, you see it is like this. You see, sir, I have to do things the way they are laid down for me. The *Savannah* could, perhaps, use that section of hose, especially if you say so, sir, but—'"

"'But what?'"

"'But if, sir, the captain of the yard *should* learn it, as he might, sir, and he *should* feel slighted, or if an inspector should happen along when it was in use, and discover that the items in the scrap-heap did not tally with his list, that there was a section of hose missing, that it was being used without authority by the *Savannah*—'"

"'Oh, you and your coulds and your shoulds!' snaps the commandant. 'Give me sea duty in place of any of these shore billets any time. Aboard ship I have only to nod my head to my executive officer and a thing's done; but here—O Lord! But go ahead, make out a request, or requisition, or warrant, or whatever's necessary, and let's have it fixed up.'"

"And Heels, who used to be in the army when he was young, but didn't like—or, rather, Mrs. Heels didn't like—to be told of it, he snaps his heels together, starts his arm as if to salute, but stops in time, says, 'Yes, sir,' goes off to his little desk, and typewrites Endorsement No. 1 to the back of the captain of the *Savannah's* letter, gets the commandant's signature, and sends the messenger with it to the captain of the yard.

"And right here was when it really got under way. You see, if the commandant had 'phoned over to the captain of the yard and said in an off-hand, fine-day sort of way, 'I suppose it will be all right to let the *Savannah* have that hose for a day or two, won't it?' why, the captain of the yard would have said, 'Why, yes, sir, let 'em have it.' But he hadn't yet sized up this new commandant. He only knew he had the reputation of being a martinet aboard ship, and now came this formal letter with its endorsement and right away the yard captain said to himself, 'He's a strict one—an endorsement on it already, and that *Savannah* captain, he must be a strict one, too. What are they trying to do—trying to catch me below when I ought to be on deck? I guess not.' He had heard of chaps that you thought you were safe with and you stretched a point or two to help them out, one of those little things that anybody would think would get by all right; and then, when something went wrong, they'd turn around and say, 'Why did you allow this?' and you had no authority to show why you did allow it. There was that last case at League Island, and a friend of his, only the year before. There were two damaged rubber raincoats and a pair of old rubber boots, and the commandant that time had said to his friend: 'See here, I'm tired of looking at those things. Why don't you auction 'em off some day and get rid of 'em?' And the captain of the yard's friend got busy and hectographed letters were mailed to all the junk-dealers in the city, and posted in the post-office and custom-house corridors, and the sale advertised in the local papers, according to the law. And after the sixty days required by the law, they were auctioned off with some other junk. There were thirteen people attended the sale, but only one bid, and that from a little stooped fellow with the beard of a prophet, who offered sixty-seven cents for the lot, and took it off in a two-wheeled hand-cart he'd brought with him. And they turned in the sixty-seven cents, together with the bill for advertising—six dollars and seventy-five cents—and considered they had done quite a stroke of business. But back comes a letter from the Bureau of Profit and Loss—or so the captain of the yard said he thought it was—wanting to know who gave them authority to advertise and sell the property of the United States without authority; and before the inquiry was concluded there were three of them rolled through a G.C.M., and the captain of the yard's friend was broke. And writing him about it, his friend had closed his letter with: 'Don't ever, on your life, have anything to do with any condemned property without you know where you're at every minute.'"

"And this yard captain didn't intend to, and so he added Endorsement No. 2, saying he had no authority, and returned it to the commandant, who sent it back, with Endorsement No. 3, asking to be informed, and so on, and the yard captain tacked on Endorsement No. 4, respectfully suggesting that in compliance with regulations, page 11,336, section 142, paragraphs 24-27, or whatever it was, that it be referred to the Bureau of Replies and Queries at Washington. Which it was, and they returned it to the yard, this time to the yard master, for further and more specific information. And the yard master, after locking it in his safe and going home and sleeping on it overnight, glued on an endorsement that you couldn't have convicted a fish of swimming by, and hoisted it over to the yard captain bright and early in the morning.

"By this time the yard captain was beginning to believe that some politician was after his job, and if so—Well, they'd have to snap 'em over pretty fast to catch him playing too far off his base, and he slid it back to the Bureau of Replies and so forth, who passed it on to the Bureau of Odds and Ends, where it steamed in and out among a lot of swivel-chairs, who were not to be upset easily. They put in a couple of heavy-eyed weeks on it, and rolled it back finally to the commandant for further information. Above all, before an intelligent judgment could be rendered, they especially desired to be informed where the hose came from originally.

"Well, the poor commandant didn't know where the hose came from originally. It might be from any one of three ships that had been lying to in the dock just before the *Savannah's* request was received; a battleship, a cruiser, and a beef-boat they were. But he supposed he had to do something about it, and so he looked up the latest orders. The beef-boat was due back in the yard in a few days; but she rated only a lieutenant-commander. The battleship had the rank: a two-starred red flag from her main. She was about as far away as she could be when last heard from; but no matter; rank had to be served. The commandant begging leave to be informed passed it on to her. Did she know anything about the section of hose in question, and if so, what? And forwarded it, care of postmaster at Manila, P.I. And when it came back—after thirty or forty thousand miles of travel that was—the battleship didn't know anything about the section of hose referred to. Nor did the cruiser, which was in the Mediterranean when caught, only she having lighter heels and hopping around more, it took eight months to get her. There was still the beef-boat, which in the meantime had gone to sea and returned home again, and was now again to sea, on her way to the China station. They went for her, and after a stern chase that lasted through six months and two typhoons and all kinds of monsoons and trades, they got her; whereat she begged leave to say that at the time of her collision with the collier *Ariadne* (for details of which see letter to Secretary of the Navy on such a day and month of such a year) many files of papers were lost. And evidently whatever pertained to the section of hose in question was among the lost files; for certainly among the existing files there was no reference to any section of condemned hose-pipe. It took three months more to get that back to the yard, and by that time the old commandant had been retired for age and a new commandant had fallen heir to it.

"The new head read all the endorsements, by now forty-eight, and pondered over them. For perhaps three days he paced the yard with it, without being able to see where it concerned him; but he was very fond of puzzling things out, and thinking he saw a way out of this, he forwarded it to the old commander of the *Savannah*, who now had a battleship, the *Texarkhoma*, which was in winter quarters with the battle fleet at Guantanamo, Cuba, from where he figured on getting an answer in three weeks at least. But before the mail reached Guantanamo, the *Texarkhoma* had been detached by cable and ordered to the West Coast by way of South-American ports. The commandant at Guantanamo thought he might overtake the *Texarkhoma* at Rio Janeiro, and forwarded the packet to the American minister there. But having meantime got another cable from the department to hurry and make a steaming test of the cruise, the *Texarkhoma* had stopped only long enough in Rio to coal ship, and so the packet missed her there. On to her next stop, Punta Arenas in Magellan Straits, the minister forwarded it, but the flying battleship, with her stops three thousand miles apart, was moving along faster than the mail steamers, which were stopping every few hundred miles. So they missed her in the Straits, and again at Callao. Not till she lay to anchor in San Francisco Bay did they overtake her, and then her commander had only to say that he didn't know where the hose came from originally; but he didn't see that it mattered, as the necessity for the use of the hose no longer existed.

"I might say that the captain's yeoman, having by now come to understand his skipper, drew up that particular endorse-ment, and he thought it pretty hot stuff", and that it would end the whole matter. And so did the new commandant back in the yard when he got it, and he shipped it on to the Bureau of Heavy Jobs with a flourish. But did it? Not much. Down there the swivel-chairs revolved a few more hundred times and they discussed it over a few dozen lunches, and then back it came with a new touch. Why did the necessity no longer exist? they asked, and shipped it by mistake to the new commandant.

"'And how the hell do I know?' says the new commandant, but not in writing, and passes it on to the old *Savannah* captain, who was now rear-admiral, with a division in the East waiting him to come and hoist his pennant. And so again it was a chase of the *Texarkhoma*, which was on her way to the Philippines *via* Honolulu and way ports. They were too late for her at Honolulu, and at Guam, and again at Yokohama; but they overhauled her at Hong-kong, where she'd been lying at anchor for a week."

"The admiral had a lot of mail that morning in Hong-kong harbor, but nothing to speed up his brain till he came to the hose-pipe thing. 'Twas then he went up on the quarter-deck and did a Marathon for an hour or so, while the officer of the deck and every blessed marine and flat-foot on duty stepped softly till he ducked below again.

"By and by, in his cabin, the admiral presses the buzzer, and in comes his trusty yeoman, the same he'd carried from the days of the *Savannah*, and to him the admiral says: 'Willoughby'—call him Willoughby—' Willoughby, how long you been in the service?'"

"'Nineteen years, sir.'"

"'Nineteen? H'm! Then by this time you probably know a little something of the ways that shore-going departments invent to worry us poor fellows to sea,' He held up the hose-pipe thing. 'You've seen this before, Willoughby?'"

"'Oh yes, sir,' says Willoughby."

"'I dare say, and so have I, and if there's a sea-going or shore-going officer in the service that hasn't bumped into it, then he must have been on the sick-list for the last few dozen years. Well, Willoughby, do you take it, this nightmare—that I thought was dead and buried a dozen times—take it and study it over, from alow and aloft, from for'ard and aft, inside and outside and topside and 'tween-decks, from mast-head to keelson, from figure-head to jack-staff; study it and stay with it, and from out of your nineteen years' experience—and you're no green apprentice-boy, Willoughby—see if you can't construct an endorsement that will lay the damned ghost of it for good and all.'"

"'Aye, aye, sir,' says the trusty yeoman, and takes it off to his office and looks it over. A wonderful thing it was by now, with its sixty-seven endorsements winged out on the back of it. Just to read them took the Admiral's yeoman an hour, and he wasn't too slow a reader, either. Well, he spreads it out and sizes it up. And sucks three pipefuls, and takes a cruise down the passageway and has a chat with his old-time shipmates, the boson and the gunner. The boson was Mr. Kiley, the same old boson of the *Savannah*, been with the Old Man when he was a middy in sailing-ship days—couldn't lose each other. A lot of things about the new Navy the boson and the gunner couldn't savvy, and when they got talking things over together they left their blue-book etiquette in their lockers. The admiral's yeoman tells 'em what the Old Man has caught in his mail, and then he asks the boson, 'Did you try to use that hose at all that day?'"

"Try to? No, but I did. D' y' s'pose I was goin' to lose out on a little thing like that 'cause of regulations? And 'specially after the officer of the deck goes inside the bulkhead to give me a chance?'"

"'He didn't go inside to give you any chance,' says the

admiral's yeoman. 'That was to write a message to the skipper.'"

"'Sho-oo boy—bubbles! He was young enough, was Mr. Renner, but not so young he didn't know enough not to bother the ship's boson when he's gettin' results. And I snakes the hose off that scrap-heap, and before he's back on the quarter I had it bustin' with navy-yard water-pressure, and you betcher he sees it over the side, but he don't look too hard at it. No, sir, he don't,' goes on the boson. 'And now take a word from me—and it ain't out of any drill-book your division officer 'll read to you. Let me have that endorsement gadjet and I'll lash it to the fluke of one of our mudhooks next time we come to anchor, and after it's laid a while on the bottom of Singapore harbor, or wherever it is we next let go, under twenty, thirty, or forty fathom of water, whatever it is, I'll let you see what it looks like.'"

"'No, no, Kiley, don't you do it,' says the gunner. 'Don't you do it. Some crazy Parsee diver might spot it and go down and bring it up; and besides, you oughtn't let it get wet—it'd spoil all that nice typewriting. Give it up to me and I'll take it up on the after-bridge, and if it's too stiff for wadding, I'll tie it across the muzzle of the first six-pounder we salute the port with, and let you see how it looks then.'"

"'What you two pirates need,' says the admiral's yeoman, 'is to learn a little respect for the shore-going departments where your orders are made out,' and goes back to his office and takes that hose-pipe communication and reads through the sixty-seven endorsements again, and then he carefully typewrites on a new leaf:

"'*Endorsement No.* 68
U.S.S. *Texarkhoma,*
Hong-kong, China,

Date So and so.

"'Respectfully returned, with the information that the need of the section of hose-pipe no longer exists, for the reason that we filled the *Savannah's* tanks with it seven years ago.'"

"'Very respectfully,'"

"'Your obedient servant,'"

"and signs his own name and rating, Percy Algernon Willoughby—call him that—Chief Yeoman, U.S. Navy, and glues that on behind the other sixty-seven endorsements and gloats over it, and for a few minutes feels like a bureau chief himself. Then for another minute or two he thought of mailing it to them. And he could see them reading that in Washington! There would be an endorsement to go ringing down the departmental ancestral halls! And as for the other yeomen, his colleagues in the service, for generations his name would resound among 'em. But he decided that that would be too much glory for one yeoman, and besides, he didn't know where he could start in at $70 a month (with additions) and all found, at his age, after being nineteen years on one job. And right here, he had to admit to himself, he didn't have so very much the best of Heels of the navy-yard. So he looks it over again; fat as a history of the Roman Empire, and hefted it and—well, there were young apprentice-boys aboard that didn't weigh any more. But to make sure, he lashes it to the butt-end of a fourteen-pound shell the gunner had once given him for a desk-weight. He hated to lose that desk-weight, a relic of the Santiago fight, but a good cause this—a good cause. He starts to unscrew his air-port, but come to think, it was still daylight, and so he waits for the shades of night to fall.

"Well, that night—three bells just gone in the mid-watch it was—the marine guarding the patent life-buoy on the port side of the quarter-deck, fell into a reverie. He ought to have been on the *qui vive*, so to speak—alert, active, wide-awake, pacing his post briskly of course, according to instructions; and if it was daylight when the officer of the deck could see him, you betcher he would. But it was the middle of the night, and a night in the Orient, with a sky of studded velvet and a sea that flowed by like a smooth roll of dark belting, and he was only—Tolliver was his name, from Georgia—only a slim young Southern boy dreaming of home and mother, and maybe of a girl he had left behind him, and he looked up at the emblazoned firmament and again at the flashing sea, and then he rested his head on the top chain-rail.

"For just a second. He had said to himself he wouldn't go to sleep; but all at once he heard a move below him, as of somebody unscrewing an air-port, and then he heard a voice say, 'Well, here goes a ghost that will stay laid!' and then a plash, a pl-m-p! and looking over quickly, he saw plain as could be the phosphorus hole in the sea, then a quarter of a second later something white as a man's face, and then it was gone into the ship's wake.

"'Man overboard!' he yells, and snaps the patent life-buoy over the side, and the marine on the starboard side of the quarter he yells, 'Man overboard!' and the marine on the after-bridge he yells, 'Man overboard!' and the two seaman on watch on the for'ard bridge, 'Man overboard, sir!' they yell, and the watch officer orders, 'Hard on your wheel, Quartermaster!' and to the bosun's mate on watch the watch officer yells, 'Pipe the deck division to quarters!' and the watch officer pulls a few bells and talks through three or four tubes, and in no time the ship is coming around in a circle, and up on deck came piling about two hundred lusty young seamen, and it was, 'boats away,' and over the side went hanging gigs and cutters and whale-boats, and then it was, 'Search-lights all clear!' and in about one minute the big ship was back on the spot, and in another minute and a half there were eight boats with half-dressed crews rowing around, and six big search-lights playing tag on the waters. An hour and a half they stood by, but no sign of him and no call from him. And then it was return to your ship, sound quarters and call the roll. But everybody was present or accounted for, and the skipper gave the captain of marines the devil, and the marine captain gave the devil to his marine guard, the Georgia boy, who by this time was beginning to doubt that he hadn't been asleep."

"Next afternoon the admiral was on deck taking the air, and after a while he asks, 'Where was that marine guard standing when he says he heard that air-port unscrewing and that splash last night?' And they dug the marine out of the brig and brought him up, and he stood on the same spot leaning over the rail, and the old man stands there and takes a look down. And he looks to see if there was an air-port handy. And there was—the air-port of the flag office. 'H'm!—h'm!' he says. 'That's all now, Lyman,' to the marine officer. Nothing more; but an hour later the marine was released from the brig—nobody knew why."

Throughout all the story Dalton had been sitting atop of the coffer-dam, hands with flat palms pressing down, and feet hanging, with heels drumming against the coffer-dam sides. After he had done he pushed himself up by the palms of his hands, rearranged his row of tin letter-files, shifted his electric bulkhead light, picked up a fat folk-lore volume and waited, with eyes twinkling down on us, for somebody to say something.

"And how long ago was that, Dallie?" asked somebody, at last.

"Five years."

"And never a word from the admiral?"

"Never a word."

"H-m-ph! Don't you suppose—"

"Suppose what, fat Reggie? D' y' mean to hint at conspiracy between a rear-admiral of the United States Navy and an enlisted man—a yeoman? Why, Reggie!"

"Of course not. But nothing more from anybody? Not from Washington, either?"

"Nothing, inquisitive child. But there's an old flat-footed friend of mine in the department—and he, whenever he writes me, never forgets to mention that every once in a while the chief clerk, or somebody or other in his division, is sure to look out the window and across the street at the White House grounds, as if trying to remember something; and whenever he takes a particularly long look he is always sure to turn around and say to the man at the nearest desk, 'What d' y' s'pose ever became of that hose-pipe spook used to haunt this place?' And the man at the nearest desk he'll look up and nibble at the end of his pen-holder, or maybe he'll get up and have a look out of the window at the Cabinet playing tennis, and after a while he'll say: 'That's so; I wonder what ever did become of that? But'—maybe another look across at the tennis court—'that'll turn up again, no fear.'"

"But it won't," concluded the flag yeoman, with a smile we could have buried one of his tin letter-files in; "for we were two hundred miles out of Hong-kong at that time, steaming 14.6 miles an hour through the China Sea, and you know it's good and deep there. And now"—he rolled flat on his back, balanced his neck on the head-rest under the bulkhead light, and his fat book on his chest—"now I'm not advising anybody, and particularly not you, Fatty, but that's the way a competent yeoman, with a little advice from a couple of old shipmates, laid that hose-pipe ghost of other days. But mind, I'm not telling you to go and do anything like that."

"No, of course not," says our captain's yeoman, and rubs his fat chin. "Of course not."

"But if you do," says Dalton, and sets his head sideways to see how Reginald was taking it—"if you do, you'd make a hit with your skipper, you betcher—only he'd never tell you."

"Why wouldn't he, if he liked it?"

"Why? 'Twouldn't be regulations. And now, you fellows, beat it. Seven bells gone and the Old Man is due aboard at twelve o'clock. And sometimes he takes a notion to go cruising around the cabin country before he turns in. Besides, I want a chance to peruse a little improving literature before I turn in myself. So beat it, all of you."

And out into the passageways and up the hatchways we beat it; all but our captain's fat yeoman, who went back to his office at a grave thoughtful pace.

# THE SEIZURE OF THE "AURORA BOREALIS"

I had no notion in the beginning of going anywhere near Newfoundland that winter, but the word was passed to me from old John Rose of Folly Cove that if I thought of running down for a load of herrin', then he'd ought to have a couple o' thousand barrels, by the looks o' things, fine and fat in pickle, against Christmas Day, and old John Rose being a great friend of mine, and the market away up, I kissed the wife and baby good-by and put out for Placentia Bay in the *Aurora*.

Now if anybody'd come to me before I left Gloucester that trip and asked me to turn a smuggling trick, why, I'd 'a' said: "Go away, boy, you're crazy." But on the way down I put into Saint Pierre. You know Saint Pierre? In the Miquelons, yes, where in the spring the fishing vessels from France put in—big vessels, bark-rigged mostly, and carrying forty or fifty in a crew—they put in to fit out for the Grand Banks fishing. And they come over with wine mostly for ballast. And in the fall they sail back home, but without the wine.

And, of course, somethin's got to be done with that wine, and though wine's as cheap in Saint Pierre as 'tis to any port in France, yet 'tisn't all drunk in Saint Pierre—not quite. The truth is, those people in Saint Pierre aren't much in the drinking line. One American shacking crew will come in there and put away more in one night than that whole winter population will in a week—that is, they would if they could get the kind they wanted. But that Saint Pierre wine isn't the kind of booze that our fellows are looking for after hauling trawls for a month o' winter days on the Banks. No, what they want is something with more bite in it. And what becomes of it? H-m—if you knew that you'd know what a lot of people'd like to know.

Well, I put into Saint Pierre, for I knew old John Rose and his gang of herring netters would cert'nly relish a drink of red rum now and again on a cold winter's night, and, going ashore, I runs into a sort of fat, black lad about forty-five, half French, half English, that was a great trader there, named Miller. 'Twas off him I bought my keg of rum for old John Rose. I'd heard of this Miller before, and a slick, smooth one he was reported to be, with a warehouse on one of the docks.

He'd been looking at my vessel, he said, had noticed her come to anchor, and a splendid vessel she was—fast and weatherly, no doubt of that. Well, that was all right, for, take it from me, the *Aurora* was all that anybody could say of her that was good. And when you believe that way, and a man comes along and begins to praise your vessel like that, whether you like his sail plans or not, why you just naturally can't help warming up to him. We took a walk up the street together.

And a master and a crew that knew how to handle her, too, Miller goes on. Now I blinked a little at that, straight to my face as it was, but after two or three more drinks I says to myself: "Oh, hell, what's the good o' suspectin' everybody that pays a compliment of trying to heave twine over you?" We got pretty friendly, and, talking about one thing and another, he finally asked me if I ever had a notion of selling my vessel. I only smiled at him, and asked him if he had any idea what she cost to build. I told him then. Fourteen thousand dollars to the day of her trial trip, and all the money my wife and I had in the world had gone into her. He had no idea she cost so much; but, on reflection, it must be so—of a certainty yes. A splen-did, a su-pairb vessel, so swift to sail, so perfect to manoeuvre. If he himself possessed such an enchanting vessel—well, he could use her to much profit. There was a way.

He said that so slyly that I had to ask him what that way was. He winked. "I deal in wines—what way can it be?" And, of course, I winked back to show that I was a deep one too. It's wonderful what things a man c'n get up to wind'ard of you after he's half filled you up. Well, no more then, but we left our caffay for a walk around the port, me looking for a little souvenir in the jewelry line for the baby. Christmas was comin', and though I didn't expect to be home till after New Year's, still I wanted the wife to know I hadn't forgotten the baby.

I was tellin' that to Miller, and a little more about them, of how I hadn't been but a couple of years married, and how I kissed her and the baby good-by on the steps, and her tellin' me the last thing not to go pilin' the vessel up on the rocks anywhere, that the baby's fortune was in her now, and so on.

Well, sir, that farewell scene, that adieu, was too touching for him—he insisted on picking out the souvenir himself, and he picked out a good one, a pretty brooch to fasten the baby's little collar, and he paid for it—forty francs—and I just had to take it.

Well, we had another drink and parted, me not expecting to see any more of him; but that night as I was down on the dock hailing the vessel for a dory to go aboard, a man stepped up to me and laid his hand on my arm. "Captain Corning?" he said, and I said yes.

Well, he was a friend of Mr. Miller—he had seen me talking to Mr. Miller, and learned that I was about to depart in the early morning, bound for Placentia Bay; he would like to ask me to do him a small favor. Could I take one package and land it on my way to Auvergne, where was one friend of his? A small matter, one five-gallon keg of rum, that rum which was of such trivial price in Saint Pierre, but on which the duty was so high in Newfoundland, and his friend was one poor man, one fisherman, who could not afford to pay the duty.

Now this Auvergne was twenty-five miles this side of any port of entry, and my first landing in Newfoundland, according to law, had to be at a port of entry. And so I told this chap that, and how I was liable to a heavy fine, and so on.

Yes, he discerned much truth in what I said, but consider that poor fisherman who could have his good rum merely for the landing—no other cost, none whatever—he, a friend of Mr. Miller, was sending it as a gift for the holiday Christmas time. And that rum—consider the piteously cold nights hauling the nets when a drink of good rum was so soothing, so grateful, so inspiring. And a little favor like that—the Colonial Government would not be—truly not—and if I did not take the rum that poor fisherman of Auvergne would have none in its stead. He could not afford it, the duty was so high—an impossible duty, as no doubt I knew.

I did know, and also I remembered many a drink of Saint Pierre rum I'd had on a cold night in Newfoundland and no duty paid on it, and many a cold night hauling herring when I didn't have it, but wished I had, and would've gone a long

James Brendan Connolly

ways to get it, duty or no duty. And then I remembered how Miller had been pretty decent to me that day—the little brooch he'd bought for the baby I could even then feel in my vest pocket—and I said all right, and when half an hour later a dory slipped up to the side of the *Aurora* and a keg was handed over the rail I didn't ask any questions, but took and stowed it under the cabin run.

Next morning we sailed, and, after a four hours' easy run, made Auvergne, a little port in Placentia Bay, tucked away between two headlands—one easterly, one westerly. Coming from Saint Pierre, it was, of course, the westward one we rounded. According to directions, I ground out two long and two short woofs on the fog-horn, at which a man pops from behind a big rock and waves a handkerchief three times.

Well, that was according to directions, too, and I drops a dory over the side with Sam Leary and Archie Gillis and the keg in it, and tells them to row over to the beach, ask the name of the lad that jumped from behind the rock, and if it was the same as on the tag to leave the keg with him. It was about a mile to the bit of beach, and the dory was almost there, when from behind the easterly headland comes the revenue-cutter. "That looks bad," I says, "but we'll say we've come for fresh water, that our tanks were leakin', and that we had to have fresh water to cook dinner, and Sam and Archie in the dory—'specially Sam—they'll have wit enough to empty the keg over the side and go on up as if they was really lookin' for water."

And that's what would 'a' happened if it'd not been for the thirst that Sam Leary and Archie Gillis most always had with them. They see the revenue-cutter, and they knew just what they oughter done, but they couldn't let go that keg without having one last drink out of it, and when they got that drink down they couldn't help thinking what a pity to waste so much good rum, and taking a look back at the cutter, and seeing she was still half a mile away—"Time enough," says Sam to Archie—"this lad behind the big rock'll have something to stow it in," and he and Archie walks without any hurry up to the rock where the man was hiding.

But instead of one man behind that rock, there was six, and right away there was a battle. Sam and Archie bowls over a couple and gets away up the beach and safe among rocks, but the revenue people got the keg. By that time the cutter was alongside us, and so they wouldn't get the little Christmas keg I had tucked away for John Rose I pulled the plug out of it in no time and let it drain into her bilge. And that was an awful waste of good liquor, and I knew John Rose would grieve when I told him.

They had a clean case against me, and I was taken with the *Aurora* to Harbor Grace for trial. When they asked me what I had to say, I told 'em that I was simply bringing a little keg of rum from a man in Saint Pierre to his friend in Auvergne. They asked me the name of the man in Saint Pierre, and I said I didn't know. They asked me the name of the man in Auvergne, and I said I didn't know. "Was this the man?" they asks, and shows me the tag on the keg. I didn't answer. And they went on to show there was no man in Auvergne by that name, and what were they to understand by that?

I told them I didn't know—it was past me. And it cert'nly was. But they knew what to make of it, they said. There were people in Auvergne doing this illegal business under false names. And I had used a false name, and to try to tell the honorable court that I did not know the name of the man in Saint Pierre who gave me the rum, nor the man I was bringing it to—why, I knew very well who gave me the rum, and I knew who I was bringing it to, and if the truth were known, I knew a lot more about the rum-smuggling traffic.

And they were going to put a stop to it.

And they laid a fine of twenty-five hundred dollars against my vessel. Maybe you might think that a pretty heavy fine, but that's nothing. Almost any little local magistrate down that way can soak an American skipper or owner for almost any amount and get away with it. And how's that? Well, we pay two or three dollars a barrel to Newfoundland fishermen for herring. Before we went down here the St. John's merchants used to pay them about fifty cents a barrel, and it's the St. John's merchants who have all the money and came pretty near running Newfoundland.

Well, when my little local magistrate fines me twenty-five hundred dollars I said I wouldn't pay it, that I'd stir things up at Washington, and so on, but they only laughed at me, and put her up for sale.

Now I'd 've bid her in myself if I'd had the money, but I only had a couple of hundred dollars in cash for running expenses with me. All my Newfoundland friends down that way were poor people—fishermen. If 'twas home we could 'a' raised plenty of money on her, but I was in Newfoundland, not Gloucester, and they rushed the thing through.

Well, the *Aurora* was bid in for just the amount of the fine, and that was a shame, the vessel she was, and she was bid in by a man nobody seemed to know. I went to the man who bid her in and told him the whole story, of what the vessel meant to me, of how I came to bring the rum over, and asked him would he give me the chance to communicate with some business men in Gloucester and buy her back, but he only laughs at me, and laughs in a way to make me think I was a child.

And in one way I was sort of a child, then, but I didn't begin to realize how much of a child till I heard a voice giving orders to make sail on the *Aurora*. A coast steamer had just come in, and from her had come a crew of men to take the *Aurora* away, and this was the voice of the man who gave me the keg of rum that night in Saint Pierre. And while I was looking at him another man came alongside from the coast steamer, and this was Miller himself. If the *Aurora* had been within distance I would have jumped aboard; but she had her lower sails up then and was moving in pretty lively fashion out of the harbor.

I sat on a rock on the beach to think it over, and, "Alec Corning," I said to myself at last—"they cert'nly tried you with the right kind o' bait—and hooked you good."

And I wondered how I could get square with Miller. No use trying to stir up Washington. There was an old skipper of mine, and they'd fined him three thousand dollars once for just a difference of opinion and he couldn't pay it, and his vessel at that moment was being used for a light-ship, and all he'd been getting out of Washington were State Department letters for ten years. And he had cert'nly as much political pull as I had, for I had none.

No, no State Department for mine, I says at last, and ships my crew up to John Rose to Folly Cove, telling them to help John with the herring, and to tell him, too, to save the herring for me, that I'd get 'em back to Gloucester some way, and myself takes passage next day on the mail packet to Saint Pierre.

It was after dark of Christmas Eve when I landed at Saint Pierre. I went up to Argand's Caffay, a place where all kinds of seafaring people used to go to get a drink and a bite to eat. There were quite a few in there now—French stokers from a steamer or two and half a dozen French man-of-war's men

James Brendan Connolly

from a French gun-boat that was lying in the harbor, I remember.

I didn't see any American fishermen in Argand's, but I knew that some of 'em would be drifting in before long. And by and by a few did, but me saying nothing to any of them, only sitting over to a table in a corner with a little bit of supper, and thinking that it was going to be a blue kind of Christmas for me, and a blue Christmas at home, too, for by this time Gloucester must've got the news of the seizure of the *Aurora*, and somebody'd surely passed the word to the wife.

I was sitting there, in the corner, figuring things out and not bothering much about the people coming and going, when somebody sits down at my table, and no sooner down than I felt his boot pressing mine under the table. I looked up, and it was Archie Gillis.

"A fine one *you*!" I breaks out—"where's Sam?"

"Gi'me a chance now, skipper," says Gillis, and orders a little something, and when the waiter was gone: "Sam's not far away. I left him up to Antone's rolling dice for turkeys. We came over, him and me, on a little French packet. Sam guessed you'd come back to Saint Pierre, and if you did he knew you'd drop in here. Sam'll be here soon, he guessed you'd come here. We've been tryin' to find out about the *Aurora*. She's in the harbor, and they're going to put out to-night."

"For where?"

"Well, it's a fishin' trip she's cleared for, but she's got more than offshore bait in her hold."

Archie had been talking straight down at his plate. Now he

stood up, and from behind his napkin said: "There's the skipper o' the *Aurora*—tryin' to collect his gang together. Don't look around. But he'll have hard work, 'cause Sam and me spent most of th' afternoon gettin' 'em drunk—specially Sam. An' Sam says don't notice him when you see him come in, for the new *Aurora* gang don't know yet that we was any of your crew." Gillis tossed his napkin down and strolled over to the bar.

By and by I heard a familiar voice at the door—could 'a' heard it a block—and pretty soon Sam himself comes rolling in. He was carrying a monstrous turkey, and he spied Archie first thing. And, "Hullo, Archie boy," he shouts. "Throw your binnacle lights on that, will you? Thirty pounds he weighs—like you see him—and twenty-five he'll weigh, or I'm no fancy poultry raiser, when he's ready for the oven."

Gillis poked his finger into the breast of the turkey. "I wish we had him for to-morrow, Sammie. He'd make a nice little lunch, that lad."

"Well, we'll have him, Archie, for to-morrow. We'll have him—the biggest turkey ever sailed out of ol' Sain' Peer. A whale, look at him."

"Aye, some tonnage to him. But y' never won him here, Sammie?"

"Win *him* here? *Here*? In Argand's? Ever know anybody win anything here? No, sir. I won him up to ol' Antone's. Twenty-seven throws at twenty-five cents a throw."

"Twenty-seven! You could 'a' bought two of 'em for that."

"Bought? Of course I could 'a' bought; but who wants to buy a turkey Christmas time? Why, any fat old shuffle-footed loafer can take a basket under his arm and go down t' the market and pay down his money and come away with a turkey or anything else he wants. 'Tain't the *getting* him. Archie—it's the winnin' him from a lot of hot sports that think they c'n roll dice. Twenty-seven throws I took and with every throw a free drink of good old cassy—"

"Twenty-seven drinks o' cassy! A lot you knew about what you was rollin' by then, Sammie."

"'Tain't what I knew, but what I *did*, that counted, Archie, and it takes more than twenty-seven glasses o' cassy to put my rail under. *You* oughter know that, Archie. I knew what I was doin'—don't worry. An' that twenty-seventh rollin'! I shook 'em up—spittin' to wind'ard for luck—and lets 'em run. And out they comes a-bowlin'. Seventeen! Cert'nly a fine run-off that, I says, and drops 'em in again, limbers my wrist a couple o' times, and then—two fives and a six— thirty-three! I gathers 'em in again, takes off my cardigan jacket, lays my cigar on the rail, jibes my elbows to each side—'Action,' I says. 'Action.' Yer could hear 'em breathin' a cable length all around me. I curls my fingers over the box, snaps her across an' back again. The len'th of the table they rolled. Three sixes—fifty-one. 'Mong doo,' yells ol' Antone—'Sankantoon—not since fifteen year do I see such play.' Well, for another hour they rolled, but that fifty-one was still high-line. I took him away. And alongside this lad when we have him to-morrow, Archie, there'll be a special bottle o' wine—some red-colored wine. I don't know the name of it. Good stuff, though, and ol' Antone gave it to me—a special bottle."

"An' well he might arter all the money you spent there, Sammie."

"An' why not there as well as the next place? Why not there

as well as here? Why not?" Sam glared down to the end of the bar, where Argand himself was taking in the cash, and his eyes, roaming round the room, caught mine and he winked. "A gen'l'man, ol' Antone, which every caffy keeper ain't—an' because he's a gen'l'man, and because some others ain't—" Sam looked around to see if Argand was getting that—"because some others ain't—because some others ain't, I say—an' I could name 'em, too, if I wanted—I could, yes."

I caught another flash from Sam's eyes, and, looking where his eyes pointed, I saw my *Aurora* captain and three or four of his crew, who had just come in.

"Name him, Sammie—name him," urged Gillis. "Name the cross-breeded dog-fish—name 'im, Sammie, name 'im."

All this was foolish enough, perhaps, but not to Henri Argand, who ran this place. He didn't have reputation enough to be able to stand off and laugh at Sammie and Archie— probably not—for by and by, with four or five helpers, he comes with a rush and in ten seconds it was a mix-up. Sam and Gillis put their backs to the bar and gave battle. There were only the two of them, and the turkey, at first. A great bird a turkey—especially when you swing him by the ankles. Down went a waiter, and down went another waiter. Sam made a couple of tremendous swipes, and then down went the *Aurora's* captain and one of his crew. The *Aurora's* captain's head, I thought, would be knocked clean off, the way the turkey hit him. Then over went a row of French stokers, and, with a back-handed sweep of the turkey, down went the bartender behind. And Sam and Archie, I could see, were working over to finish the *Aurora's* new crew, and would've got 'em, too, but Argand, inside the bar, picks up a bung-starter, sneaks down and gives Sam and Archie a couple of slick taps over the ear, and down they went—just slid feet first away from the bar and on to the floor, flat—and

　　　　　James Brendan Connolly

as they slid Argand reaches over and grabs the turkey out of Sam's hand.

That sort of put it up to our national pride—there was six or seven American fishermen in the place—and we waded in, and the French man-of-war's men, they waded in, and it was one fine battle for maybe ten minutes, with nothing in the way of empty bottles, or full ones either, being overlooked. And when we couldn't reach any more chairs or table legs we pulled off our sea boots, and, believe me, a big red jack with a three-quarter-inch sole and an inch and a half of heel—you grab a sea boot o' that size—it don't weigh more than four pounds or so—you grab it by the ears and get a full healthy swing on it and let it hit a man anywhere above the water-line, and he won't mistake it for any sofa cushion.

It was a fine fight, and I think we'd 'a' won out only for the re-enforcements from outside. A liberty party of French man-of-war's men come first, and then the police lads with the red trousers and the swords, and out we went into the street.

And when they got us out they locked the doors and barred the windows.

While I was pulling on my red jacks again, out under the lamp, on the corner of the street, up comes Sam and Archie. "Say, Alec," begins Sam, "but you cert'nly laid 'em out with your sea boot."

I thought Sam and Archie would be pretty well smashed up, but there wasn't a mark on 'em except a couple of lumps behind their ears.

"Not us," explained Sam. "Nothin' happened to us except bein' stepped on a few dozen times. But did y' land the rest o' the *Aurora's* crew, Alec?"

"I don't know. I swung for 'em, Sam."

"You got 'em all right, and that'll put it out o' their heads to bother with the *Aurora* to-night, though"—he cocked up an ear to the whistle of a rising breeze—"it begins to feel like they wouldn't 'a' gone out anyway—it's breezing up so."

"Where's she layin'?"

"Off the end o' the big dock. An' if it keeps on breezin' they won't be goin' out in the mornin' either. A bad time anyway to put out on a cruise—Christmas Day. But what d'y' say, Alec, if we take a look around the place?"

We'd got a pretty good start for Christmas Eve, and around Saint Pierre we went, Sam and Archie and four men of the *Lucy Foster's* crew who'd been in the mix-up. They were ready to tear things up, but there wasn't much to tear up, because everybody heard us coming, and whenever we'd get to a place, we'd find the doors locked and the windows barred. The only place not locked that night was the little cathedral, and by and by, when we found there was no place else to go, we all went in there.

It was a midnight mass being celebrated, and it was the sound of the choir voices coming from there that got us, and, Catholics or no, no matter, we all went in and heard mass, too, and when we came out, not feeling like trouble any more, we all went down to old Antone's and turned in.

Christmas morning everybody was feeling better, all but Sam Leary and me. I was thinking of my vessel, and Sam of his big turkey. He wanted to get that turkey. He wasn't going to leave Saint Pierre till he got it back. No, sir, he wasn't. And he had a pretty good notion just where it was then. Up to Argand's, cooking for Henri's Christmas dinner. Or maybe him gettin' fifty cents a plate for it for customers' dinners. And he'd cut up for about forty platefuls. And for forty plates at fifty cents or two francs a plate. "Mong doo an' sankantoon," yells Sam all at once. "Come on, Archie—come on, fellows"—and up the street went Sam and Archie and the four of the *Lucy Foster's* crew to see about the turkey.

But that wasn't getting me my vessel, and I went down to the water-front to look for her. There she was, my lovely *Aurora*, to anchor in the stream, and there was me on the end of the dock looking at her, and that's all I could do—look at her. She was lying to two anchors and with her mains'l standing. A little further off shore and even her two anchors couldn't 've kept her from dragging and piling up on the rocks with that mains'l up, for a rocky harbor is Saint Pierre, and now it was blowing a living gale of wind.

While I was standing there on the big dock, along comes the trader Miller with another chap. He must 've seen me, but he pretended not, and I didn't make any sign I saw him. He pointed out the *Aurora* to the man, saying a few things in French. And then he raised his voice.

"When it moderates she will depart—and with a car-go," he said—the last in English, and by that I knew he meant it for me. "Go on," I grit out, "go on, have your fun."

"Yes, I pur-chased her ver-ry cheap," goes on Miller, and then a great racket, and down the dock on the run comes Sam with his big turkey, which was all cooked, I could see, fine and brown—and Archie behind Sam and the four *Lucy Foster* men behind Archie and behind them again a bunch of Argand's waiters and the gendarmes with the red trousers and swords.

There was a dory tied up to the end of the dock; I don't know who owned it, but there it was. "Come on, jump in." I yells, and all hands piled in, and we shoved off; all in one motion almost, and by the time Argand's crowd got to the stringpiece we were a vessel length away, and pulling like homeward bound.

"Lay to it." I kept saying to them.

"Aye, lay to it, and we'll eat that turkey for Christmas yet," yells Sam.

"Lay to it, and we'll have more than the turkey." I says.

"What's that we'll have, Alec?" hollers Sam.

"Pull to the Aurora and see." I hollers back. It was blowing so hard we could hardly hear each other, and what with the chop we were driving the dory through we might well have been in swimming.

We made the *Aurora*, and, looking back as I leaped over her rail, I could see Miller running back up the dock.

"Hurry, fellows." I yells to them, "Miller's gone to head us off."

As we drops onto the *Aurora's* deck a head pops out of the fo'c's'le companion-way. He looked like he'd just come out of a fine sleep. "You," I yelled, "allay you—rauss—beat it," and rushed him to the dory we'd just come aboard in. He looks up at me in the most puzzled way. Two more heads popped up out of the companion-way. "And allay you two," yells Sam and Archie, and grabs 'em and heaves 'em into the dory, casts off her painter, and they drifts off like men in a trance. One minute they were sound asleep in their bunks and the next adrift and half-dressed in a dory in the middle of the harbor with a gale of wind roaring in their ears and a choppy sea wetting 'em down.

"In with her chain-anchor slack," I calls, "and then up with her jibs," which they did. "And now her fores'l—up with her fores'l." Then we broke out her chain-anchor. I was to the wheel and knew the second the anchor was clear of the bottom by the way she leaped under me. "Don't stop to cat-head that anchor," I calls, "but cut her hawser." They cut her hawser free, and with the big anchor-rope kinking through the hawse-hole, away went the *Aurora*, picking up, as she went, the chain-anchor with its eight or ten fathoms of chain still out and tucking it under her bilge; and there that anchor stayed, jammed hard against her bottom planking, while she rushed across the harbor.

"Now," I said, "let's see if we c'n work out of this blessed pocket without somebody having to notify the insurance companies afterward."

All along the water-front the people by now were crowding to look at us. All they saw was an American fishing schooner with a crazy American crew trying to pick her way through a crowded harbor with her four lowers set in a living gale.

We were across the harbor in no time. "Stand by now—stand by sheets," I sung out. Steady as statues they waited for the word, and when they got it—"Har-r-d a-lee-e!" Whf-f the steam came out of them, and the busiest of all was Sam Leary, with the big turkey between his feet.

As she came around I was afraid her anchor would take bottom and her way be checked. It did touch, but the *Aurora* spun on her toes so quick that before that anchor knew it was down she was off and flying free again.

All this time I was looking around for Miller and at last I saw him in a little power boat. He had the French gun-boat in mind that was sure, but his craft was making heavy weather of it, and before he was half-way to the gun-boat we were under her stern, on our shoot for the harbor entrance, and from the gun-boat's deck they were peeping down on us, grinning and yelling the same as everybody else, waiting to see us pile up on the rocks somewhere.

But no rocks for the *Aurora* that Christmas Day. She knew what we wanted of her. There's a spindle beacon in Saint Pierre harbor, white-painted slats on a white-painted rock sticking out of the water, and there was a French packet lying to the other side. We had to go between. I knew they were betting a hundred to one we'd hit one or the other.

We weathered the packet and squeezed by the beacon. The end of our long bowsprit did hit the white-painted slats, gave 'em a good healthy wallop, but that wasn't any surprise—we figured on going close. We were by and safe, and looking back from the wheel to mark her wake swashing over the very rock itself, I had to whisper *to* her:

"*Aurora*, girl, you're all I ever said you were." But if you'd seen her, the big spars of her, the set of her rigging, the fine-fitting sails, the beautiful line of the rail, and the straight flat deck, you'd have to admit it wasn't any surprise. You couldn't 've done it with every vessel—but the *Aurora!* A great bit of wood, the *Aurora!*

And looking past her wake, I picked out Miller's motor boat along inside the French gun-boat. But no gun-boat was worrying me then. They might chase me, but the gun-boat wasn't afloat that could 've chased and caught the *Aurora* in that gale. A man didn't need to be a French captain to know that.

James Brendan Connolly

But for fear they might chase us, I kept her going. And after we'd had time to get our breath, we took a peek into her hold. And it was loaded with cases—wine, brandy—liquors of all kinds. And the gang said: "How about it, skipper?" And I said: "Help yourself—you've earned it," and they helped themselves.

And they had their promised Christmas dinner. The turkey had only to be warmed up. After it was warmed up, it was fine to hear Sam telling about the recapturing of it. "He was in the kitchen—just been hauled out the oven—and the chef, he was standing over him with a big carving knife, when I spots the pair of 'em through the window. 'Stand by, fellows,' I hollers, and jumps through the window and grabs the carving knife and chases cheffie out the room with it. And back through the window comes me and the turk. An' they all hollers murder and comes after us. And look at him now! Twenty-five pounds he weighs—the biggest turkey, I'm tellin' you, ever sailed out of ol' Saint Peer. A whale, twenty-five pounds as he lies there. And four kinds of wine—four kinds. Cassie, champagne, claret, which you don't have to drink 'less you want to, and that red-colored wine I don't know the name of, but good stuff—I sampled it. And that's what I call a Christmas dinner."

And I guess it was. Pretty soon they were hopping around like a lot of leaping goats. The best-natured crowd ever you see, mind, but it was Christmas Day, and they'd done a good job; the blood was running wild inside them, and I let them run a while. And then when I thinks it time to begin to straighten them out, I looks them over and finally picking out Archie Gillis I says, 'Archie, I think you're the drunkest! Take the wheel and soak it out.'

And Archie stood to the wheel, and up the cabin steps the rest of the gang kept passing him drinks of champagne when they thought I wasn't looking.

By dark of that Christmas we shot into Folly Cove in Placentia Bay and came to anchor off John Rose's wharf. And the *Aurora's* crew were there helping John, and there was the load of herring John had promised. And he thought I'd come for the herring, but I hadn't—not yet. I had a word in private with John, and he found a nice little place among the cliffs, and with John Rose and the *Aurora's* crew it didn't take long to stow those cases of wine where no stranger would find them in a hurry.

And when that was done I goes over the papers again. And sure enough, her papers read for a fishing trip to the Grand Banks. Her crew had been shipped for a fishing trip. Her gear, dories, bait (not much bait though) was all for a fishing trip. It was plain as could be, I had Miller under my lee. And so we put out again into the night, and before daylight we were back in Saint Pierre harbor again, and all hands ashore.

And when Miller woke up in the morning there was the *Aurora* laying to anchor in the stream just where she'd been the morning before. And we were having a nice little breakfast up to Antone's when Miller and the governor and the gun-boat captain comes to get me. And Miller was going to arrest me, put me in irons, not a minute's delay, not one, and I says "For what?" And Miller throws up his hands and repeats: "For what? He says for what? Mong Doo, for what?" And I says: "Yes, for what? What are you going to arrest me for? For a little excursion trip, a little run off shore, is it?—so's to eat our Christmas turkey in peace?" I see that my play lay with the French naval officer, so I turns to him. "There was a turkey. Old Antone here will tell you that it belonged to one of my men, Mr. Leary here—that he won it fairly, and that the same turkey was stolen from him in Henri Argand's. And Mr. Leary got it back. And they would not let him have

James Brendan Connolly

it in peace, and so, to escape mistreatment, we jumped aboard the first vessel we saw in the stream and put out the harbor. You yourself doubtless, saw us." He nodded. "Your whole crew saw us. The whole harbor saw us. There was no concealment." I stopped for the French captain and the governor to get that. Miller was looking at me goo-goo-eyed, but both the officials nodded and said: "That is true."

"And when we found ourselves safe out to sea, we had our dinner, our Christmas dinner—in the peace we had sought. And surely these gentlemen"—I bowed my best to the gun-boat captain and the magistrate—"do not consider that a crime—to ask to be allowed to eat our Christmas dinner in peace."

Miller was fair up in the air by then—"You pi-rates—pi-rates."

I leaps to my feet. "Pirates—to me? To these men? Simple honest fishermen who know only toil? Who toils harder than they? Pirates—to them! Why, if they were anything but the simplest and honestest set of men, they would have taken that vessel out of my hands and sold her—sold her in the States—and what could you or I or anybody have done about it? But did they—or I? No, sir. As soon as we had finished our Christmas dinner we brought her back."

"But the wine?" shrieks Miller.

"What wine?"

"The wine—the wine—her cargo of wine."

"Wine? Cargo of wine—what's he talking about?" I looks at my crowd, and they all says: "Wine? Cargo of wine?—he's crazy."

I turns impatiently to the governor and French captain. "Gentlemen, this is a serious accusation, but easily settled. If there was wine in that vessel, surely her papers will say something of it. It will be on her manifest, that is certain."

Now these two, the governor and the French naval officer, were honest men. "That is so," they said. "He is quite right— quite right," and looked at Miller, and Miller, with his eyes like door-knobs, looks at me. And I gives him a wink with my wind'ard eye and he near blew up.

But he begins to see a thing or two, so he goes off with the French officials, but before we had finished smoking our after-breakfast pipeful he comes back—alone now—and says: "What do you propose?" And I said: "Within a thousand miles of here is a friend of mine with a lot of wine—as good a lot as the *Aurora* had in her hold yesterday—maybe a couple of dozen quarts shy—you know, a Christmas dinner, and so on—and only last night my friend was figuring it up, and he thought there was twenty thousand dollars' worth in this lot of his, and that without figuring in the duty—but he don't care for wine much—but he does love a good Vessel, and he was looking the *Aurora* over and he said he'd be willing to exchange all that wine for the *Aurora*. I told him that the *Aurora* only cost you twenty-five hundred, but he said, 'No matter, I have a weakness for the *Aurora*,' this friend of mine. Of course there'll be a few little extra expenses you'll have to pay for, like the hawser and the big anchor cut away and the keep of a crew for a week over in Newfoundland, and so on, but that won't be much—five hundred dollars ought to cover it all."

And Miller gave back the *Aurora* and paid over the five hundred, and I gave him an order on John Rose for the wine. And then I took the little baby's brooch out of my pocket and handed it back to him.

And then I sailed over to Placentia Bay in the *Aurora* and took twenty-one hundred barrels of herring off John Rose and put out, and, getting the first of a stiff easterly, the *Aurora* carried it all the way to Gloucester. And I was home to the wife and baby by New Year's. And the baby got a good brooch. I could afford it. From the profits of twenty-one hundred barrels of fine fat herring I could well afford it.

I haven't seen Miller since, but they say he's shyer than he used to be of simple American fishermen.

# LIGHT-SHIP 67

I

Perrault was the good old Frenchman who kept the general store just across from the Navy Yard gate, and Baldwin was the chief boson's mate, U.S.N., who commanded the *Whist*, the little tug which was used as a general utility boat by the Navy Yard people.

Old Perrault was born in Paris, and, in God's goodness, hoped yet to die there. And Baldwin had been in Paris, more than once in his cruising youth, and could converse of Paris; and to converse of Paris, in such loving language, was it not to win one's heart?

Old Perrault had never dissembled his regard for the sailor. A pity he viewed life so carelessly, the brave-hearted Baldwin. So excellent in many respects, if he had but a little ambition for himself! If he but hearkened a little for the world's opinion. But such a man! Sometimes old Perrault wished that his motherless Claire would disregard all his wordly homilies, fall in love with the rugged Baldwin, and marry him.

Baldwin himself maintained no such exalted hopes. A fine

James Brendan Connolly

husband he'd make after his riotous years! But he had a friend, recently detailed to the yard, and warmly recommended by the boson's mate, this friend Harty, chief wireless operator, soon came to be the most regular of all the Saturday night attendants at old Perrault's store. It was on Saturday nights that the unmarried foreman on the breakwater job came up to see old Perrault. If you stood well with the old fellow, like as not he would ask you to the house of a Sunday afternoon, and then you could sit around and rest your eyes on the lovely Claire while she played the piano.

One might think that old Perrault, who so casually picked his company, was a careless sort of parent; but not so, as witness his questioning of Baldwin, when it began to dawn on him that this wireless operator was becoming a distinguished member of the Sunday afternoon parties; and the boson's mate, who revered old Perrault, but who also thought a lot of his friend Harty, spoke judiciously.

"He's all right," he replied to old Perrault, "all right. Yes, I know he used to drink an' was generally wild once; but he's over that. Oh, sure, all over that now."

It was beginning to look like Harty for Perrault's son-in-law, when Bowen came along. Bowen was the expert who came to overhaul the wireless plant in the yard. An easy-going, but wide-awake sort, Bowen, who seemed to have been everywhere and who could talk of where he had been, talk without end, and always with the intimate little touches which you never found in the guidebooks. He captured old Perrault at the first assault. Old Perrault from behind his counter happening to catch a stray word, listened, looked up, and, noting the animated features, hastily signalled the newcomer to come out of the crowd. One minute later he had put the vital question: Had Mr. Bowen ever been to Paris?

To Paris! Bowen started to touch the end of a finger for every time he had been to Paris. Old Perrault could not wait for him to finish. "And the Champs Elysees, Mister Bowen, you have been there?"

"The Champs Elysees? If I had a dollar, M'sieu Perrault—"

"Eh?" The old man wanted to hear him say that "M'sieu" in just that way again—"if you had one dollar, Mister Bowen?"

Bowen understood. "Yes, if I had a dollar, M'sieu, for every time I sat on one of those chairs inside the sidewalk—in under the trees, you know, M'sieu—and watched the autos go by! Talk about autos!—there's the place for autos, coming down from that big Napoleon Arch. Some arch, that, isn't it? Yes, sir—down from there to the Place de la Concorde and back again, around the Arch and on to the Bois. And there's a sight for a man, too! To sit out on the Bois sidewalk, M'sieu, your chair almost under the bushes, and watch those cabs and autos in the late afternoon, coming on dark. Count them? No more than you could count fire-flies of an evening in the West Indies—like one string of light."

"Mon Dieu! Come to the inner room, if you please, sir, and tell me more. What a good angel which has sent you here! Twenty-five years since I have seen my Paris. And the Tuileries, my friend, is it yet the same?"

"Just the same, M'sieu, a million bare-legged children with short white socks running wild, and another half a million nurses with white caps running wild after them. And the Eiffel Tower! But that's since your time, M'sieu Perrault?"

"Ah—h, but have I not heard? Continue, continue, if you please, sir. You bring a strange joy to my heart. The Louvre, for example—you have been there, yes?"

"Been there? Yes, and 'most googoo-eyed from looking at the pictures there—miles of 'em, aren't there?"

"Oh-h! and Mona Lisa—yes!"

"That dark one with the queer kind of a smile? She must have had green eyes, that one—green eyes with lights in them. And she kept them all guessing, I'll bet a hat, when she was alive—" and Bowen ran on till every blessed breakwater man silently stole away. Bowen and old Perrault had a three o'clock session that first night; and within the year he had married Claire.

## II

Having completed his work on the wireless plant at the Navy Yard, Bowen thought himself due for a lay-off. And he did want to be home for a while, but orders came to have installed before the end of the year an experimental plant on Light-ship 67, which guarded Tide Rip Shoal to the eastward.

Bowen, with his two helpers and his apparatus, took passage with Baldwin on the wheezy little *Whist* to where, twenty miles east by south from the end of the breakwater, lay the tossing light-ship.

Baldwin was well acquainted with old 67. Every once in a while the commandant would order Baldwin to make this trip for the accommodation of somebody or other in the yard. "But a wonder," he observed now, as he had observed a score of times before on nearing her—"a wonder they wouldn't put one of those new class o' steam lightships out here. If I was you, Bowen, I'd have an eye to the life-boat you see hanging to her stern there."

"Why?"

"Well, if the old hooker went adrift, you might need it."

"What's her sails for?"

"I dunno. I often wondered, though. They've been tied up, just like you see 'em now—stopped snug and neat between gaffs and booms—for, oh, I dunno—twenty years now, I reckon. I know I've yet to see 'em hoisted. But when'll I come and get you?"

"I'll send word to the yard station by wireless, to Harty or whoever's on watch there, when we get it rigged."

"All right. And say, a great thing that wireless, ain't it? Well, good luck." Baldwin gave the bell and the *Whist* backed away. He rolled his wheel over, gave her another bell and around she came; then the jingle and ahead she went full-speed, which in smooth water was almost eight knots.

The light-ship crew, headed by her yellow-haired keeper, stood around and watched Bowen and his helpers assembling the parts of the wireless. A momentous occasion for the light-ship crew, for nobody bothered them much. Once every two months the supply ship came around, and sometimes, if the weather was fine, some unhurried coaster would stand in and toss them a bundle of newspapers. But no running alongside old 67 by any big fellows. A good point of departure, Tide Rip Shoal! Sight it over your stern and lay your course by her, but otherwise give her a wide berth; for you could pile up a ten-thousand tonner on that shoal or the beach to the west and—yes, sir, high and dry, before you knew it, especially if it was thick and you were coming from the east'ard. No, the big fellows were satisfied to have a peek at Tide Rip through a long glass; and so on 67 anything at all except a spell of bad weather stirred them deeply.

In the daylight hours Bowen and his helpers worked at their wireless, and at night they sat in with the light-ship crew. Bowen usually played checkers in the cabin with the keeper, Nelson, and while they played the keeper gave him the gossip. He had been nineteen years on Tide Rip Shoal light-ship, had keeper Nelson.

"No, no things never happen. He blow and she tumble about and her chain chafe—chafe tarrible sometime. Nineteen year those chain ban chafe so. One time he blow ten day without stop, but" (he removed his big pipe to laugh aloud)—"but ten day over and she right dere. Good ol' 67, she ban right dere. I axpect ol' 67, she be here on Yoodgment Day." Old Nelson put his pipe back, puffed three times, frowned at the checkerboard, scratched his yellow head, let drop his eyelids and pondered. At about the time Bowen began to think the keeper must be taking a nap, a long arm swooped down and moved a black checker one square north-easterly.

Now, if Bowen had been riding to anchor in that one spot with old 67 for nineteen years, perhaps he, too, would have paid small attention to a gale of wind and a high sea; but he was a shore-going man, and he grew very, very weary of the jumping and the rolling, and of the everlasting rattling and chafing of the iron chains in the iron hawse-holes.

Two chains there were, like double-leashes to a whippet's throat. The heave of the sea would get her and up she would ride, shaking, snapping, quivering to get her head. Up, up she would go, and as she struggled up, up, Bowen, watching, would find himself crying out, "By the Lord, she's parted them." But no—Gr-r—the iron chains would go, Kr-r the iron hawse-holes would echo, and, suddenly brought to, dead she would stop, shake herself, and again shake herself to get free; but always the savage chains would be there to her throat, and down she would fall trembling; and the white slaver would scatter a cable length from her jaws as she fell.

Bowen, with an arm hooked into a weather-stay, would stand out and watch her by the hour; and "Some fine night you'll break loose," he would say over and over to himself, "and then there'll be the devil to pay around here," and on returning to the cabin he would tell Nelson about it.

"No, no," Nelson would shake his head, and after he had had time to think it over, he would smile at Bowen's fears. On nights like these, when he couldn't have his little game because he couldn't keep the checkers from hopping off the board, Nelson liked to lie in his bunk, within range of the big, square, sawdust-filled box which set just forward of the cheerful stove. With eyes mostly on the oil-clothed floor, the light-keeper would smoke and yarn unhurriedly. "No, no," Nelson would repeat. "For nineteen year now she ban here, yoost like you see now. No drift for ol' 67. She ban too well trained."

But the chafed-out chains gave way at last. Christmas Eve it was, the night when Bowen had hoped to be through with his work. It was also the third and worst night of the gale, and Bowen, restless, homesick, was on deck to see it. She leaped and strained as she had leaped and strained ten thousand times before—and then they writhed, those chains, like a stricken rattlesnake, for perhaps three seconds, and S-s-t!— quick as that—they went whistling into the boiling sea. Off she sprang then—Bowen could no more than have snapped his fingers ere she was off—foolishly, wildly, and then, almost as suddenly as she had leaped, she fetched up. It was as if she didn't know just what to do in her new freedom. And while she paused, the sea swept down and caught her one under the ear. Broadside she broached and aboard her foamed the ceaseless sea, and the wind took her. And whing! and bing! and Kr-r-r-k!—that was the life-boat splintered and torn loose. And sea, and wind, and tide, all working together on old 67, away she went before it.

Inshore, they knew, the high surf was booming; and they made sail then, and for a while thought they could weather it; but when the whistling devils caught the rotten, age-eaten, untested canvas—whoosh! countless strips of dirty, rusty canvas were riding the clouded heavens like some unwashed witches.

Tide and wind were taking her toward the beach, and Bowen, everybody, even the unimaginative viking in command, could picture that beach and the surf piling up on it. High as the light above their heads it would be, and they would live just about ten seconds in it. Yes, if they were lucky, they might last that long.

Bowen was one of those workmen who like to make a good job of a thing. He was not ready to send his first wireless message. Another morning's work and he had hoped to be ready, and that first message was to be a Christmas greeting to his wife; but now he made shift to get a message away in some fashion. With limber wrist and fingers he began to snap out his signal number. A dozen, twenty, surely a hundred times he repeated the letters, holding up every half minute or so to listen. By and by he caught an answering call. It was the Navy Yard station. Feverishly he sent:

"Light-ship 67. Tide Rip Shoal. Have parted moorings. Drifting toward beach. Send help."

He waited for an answer. None came. He repeated. No answer. Over and over he sent it. At last he caught: "OK. Been getting you. Go on."

"Drifting fast. West by south. Before morning will be in surf."

Again Bowen waited, and then the answer came: "What do you want me to do?"

"Do something to save us."

"Why don't you do something to save yourself?"

"Sails blown away. Life-boat gone."

"Haven't you got a chart of Paris?"

"Chart of what?"

"Paris? With a few M'sieus on it? Good night."

Bowen let go the key, leaned back in his chair, rubbed his eyes, took off his receiving gear and stared at the wall.

"What answer?" Nelson and his peering crew were at his shoulder.

"No answer."

"Dan we moost go up and dowse dose signal light, so no ship t'ink we ban on shoal yet," and out onto the deck the impassive Nelson led his men.

"Good old squarehead—you're all right," muttered Bowen. "But as for you," he gritted, "if I could only—just one grip of your throat is all I'd ask for, and then, you dog!"

III

Harty closed his wireless office and headed for the water-front. Near the shore-end of the breakwater he came to a halt. He could but dimly see the beginning of the outstretching wall of concrete, but plainly enough he could hear the combers thundering over the crest of it.

A proper night for an enemy to be adrift in a powerless hulk. Sea enough to suit any purpose out there. And wind! From where he stood in the lee of the donkey-engine house, to the water's edge was a full hundred feet, and yet even so, whenever he stepped out into the open, it was only to be drenched with spray. And out there in the blackness, twenty miles offshore, it would be blowing good; out there on the edge of that bank, in the hollow of the short, high, ugly seas, was a rolling, battered light-ship; as helpless as—well, there was nothing ashore to compare to her helplessness. And when she hit in on the beach—when she hit the sand—it would be over and over she'd roll, and out of her he would come and be smothered. For a second he'd be smooth and sleek as a wet rat and then—Oh, then!

Even in moderate weather, what chance would they have in that surf? And to-night it would be to her mast-head, with combers curving like a rattlesnake's neck, and twisting, and hissing, and they would catch him up, and ten ways he'd go then, gurgling, smothering, drowning, and his body, if ever it did come ashore for anybody to find,—after a December night,—they'd find it frozen stiff.

The walls of the little engine house were icing up, the spray was freezing on his moustache—surely a proper night for a man's enemy to be lost. In the lee of the little shack he lit a cigar; but it would not stay lit, and he threw it from him. The curse which he hove after it brought an answering hail from across the dock, "Hullo there"! Harty drew back, but the hurrying step drew nearer, and suddenly the hurrying form was beside him, and a pair of eyes were peering at him.

"Who's this? Why, hullo, Bud! What you doin' here?"

"Who's that? Oh, hello, Baldy. Where'd you come from?"

"From the *Whist*—where else? Told the crew to beat it—all except old Pete. Holidays don't mean anything to Pete, so he's sleeping aboard. A wild night, Bud. Maybe we wasn't glad not to be caught outside! The old *Whist* she'd sure have a fine time outside to-night. She'd last about half a night-watch out there—say out where old 67 is to-night. But where you bound, Bud?"

"Nowhere—anywhere."

"Well, what d'y' say if we take a look in on old Perrault?"

"What do you want to go there for?"

"Oh, forget that. Come on. Every Christmas Eve since I've known him we've drunk a Christmas health together. A good old scout, Perrault, and you and me, Bud, we ought to be ashamed the way we kept away from him lately. Passed him on the street the other day. 'Ah-h, dear Baldwin, you have time for the Port Light saloon, but not for your old frien'", and he shakes his old head. 'Please, do not fail, Cap-tan, on this Christmas Eve!' he says to me. 'And Mr. Harty also.' Come on now. Be good. 'Twarn't him didn't marry you, mind. Come on, Bud and forget it."

"All right—go ahead."

It was old Perrault himself who spotted Baldwin coming in the door of the store. His joy was bursting. "Ah-h, Cap-tan! Ah-h, you come once more to see your old frien'. And you also, Mister Harty. Now then—and you shall also, Mister Harty. Yes, yes, I say it—drink with me to the Christmas."

Baldwin filled his glass. Harty made no move.

"Come on, Bud, you too. What's the matter with you? Here, fill her up. What's the matter with you, anyway, to-night?"

"I'm on the water-wagon."

"Since when?"

"Since to-day."

"Sufferin' Neptune! Who ever heard of a water-wagon doin' business on Christmas Eve? I think if we looked it up, you'd find a law against it, and if there ain't, there ought to be. Come on. No? Well, all right, stay on it. Mo-sher Perrault—" and, as he had done for many a Christmas Eve before, Baldwin touched his glass to old Perrault's, and gave the toast.

"A fair, fair wind to you and yours,
No matter the course you sail!"

Ere they had set their glasses down, Harty was making for the door. Old Perrault entreated. "Why, Mister Harty!" and Baldwin whispered, "What's your hurry, Bud?"

"I've got to go," he said to Perrault; to Baldwin he whispered, "Somebody's coming in—I heard her voice."

"Oh, varry well, if you will not stay," sighed old Perrault.

"But hark! Attend one moment, gentlemen. She comes." He lowered his voice. "She goes to-night to the church. She has, you understand, gentlemen, fears. And also—" he leaned over and whispered into Baldwin's ear.

"No!"

"Truly."

Baldwin took off his hat and clasped the storekeeper's hand. "God keep her."

"Sh-h—She is here."

She stood in the doorway. It was Harty's first chance in months to look her fairly in the face. She smiled on Baldwin, bowed, but without smiling to Harty, kissed her father, whispered a word in his ear, and turned to go. Baldwin jumped forward. "Mrs. Bowen, hadn't me and Mister Harty better see you to the church—might be a drunken loafer or two on the street—and a blowy night."

"I shall be most honored, Captain."

They went out; but from them all not a word, until they were at the church door, and here it was she who spoke. "Captain Baldwin, is it not a dangerous night?"

"Meaning at sea, Mrs. Bowen?"

"At sea—on the light-ship."

"Why, bless you, no. Old 67, she's been out on that spot— Lord knows how long she's been out there. She's sort of a part of the furniture out there now. Why, the very fishes that come to feed on South Shoal, Mrs. Bowen—they'd think they was on the wrong bank if they couldn't look up and see the barnacled bottom of old 67 over 'em. Rough? Lord, yes, plenty rough out there t'night, but not dangerous. Lord, no, Mrs. Bowen, not dangerous. All she's got to do is to hang on to her moorin's."

"You are a kind-hearted man, Mr. Baldwin, and a good friend. My husband, he thinks the world of you. I go in now, to pray for him, to bring him home to us. Good-night, and a happy Christmas to you." She hesitated, "And to you, Mr. Harty, a happy Christmas also."

Harty did not close the door behind her until he had seen her kneel at the altar-rail. Out in the street again, he turned abruptly to his chum. "Look here, Baldy, what was it her father whispered to you—just before she came into the backroom?"

"What? Why-y—I—Well, no harm telling it, I reckon, though I don't know why he didn't tell you, too, Bud—she's goin'—" Baldwin lowered his voice—"she's goin' to have a baby, and—what's it?"

"Nothing."

"Oh-h! And her old father, you'll be hearin' no more from him about goin' back to Paris to die. Gee, but this wind is fierce, ain't it? Say, Bud, but d'y' b'lieve that some people, especially women, that they know without bein' told when people they think a lot of is in danger?"

"I don't know. Do you?"

"M-m—sometimes I think there's something in it. Did you notice the look in her eyes to-night? But—" the red lamp of the Port Light saloon loomed brightly ahead—"it's a pretty cold night—a toothful o' something, what d'y' say?"

"Nope."

"Then where you bound?"

"I don't know—take a walk, I guess."

"Well, you sure picked a fine night for a walk. Better lash your ears to your head, if you're heading for the beach-side. Be back this way soon?"

"I don't know."

"You don't know? What's got into you to-night, Bud?" Baldwin stared at his chum. He stepped nearer and laid a hand on Harty's arm. "You ain't sick, Bud?"

"God, no! I'm all right. I'll take a walk and come back."

"All right, but hurry back, won't you?"

IV

The Port Light saloon was doing a fine business. The swinging doors between the backroom and the bar were swinging all the time—and at the various tables a score of young men and a dozen or so of young women, and one stout fellow at the piano, were roaring dull care away.

The piano occupied one corner of an alcove off the large backroom. In the other corner of the alcove Baldwin and a few friends were sitting into a quiet little game. Things had been breaking well for the sailor, and it promised to be a blissful night, for when luck came his way in a poker game, Baldwin could fall into a trance, if nobody disturbed him.

It was Hatty who came bursting through the swinging doors to disturb him. One peek at his chum's face and "O Lord!" murmured Baldwin, "still on it." Aloud he added, "Sit in, Bud," and Harty sat in, after first ordering a round of drinks.

Baldwin lifted his drink. "Fell off that water-wagon kind o' sudden, didn't you, Bud," but without even a curious glance emptied his glass.

Four or five hands were played, and, luck still running the sailor's way, he was smiling like a moonlit sea, when, "Say, Baldy," shook him out of his revery.

"Lord, Bud! What?"

"A hell of a fine bunch we are."

"Fine how?"

"To be spending our Christmas here."

James Brendan Connolly

"Why, where else would we be?"

"Where but home?"

Baldwin smiled broadly. "Say, Bud, I don't see you logging any record-breaking runs for home.

"Blast it!—I've got no home."

"Well, who has?"

"But—" Harty took the spare pack which he had been riffling and slammed it down on the table—"there's men who've got homes—good homes—who're going to their death to sea to-night."

"What's the matter, Bud? Sit down. Sure there are. They're there every night, goin' to their death somewhere out to sea, but how c'n we help it?"

"We *can* help it." Harty stood up "Fine men we are, all of us."

Ting-a-ling-a-ling-a-tump-ti—
Ting-a-ling-a-ling-a-tump-ti—

came from the piano.

Harty whirled around. "And as for *you*!" He picked up the spare pack and hurled them at the fat piano-player. "Blast you! Yes, *you*—I said *you*, didn't I—shut up! It's petticoats you ought to be wearing."

The piano-player's lower lip fell away from his teeth. His wall eyes opened abnormally. "Why, what did I do to you?" he gasped.

"Nothing. You couldn't do anything to anybody. You haven't the gimp. Shut up."

Harty faced Baldwin. "The hell we can't help it. The light-ship to South Shoal could be going to her death with all hands, and we're sitting here and guzzling rum."

Baldwin was holding his cards up in front of his eyes. He riffled the close-set edges with a dexterous thumb, took another squint, pursed his lips, said softly—"M-m—yes, I'm in," dropped two white chips onto the little pile in the centre, then, looking up, laughed tolerantly at Harty.

"Rum? Mine's rye, Bud, when there's any choice, but what's wrong with you to-night? Sit down. Maybe you've got it right, Bud, but what's the use of gettin' highsterics over it? Maybe some of us could be a lot better than we are, but I don't know's any of us ever pretended to be anything great, did we?"

"Great? I didn't say anything about *great* men. We're not half men, Baldy—the light-ship is going with all hands."

"One card," Baldwin scaled his discard to the table and stuck the new card in with his others before he answered. His voice was now less patient. "Say, Bud, maybe we're not half men, but don't rub it in—don't. If anything's wrong with the light-ship, how'd you know?"

"I know."

"But how?"

"Wireless."

"Wireless?" Baldwin was peering at his cards. Suddenly he

looked up. "Hah—wireless? Eheu-u—" he whistled softly, gently laid his cards face-down on the table. "You got word, Bud?" He half-turned to the man on his right. "Do I see you, Bo, did you say?" He picked up his cards. "Sure I'll see you—and two more red lozenges to come along. But what can we do about it, Bud?"

"There's the *Whist*, Baldy."

"What, her? Send her to sea to-night? We couldn't if we wanted. She only goes out under orders from the commandant, remember. And the commandant, he's on leave, visitin' his married daughter somewhere over Christmas."

"And a G.C.M., too, wouldn't it, Baldwin?" put in the man called Bo, "without orders."

Harty whirled on Bo. "Who the hell gave you a rating to butt in on this? Orders? To hell with their orders, and to hell with their general court-martials. Orders, Baldy, when it's lives to be saved? Christ, Baldy, you haven't forgot, have you? Bowen's on her. Bowen, man, and remember she's going to—"

Baldwin held up one wide-spread hand palm out. "That's enough, Buddy. You've said enough. I don't know what the poor old *Whist* will do once she finds herself away from the lee of the breakwater t'night, Bud, but we'll go, and if they're there and we stay afloat, we'll get 'em. And Bo, I could play this hand all night, but two round blue moons to see what you got. Hah? King full, eh? The nerve of you! What did y' think I was only taking one card f'r? There, feast your eyes on that fat black collection, will yuh? In a row? Sure in a row. Look at 'em—a three-toed black regiment of 'em. And these other little round red, white, and blue boys, cash 'em in, will yuh, Bo? And put the money in an envelope for me?"

"And for me too." Harty had drawn out a roll of bills and laid them on the table. "I don't know how much is there—count it, you. And if I don't come 'round again, here's an address—South Boston, yes—where you can send it. A little nephew of mine, a fine fat little devil who thinks his uncle's the greatest man in the world. The poor kid, of course, don't know any different. So long, fellows. All ready, Baldy?"

"All ready, Bud—head away."

Through the streets, past the Navy Yard gate and through the Navy Yard the two friends tramped silently.

"Won't you need more than the three of us to handle that tug?" asked Harty.

"Three's plenty, Bud. You and me an' old Pete, we can make out. What's the use of risking any more, though if we did need 'em, we'd get 'em. We'd only have to beat up the water-front, and volunteers! They'd come a-running, Bud, from every joint and dance-hall, enough to run a battleship—in no time, yes, sir. Why, Bud, even that squash-head of a piano-player would 'a' come if we'd ast him."

"H-m-m—you surely think well of people, Baldy."

"No more strain than to think bad of 'em. But what'd be the use? Us two an' old Pete, who'll be sleepin' aboard, c'n run her, Bud."

And they had put out in the *Whist*, and now down in the combined engine and fire-room of her were Harty and old Pete toiling to keep steam up. A notorious little craft, the *Whist*, one of those legacies which sometimes fall to the Service; the department always going to fix her up, and always putting it off until the next appropriation. Her old boilers leaked, and in a sea-way her old seams gaped, and what between keeping steam up and her bilge pumped out, Harty and Pete could hardly find time to brace their feet whenever she attempted, as she did about every fifteen seconds, to heave them across the floor.

To the wheel of the *Whist* was Baldwin, and as with every dive of the plunging *Whist* the spray scattered high above her bows, so through the open windows of the pilot-house came barrels of it, and not a spoonful that didn't go to his drenching.

"But it's a good thing to get good and wet at first," reflected Baldwin, "then you won't be worryin' any more about it." It was not only wet, but cold. But naturally, too, when you're a-wrecking to sea of a cold winter's night you just got to expect a few little discomforts.

The ancient *Whist* rolled down, down, down, and jumped up, up, up; but mostly she went down, and while she was down the swooping seas piled over her. However, all right so far; an hour now since she had left the breakwater, and there she was still afloat. No telling always about those wheezy little wrecks of tugs. Baldwin looked out and back toward her stern, almost with pride. Going since the Civil War, she'd been, and still afloat. Must have been some little original virtues in her planks that pleased old Neptune, and so he passed her up. Maybe she'd never been caught in the open seas on a night like this; well, maybe not, but you betcher she wasn't afraid of it.

Straight out from the breakwater Baldwin kept her going. Slow, heavy, pounding work; and now two hours gone, and no light-ship yet. He swung her about, a ticklish feat, and paralleled the beach to the north, and just off the beach, after an hour of northing, he spied the distress signals—two, three, yes, and four big torches.

The countless white-plumed riders were charging by, but straight for the drifting lights, straight down the line of roaring troopers, Baldwin paraded his little *Whist*; and when he was near enough, "We'll heave you a line!" he hailed. "And in God's name get it, for there mayn't be a chance for a second one afore the breakers 'll get you."

He placed his mouth to the engine-room tube "Ho-o, Buddie. On deck with your line now."

"All right, Baldy." Harty turned to his working mate. "So long Pete, see you later."

"So long, son, and have a care on that open deck."

Harty climbed the iron ladder to the deck, shouldered his way through the wind-pressed door and onto the deck, and started aft.

It was cold. Under his thin suit of dungaree Harty was rolling in sweat. The winter wind whipped him like a cat-o'-nine-tails. He crept aft, coiled his heaving line and waited in the stern for the word. She was jumping so that to hold his feet on her open, icy deck aft, he was compelled to hook one hand to the towing bitts.

"Only time for one try, so don't let nothing go wrong. An' watch out for any of those big fellows comin' aboard, Bud," came Baldwin's last warning.

# V

On Light-ship 67, drifting broad onto the breakers, all hands were perched high in her rigging, safe above any stray seas; all but Nelson and Bowen, who were hanging on to her weather rail forward.

Bowen was the first to realize what the figure on the after end of the tug meant to them. "Heave for here!" he shouted, and Nelson, also awake to the situation, held up one of the torches for a mark.

Nearer and nearer butted the tug. "Stand by!" they heard the call from the forward end of her. Looking up, they could see the shadow against the pilot-house light. "By!" came the echo, and the man astern stepped on to her open quarter and balanced himself to heave.

A note in that answering voice caught Bowen's ear. "Say, Nelson, that's not one of the tug's regular crew!"

"I don't know. I don't t'ink, but he ban a foolish man," replied Nelson—"he should lash himself."

"Stand by with the line!" came again.

"By!" echoed tensely from astern.

"Ready!"

"All ready!"

"When she lifts! Now—w—"

From the top of a sea the line came whistling down to the

light-ship rail. "I'll take it," called Bowen, and, loosing his hold of the stay, he reached out and caught the flying line to his breast. "A good throw," he muttered, and hauled it in.

The hawser followed the heaving line, and Nelson and Bowen, with life-lines about them, bent the stubborn end of it around the windlass. It was heavy work, even for two men, on the tumbling, slippery deck, and, that done, they turned, anxiously, to see how the man in the stern of the tug was making out. He was there, back to, bending the thick stubborn bight about the towing bitts with slow, heavy motions. They saw one great sea break over him; and another: but when the seas were past there he was still working away.

"Won't he never mak' him fast?" wailed Nelson.

"Give him time," snapped Bowen. "He's doing well. He's got to do it right. If his end came loose, where would we be? Give him time."

Nelson looked significantly shoreward. "Time?"

"How's she coming, Bud?" they heard then.

"Bud? And that sounds like his voice, too," muttered Bowen.

"Wa-atch out!" Even with the roar of it Nelson and Bowen could hear the warning from the pilot-house to the man in the stern of the tug. A tremendous sea it was and the little *Whist* went over—over. Over until her side-lights were under. There she held for a moment, started to rise, and then a following sea caught her and overbore her and that time she rolled low enough to take salt water down her funnel.

She came back—after a time. Up, up, nobly; but when they

James Brendan Connolly

next looked from the light-ship they could see no figure in her stern. Bowen leaned far over the light-ship's rail. Nothing there, but he called to Nelson for the torch, and Nelson let it flare out over the water.

Then Bowen saw him. Almost under the bow of the light-ship he was, and the big torch was throwing a light like blood on his face. "It is him!" cried Bowen.

"Vat iss?" demanded the puzzled Nelson, and then under the light he, too, saw the face in the tossing waters.

Bowen, with a life-line under his arms was already over the side. But his plunge fell short. Nelson heard a sound as of a man's voice smothering, saw a hand raised and lowered, and then into the tossing blackness the lone figure was swept.

Nelson hauled Bowen aboard. When he recovered his first word was, "God, Nelson, that was Harty!"

"Harty, wass it? I don't know him, but he was one goot man."

The big hawser strained and groaned, chocks and bitts crooned their song of stress, the wind whistled its dirge, while out from the breakers the *Whist* hauled her tow.

To the wheel of the tug Baldwin glanced ahead and behind, pointed her nose for the breakwater, gave her four bells and the jingle, put his mouth to the tube, and answered, "Yes, Pete, that's right—'twas Bud went. And now it's up to you, son. Keep steam on her, and if the hawser holds and nothing else happens, she oughter stagger home all right."

Nothing more happened and the *Whist* staggered home. The morning light saw her safe to the Navy Yard with the light-ship moored alongside.

Bowen stepped from the light-ship to the tug. Up in the pilot-house he found Baldwin. The sailor was staring through a window, staring out to sea. Bowen waited.

Baldwin turned inboard at last. "I s'pose you're wonderin' how we knew. Well, 'twas Bud passed me the word, and more than that, 'twas Bud broke me out of as promisin' a little game as ever a man sat into. Chips? Enough to fill my service cap afore me, and not all white chips either. And he comes along and just the same as yanks me up by the collar an' says, 'You got to go!' and I had to. And of course where I go Pete goes."

"And a game thing, Baldwin."

"Game hell. It's our trade—Pete's and mine. But it wasn't Bud's. But he was bound to go. And when he went under, when I woke up to it he was gone, I looked out. The sea was still rolling up to the clouds. I sticks my head out the window to cool it, and to myself I says: If there was only somebody else in this watch so I could take five minutes off somewhere and lie down and cry. That's the way I felt about it. Yes, sir, if it wasn't for you fellows behind and good old Pete below, I believe I'd let everything go. Yes, sir, government property or no, I believe I'd a let the old *Whist* roll up on the beach and been glad to roll up with her. And Bud—" Baldwin came suddenly to a full stop and stared out to sea. After a time he turned and asked: "Did you see him when he went?"

"I did. And that time I grabbed for him and missed and he went by me, he half-turned and looked at me, and I thought he said, 'I never meant it.' Just that I heard, when the sea washed over him, and when he came up again he must've thought that I didn't understand, and he waved one arm. It was like he was saying 'Good-by!'—the way he did it. Yes, he was all right—Harty."

James Brendan Connolly

"You betcher he was all right. An' more than all right. As for that, it's a damn poor specimen' that ain't all right when it comes to a show-down. I've known Bud—I can't remember when I didn't know Bud Harty. And, Bowen, he was a better man than you or me. Bud always let you see the worst of himself, but you had to guess at the best of him. Bud, he sure could hate a man—but, son, he could like you a lot better than ever he hated you."

The two men sat and looked out to sea in silence. At last Baldwin, with a heavy sigh? stood up, and, reaching into a locker, brought forth a bottle and two glasses. "I s'pose we oughter try to forget it for awhile. This stuff here, it's against regulations havin' it aboard, but lots of things against regulations never hurt anybody. It was against regulations our takin' out the *Whist* last night. And when the commandant's back from leave I reckon I'll get mine. For you"—he laid a forefinger against the big rating badge on his coat sleeve—"that I've been shipmates with for fifteen years—off and on—I reckon will be detached. But I've been disrated before and we'll let that pass. But you an' me and Bud, we ain't been the best of friends we used to be since— well, you know when, but you're goin' to drink for him now the toast he wouldn't drink last night, but the toast that if he was here I know he'd drink now, for it's a sure thing that when he went into the breakers he didn't go out of hate. So you drink for Bud, and I'll drink for myself. Here's to you and yours, Bowen, your wife and the baby that's comin'—"

"And that baby—if it's a boy, Baldwin, I'll name after him."

"Will you? God, but he'll like that—Bud'll sure like that. And now, here you go—

"May the wind be always fair for you
Whatever the course you sail!"

"An' you an' me and all of us we'll be like we used to be, an' Bud'll like it, I know. An' now one to Bud himself. I know 'twill please him to see us doin' it. Here's to Buddie, Bowen. Is it a go?"

"Let her run!"

"Run it is, and a gale behind her—Christmas to Bud!"

# CAPTAIN BLAISE

## I

Two years now since Mr. Villard had come home, and not a soul on the plantation but believed that at last the new master had given up his mysterious voyages and was home to stay. But one day I had business in Savannah, and while there, hearing that the bark *Nereid* was in from the West African coast, I strolled down to the river front; and presently I was approached and addressed by the master of the *Nereid*, a seaman-like and rather shrewd-looking man who had a message for Mr. Villard, he said—from the West Coast.

"I am charged to ask him to pass the word to Captain Blaise," said the *Nereid's* master, "that an old friend of his lies low of fever into Momba. Captain Blaise would know who. We were putting out of Momba lagoon and I was standing by the rail, when a nigger came paddling up and whispered it. Like a breath of night air it was. 'Tell Master Captain that Ubbo bring the word,' said the nigger, and like another breath of wind he passed on. No more than that. A short, very stout, and very black nigger. And I was to pass the word to Mr. Villard, a gentleman of estate near Savannah, Georgia, and if you, sir, will attend to that, my part's done."

After my dinner in town was through with, I rode hard; but it was late night by the time I reached the manor-house. I found him sitting out under the moon, smoking a cheroot as usual, and he continued to smoke immovably for some minutes after I had delivered the message; but by and by he stood up and took to pacing the veranda, and presently, after his fashion, to speak his thoughts aloud.

"A hundred thousand acres and a thousand slaves, good, bad, and indifferent—surely a man does owe a little something to his manorial duties. At least, so all my highly respectable and well-established neighbors tell me. What do you say, Guy?"

"I never gave much thought to the matter, sir."

"No? Well, doubtless you will—some day. But d'y' remember Kingston Harbor, where the black boys dive through the green waters for the silver sixpenny pieces, and Kingston port, where the white roads and the white walls throw back the tropic sun so that it seems twice as hot as it really is—Kingston, Guy—in Jamaica, where the sun sets like a blood-orange salad in a purple dish? D'y' remember, Guy, and the day we were lying into Kingston in the *Bess* and the word came that my uncle was dead? Aye, you do; but don't you remember how he used to rail against me? To be sure—you were too young. And yet a good old uncle, who gave me never a mild word in his life but left me his all at death."

"And why shouldn't he, sir?"

"Why not? Aye, that is so. Why not? And yet he could have left it to anybody—to you, say."

"Why to me? Who am I?"

"What? Who are you?" He ceased his pacing. "That is so, Guy—who are you? You with the strange, quick blood writ so plain in your countenance that there—"

"Isn't it good blood, sir?"

"Aye, Guy, be sure it is good blood. But often have I thought how he would have stormed if—" He gazed curiously at me.

"If—"

"Aye, if—but no matter." He resumed his nervous pacing back and forth, back and forth, hands in pockets, head up, chin out, and face turned always toward the river, past the moss-hung cypress trees to the yellow Savannah flowing swiftly beyond. The salt tide-water made as far as Villard Landing, and when it was in full flood, as now, it brought the smell of the sea strongly with it.

"No matter that now, Guy. A good old soul, my uncle, d'y' see; but the blood was everything to him. And he put it in the bond and I am bound by it: that only the lawful issue, a son of the house, shall inherit. 'I'll have no strange derelict child inherit my estate.' His own words. So this fair estate, lacking lawful issue of my body or my old uncle's son—and he is dead—it goes out of the family. Oh, a stormy, intolerant, but well-meaning old uncle, who would have none of his property left to—Oh, but not that, Guy—no, no, lad." He laid a restraining hand on my shoulder. "No, no, lad, you must not take that to yourself; for you are, no fear, honest born."

"I've waited long for you to tell me even that. Won't you tell me more, sir?"

"Enough for now. But whatever my uncle thought or wished, here, Guy, is an estate to your hand to enjoy. What d'y' say, eh, to the life of a Southern gentleman on his plantation? A hundred thousand acres, a thousand slaves, a stable of the horses you love so, upland and river bottom to hunt, dancing, riding, balls, the city in winter. Is not that something better than the hard, uncertain sea, Guy?"

He had paused for my answer, but I made none. He was standing motionless, except for the backward toss of his head and the deep inhalation, three or four times, of the briny air from the flooding river. There was disappointment in his voice when he took up the talk again.

"Oh, Guy, between us two what a difference! I was born ashore, you at sea, and yet

> "'It's you for the back of a charging barb,
> And me for the deck of a heaving brig!'"

In a lower voice he repeated the couplet, and was plainly vastly pleased with it. "Faith, and I wonder is that my own, or something I read somewhere. Something of the lilt of a Scotch strathspey to 't, shouldn't you say? You know more of such things. What d'y' say—shall I claim that for my own, Guy?"

"You do, sir, and it's not Homer, nor Dante, nor Keats who will rise up to accuse you of plagiarism."

"Bah! You would no more allow me the merit of a poetic vein than—"

"Poetry, sir?"

"Poetry—why not?" and suddenly bending sidewise and forward, he essayed to obtain a fuller view of my face. And it is true that I was thinking of anything but poetry.

His face darkened as he gazed. "A hundred estates and plantations were nothing to me against—" he burst out passionately, but no further than that. He checked himself and went inside, and with no good-night going.

In the morning he was gone. I waited—one, two, three days, and then I went also—to Savannah, where I saw the *Bess*, but so altered that it needed a lifetime's intimacy to hail her in the stream. Her spars had been sent down and her name was now the *Triton*, and to her bow and stern was clamped the false work which left her with no more outward grace than any clumsy coaster; and by these signs I knew that Mr. Villard of Villard Manor would once more disappear and that Captain Blaise would soon again be sailing the *Dancing Bess* overseas.

Captain Blaise had not yet come aboard; but whatever ship he sailed the full run of that ship was mine, and I went into his cabin to wait for him.

It was after dark when he came over the side. It was always after dark when he boarded the *Bess* in home ports. His words were colder than his expression when he addressed me. "And where are you bound?"

"I don't know yet, sir."

"And why not?"

"You have not yet told me, sir, where you are going."

"Suppose it should be the West Coast and the old trade?"

"I'm sorry, sir, but even so I go."

"And leave all that good life you love so at the Manor?"

On his face was still the stern look. I could not stand it longer and I stepped closer to him. "You have not turned against me, sir?"

He softened at once. "Guy, Guy, don't mind me. I meant well. I thought you might prefer the shore to living on the sea."

"I do, sir, but when you are at sea it's at sea I'd rather be too, sir."

"Ah-h—" and when he looked at me like that it mattered not about his law-breaking—he was the bravest, finest man that ever sailed the trades. "Guy, my boy, if you'll have it so, why come along. And once more we'll cruise together; but you won't judge your commander too harshly, will you, Guy?"

We took the ebb down the river. Our papers read for a West India trading voyage, but we lingered not among the West Indies. Four weeks later we raised the Cape Verdes, and an islet rose like a castle from out of the mists. Abreast of a pebbled beach we came to anchor and waited.

## II

A boat scraped alongside, and the agent Rimmle came aboard. He came out to have a chat for old time's sake; and yet not so old either, he corrected, and would Captain Blaise come ashore and have a drink or two of good liquor? And Captain Blaise replied that he carried as good liquor in his locker as ever graced any sideboard ashore. And they dropped into the cabin, where I happened to be, and had a glass of wine and a word or two, and another glass and a few more words; and at last Rimmle put the question: Would Captain Blaise run one more draft?

Long ago, Captain Blaise promised me that there was to be no more slave-running, and as he never lied to me, I wondered now why he paused and pondered as if debating with himself. At last he looked up. "It doesn't pay any more, Rimmle."

"Well, in these days," observed Rimmle, "I don't blame you, with the bull-dogs of men-o'-war making it so hot."

We all had to smile at that, and Rimmle, seeing that Captain Blaise was not to be shamed into it, went on. "But suppose there was larger head-money than ever was paid before, Captain? And if half the head-money and the crew's pay were laid down in advance? For it is hard, as you have often said, Captain, that anything should happen to brave and willing men on such a cruise and they have neither profit nor safety of it." It was the old talk all over again, the agent urging him once more to take to slave-running, except that in other days Captain Blaise had displayed less patience.

The wineglasses had already been filled too frequently for me, and, pleading business, I had spread out a coast chart on the other end of the cabin table and was studying it, this by way of removing myself from a conversation which I saw was not to end with trading or slave-running.

This Rimmle was one of those who held Captain Blaise for a sort of idol. I had seen dozens of the kind before. Great hours for them when they could sit in with the famous Captain Blaise, and so now, with the agent bound to talk of the West Coast trade, lawful and otherwise, Captain Blaise was making but slow headway.

I was thinking of stepping up on deck to stretch my legs, when the conversation took a sudden shift. "Captain"— Rimmle put the question hesitatingly—"I thought I had seen the last of you. May I ask what lured you back?"

Captain Blaise had decanted another bottle and was viewing the rich-colored bubbles as he held the carafe up against the light. Such little things afforded him keen pleasure. He set the carafe down—softly—only to ask by way of reply: "Rimmle, what is it always brings men back?"

Rimmle laid his head to one side and nodded shrewdly. "As far as my experience goes, Captain, it is one of three things."

"And which of the three is my failing?" Captain Blaise was absently filling their glasses.

"M-m—It cannot be money—you never cared for that. You who have made fortunes and spent them as fast as you made them—no, it cannot be money. And then your newly acquired property in the States—"

"*My* newly acquired—What of that?"

"Why, the rumor is out that you fell heir to a great estate in

James Brendan Connolly

the States—on the banks of the Mississippi or the Ohio, or some outlandish name of a river in the States."

"Oh, a rumor! Go on."

"And as for the drink—it must be a great occasion, indeed, Captain, when you take more than is good for a man. And so—"

"We can never take too much drink in good company, Rimmle. And so drink up—here's health! And so you think it must be—" He smiled faintly at the agent. "And yet who should know better than you that all the gold I ever gave for a woman's favor would not suffice to keep the poorest of them in cambric handkerchiefs."

"As to that"—the agent pursed up his full moist lips—"it is true; the kind who looked for money were never your kind. And yet that kind sometimes cost men a hundred times more in the end."

Captain Blaise bent deferentially toward the agent. "You think that, Rimmle—truly?"

Rimmle bowed wisely.

Captain Blaise continued to regard him in the most friendly way, and yet with an air of doubt, as if debating how far to discuss matters of this kind with him. And then, leaning yet further forward and speaking rapidly, energetically: "And agreeing that it is so, who is it that ever regrets the price? D'y' think that I, even though I be what I be, that I—Why, Rimmle, even you who live to amass money"—Rimmle flushed—"even you have had your days when—To be sure you have had." Rimmle beamed. "And so, Rimmle, you can believe possibly that Captain Blaise may yet have his immortal hour, and cherish the hope none the less dearly in his heart because his head, from out the experience of bitter years, tells him that it can never be. And it may be that I go this time for neither money nor drink, nor anything else in which traders ashore or aship commonly bargain. But, hah, hah!"—he grinned suddenly, sardonically, at the agent. "Think of us, Rimmle, sitting in the cabin of a West Coast slaver and smuggler discoursing in this fashion—two gallant gentlemen who trade in human misery."

Ten years since Captain Blaise had done any slave-running, and Rimmle, who knew that, was slave-running still, and so he did not quite know how to take this outburst.

Neither did I. Where Captain Blaise was sincere and where talking for effect I could not have said; but surely he was moulding Rimmle like jelly; and now looking out from under his eyebrow at Rimmle, but his lips curved in a smile, he selected a cheroot and lit it, and lit another for Rimmle, who now smiled too. And cheroot followed cheroot, and story story, and drink drink, and the agent gurgled with joy of the intimacy. "What adventures you have had, Captain, and"— he blew a cloud to the cabin roof—"what stories!"

"Adventures? Stories?" Captain Blaise shrugged his shoulders. "Well enough, Rimmle, in their way. 'Tis true I can tell of blockades evaded and corvettes slipped, of customs officers bedevilled, of tricks on slow-tacking junks, and of dancing with creoles under the moon. But what is that? The heedless, unplanned adventuring of an irresponsible American captain. Now you, if you cared to talk, Rimmle, you, I warrant, could tell of big things, things which concern great people—of admirals and governors and what not; for you, it is well known, Rimmle, have your own bureau of information."

Rimmle chuckled. "It is true"—and then he paused. Captain

Blaise refilled their glasses. In courtly imitation of the Captain, Rimmle raised his and they drank.

Captain Blaise filled them up again. "Men like myself, Rimmle, are but pawns in this trading game. It is the people on the inside, the Governor of Momba and gentlemen like you, who direct the play."

Rimmle smacked his lips. "M-m—To be sure, the Governor of Momba—"

There was a half-hour of anecdotes of the Governor of Momba and his son before Cunningham's name was even mentioned; and when the question of him was slipped, so casually was it slipped that I, with senses astretch, did not realize that this must be the sick man at Momba—not until the next question was put.

"But there must have been something else, Rimmle, between the Governor and Cunningham?"

Now, had they been drinking ordinary wine or heavy ale, Rimmle might have held his own. But this was a rare vintage, a delicate bouquet meant for a finer breed than Rimmle. His tongue was still limber but his wits were fled. He was vain to display to the famous Captain Blaise his knowledge of secret affairs. "Yes, it is true, Captain, there was more than showed on the surface there. And that insult to Cunningham was no accident. No,"—he winked,—"not at all. He had insulted and shot men before, but he never knew that Cunningham was a professional duellist himself. None of us in Momba knew. Did you, Captain?"

"He was not." Captain Blaise banged his hand on the table. "He killed three men, yes; but bad men, and killed them in fair combat."

"Hm-m. A man to let alone that; but nothing of that was known—not then. However, he took the Governor's professional duellist out behind a row of palms one sunny morning and shot him—a beautiful bit of work. It was the vastest surprise—a shock. But a duel, lawful possibly in your country is not so in ours, Captain, and—"

"And is his daughter with him?"

"When she is not at the Governor's house—yes."

"What! Why there?"

"I don't know, unless it is the only house in that country where a young lady of her position—and then her beauty—"

"Under that old satrap's roof? But here, Rimmle, what is the Governor going to do with Cunningham?"

"Well, Captain, if it should happen that she will marry the Governor's son, why Cunningham might be allowed—you know how, Captain, ho! ho!—surely, to escape. Especially as nobody seems to mourn the man he shot. But when she seemed slow to fall in with their wishes, and as Cunningham had converted all his property into gold and diamonds and shipped them or hid them—though no search has unearthed them—preparatory to shooting the Governor's friend, why they grew suspicious and threatened to push matters. Cunningham was nominally under arrest always. And then he fell sick. How sick? Hard to say. But should he die, or be punished—imprisoned, say—for the duel, consider it. She is a beautiful girl, true, but human, and in time in that lonesome country where white gentlemen of social position are so scarce—! And, after all—the Governor of Momba's son and—"

"Rimmle"—Captain Blaise had stood up to look through an air port—"it's a fair wind for me. Shall I put you ashore?"

"Ashore? Why, yes, yes! Bless me, I've had quite a stay, haven't I? But if you care to try again, Captain, my friend Hassan is into Momba. He will be aboard, no fear. If you do business with him, Captain, why, draw on me, and it's money in my pocket."

"If I do business of that kind this cruise, Rimmle, I promise you I'll do it with Hassan."

"Thank you, Captain. Speedy voyage to you, and don't forget Hassan. Good-by, sir, to you."

Within the hour we sailed for Momba.

## III

A squadron of corvettes and sloops o' war put their glasses on us lazily as we neared Momba; but with our Dutch bow and stern, our stumpy spars, no self-respecting war-ship was bothering the *Triton*. They let us pass without so much as a hail.

Captain Blaise planned to cross Momba Bar that night, all the more surely to cross because the watchers ashore, seeing us hang on and off in the late afternoon, would probably report that we were waiting for morning. So we hauled her to in the dusk where, were it light, we would have seen, under its three fathom of water, Momba Bar lying white and smooth and quiet as a sanded deck as we passed on. With the wind coming low and light from the land that was; but were it a high wind and from the sea, there would be no going over that bar at night or any other time.

We slipped silently up the inside, the northerly passage, to the lagoon, and crept up the lagoon just as silently, but even as we were mooring the *Bess* in a nook at the head of the lagoon, a tall Arab was alongside. With him Captain Blaise and I went ashore in the ship's long-boat, and to avoid suspicion we took no arms. An hour of camp-fires and shadows under the trees we wasted then with this sharp trader Hassan. No printed calicoes, or brass rings, or looking-glasses for him, nor rum, he being a true believer. Nothing of that; but of gold paid into hand, and plenty of it there must be. And Captain Blaise, to allay suspicion, discussed matters hotly. Finally he agreed to the Arab's terms, and Hassan salaamed, and out under the open sky we went again.

"A proper villain, Guy, is that fellow. Did you ever see so

wonderfully cunning a smile? And in the morning I am to give him a draft on Rimmle! Sometimes I think there must be something infantile about me, strangers do pick me up for such an innocent at times. But in the morning, my shrewd Hassan—"

Naked feet padded beside us. "O Marster Carpt'n, Marster Carpt'n, suh—"

"You, Ubbo!"

"Yes, suh, Marster Carpt'n." It was a short, very stout, and very black negro who stood at attention before Captain Blaise.

"Where's your master?"

"Waitin', Carpt'n, suh. He sick, suh, but not so he die, he say, suh."

"And Miss Shiela?"

"Missy Shiela at de Governor's, suh. An' de missy know you come too, suh. I been watchin', suh, for long time. I see de ship, suh, an' I know you come over de bar, suh, to-night. An' I tell de marster, suh. An' marster waitin', an' Missy Shiela waitin', Marster Carpt'n, to take um away—to take um home, suh. He very sick, suh."

"After us, Ubbo."

We raced to where was the long-boat, screened under a bank. From her crew we took four good men and followed Ubbo.

The roof of a low building loomed above the jungle growth. Ubbo uttered a warning sound. We could hear the regular tread and presently a form showed around the corner of the house. It was a negro in uniform with a musket held carelessly over his shoulder.

Captain Blaise whispered to his men: "When he comes around again get him. No noise. Choke him first." The four sailors leaped together when next he appeared. In an instant almost it was done. They laid him on the ground, threw his musket into the brush, and we entered the building.

On a cot beside an open window, with a reading-lamp at his head, lay a tall man.

"Still alive, Gad," called Captain Blaise cheerily.

"Still alive, Blaise, and I reckon you did a neat job on that nigger guard, for all I heard was a little gurgling. Yes, still alive. Still alive, Blaise, thanks to Shiela's discrimination in the selection of the Governor's nourishing cordials, and thanks no less to my boy Ubbo's sleepless habits. But, old friend, you're none too soon. And don't waste any time in getting Shiela. She is still at the Governor's. I bade her stay there so they would not suspect. She has my sabre and duelling pistols with her, by the way. And she'll bear a hand with them, if need be. But who is this? Oh, this is Guy? I'm glad to know you, Guy."

A wreck of a tall, slender, handsome man, such a man he may have been in his prime as was Captain Blaise, but older. A sporting, reckless sort he may have been, but a man of manner and blood. Two of the crew bore him out, though one would have sufficed. "Ubbo will show you where the strong-box is, Blaise," he called on being borne off; and Ubbo led us through the thick jungle to where, under a rock over which a little water-fall played, a massive iron chest was buried. It took two stout men of the crew to handle it.

We saw Mr. Cunningham and the strong-box safely to the long-boat and then, with Ubbo, took station behind a hedge which bordered the Governor's grounds. There was much going on there—music and people strolling on the lawn. Captain Blaise pointed out the Governor to me, and his son, and bade me notice also fifteen or twenty barefooted but armed and uniformed negroes clustered between two rows of palms on the farther side of the lawn.

"We'll wait here, with the hedge to protect us," said Captain Blaise, and motioned to Ubbo. "Tell Miss Shiela that all's ready."

The negro slipped away. A short minute or so and Captain Blaise, who had been peering like a man on watch on a bad night, gripped me nervously. "Look, there she is!"

I looked. Never again would I have to be told to look. She was framed in a low window off the veranda. The Governor's son was now close behind her. Ubbo was standing on the lawn over near the musicians. We crept nearer. Turning, as if accidentally, she saw him and called to him. "How is your master, Ubbo, to-night?"

"Marster tell me to say he more happy to-night, Missy."

"Told you to say, Ubbo?"

"Yes, Missy, marster tell me to say."

"That's the signal, that sentence," whispered Captain Blaise.

"That's good. You can go, Ubbo." She smiled and chatted with the Governor's son then.

"She can't have interpreted the message aright," I panted.

"Because she did not leap into the air? Trust her—she's Gadsden Cunningham's, her own father's daughter."

In a few minutes she turned from the Governor's son to his father, from him to her ladyship, and from her without haste to some less distinguished member, and then in the most casual way in the world she strolled inside and from our sight.

Hardly a minute later the signal came: a firefly's flash five times together and three times repeated from the darkened upper story.

Ubbo was with us when the signal came. "Marster Carpt'n," he whispered, and handed him a sabre and a pair of duelling pistols. "Missy send um—an' dey loaded, both um, suh."

Captain Blaise, taking the sabre and passing me the pistols, ordered Ubbo to show the way.

We skirted the grounds and entered by a rear gate a garden where were all sorts of low-growing trees and high-growing shrubs to screen us as we drew near the rear veranda. I saw the white gown with the dark blue sash shining out from the shrubbery, and then the white and blue drew back. I would have leaped out on the path to follow, but a restraining hand was on my arm. "Wait, wait!" warned Captain Blaise.

It was the Governor and his son hurrying around the corner of the veranda. "I do not believe it," the Governor was saying. "I cannot credit it. That could not have been his ship which was reported still off the bar at dark—a clumsy galliot of a craft she was described; and besides, he would not dare, a whole squadron cruising within an hour's sail."

"But he is gone, and we found the guard was overpowered.

He does not even know how it happened, and his ship is even now moored in the lagoon, and he himself was with Hassan less than an hour ago. Hassan will say no more until he gets his advance money in the morning. But if we move now, he is caught like a rat in a trap. Why not send word to the squadron? The wind is from the sea again and increasing, and he cannot now recross the bar. If we could get hold of Cunningham's nigger, he'll know something. Perhaps we can make him tell. I've sent Charlotte to watch her." He ran to the corner of the veranda. "O Ubbo! Where in the devil is he? O Ubbo! Only a few minutes ago he was talking to her out front. Ubbo! O Ubbo!"

A mulatto girl came hurrying from within the house. "The American missy, I cannot find her. She not in her room, suh."

"What!" The fat old potentate almost jumped into the air.

But the son kept his head. "Not in her room, Charlotte? And Ubbo gone, too? Had I not better make the guard ready, sir?"

"Yes, yes; have the guard fall in."

They rushed around the corner of the veranda and we leaped into the lighted path. She, too, stepped out into the light. "Captain Blaise, oh, Captain Blaise, you don't know what courage you give us."

"Miss Shiela, you don't know what joy you give us."

"Still the same—but—but who is this?" she cried out like a surprised child. And then she seemed to know without being told, for "Oh-h, of course, this is Guy," she said, and smiled as if she had an hour to smile in, and gave me both hands.

"Come," said Captain Blaise abruptly. And down the rear path we hurried, and, circling the garden, entered the hedged path to the lagoon bank. All went well until we had to pass the walk which crossed our path from the front lawn. Here the light of a row of hanging lanterns fell on us.

And they saw us, the Governor and his son and the assembled guards, and came charging down across the lawn after us. But only two abreast could they come down the path.

"The boat is now but a hundred yards away, Miss Shiela," said Captain Blaise. "Guy will take you there. Go you, too, Ubbo." I took her hand and we raced to the bank, where I handed her to a place beside her father in the boat.

"And what are you going to do now?" she asked.

"I? Why, I must go back to help Captain Blaise."

"Oh, of course. But hurry back. And be careful, won't you?"

I ran up the path and was soon at his elbow. The column was crowding down the path, and so soon after coming from the bright light, possibly they could not see clearly when he swung. However it was, one groaned and slid down. He cut again and the head of the column stopped dead. "What's wrong?" came a voice, the Governor's. "What are you stopping for?"

"Won't you step this way and find out?" jeered Captain Blaise.

"What! only one man?"

The hedge lining the path was waist high, trimmed flat and

wide, but I never suspected what was coming until I saw the flash and felt the ting of the bullet on my cheek. "Drop!" warned Captain Blaise, but I had no mind to drop. I held one of Mr. Cunningham's duelling pistols ready for the next shot. I saw it and fired, to the right of and just above the flash. I had half seen how he had rested his elbow on the hedge and carried his head to one side when he fired that first shot. There was the crash of a body through the hedge. And then a silence.

"You got him, I think," said Captain Blaise.

I had been spun half around by the shock of something or other, and now I was once more facing the path squarely, and a thought of those red and blue and gold uniforms jammed in there gave me an idea. "Ready, men!" I called out. "Steady! Aim!—and be sure you fire low." No more than that, when in the Governor's guard there was the wildest scrambling and trampling to get to the rear.

And we left them falling rearward over each other and ran for the landing. The men were waiting on their oars. We leaped in, and Captain Blaise took the tiller ropes. "Give way!" he ordered.

Mr. Cunningham was lying on cushions in the bottom of the boat. I was still laughing, and he rolled his head, I thought, to look at me.

"Where did that skunk get you, Guy?" asked Captain Blaise.

"Why, I didn't know that he got me at all."

"Feel on your cheek."

There was blood, not much, trickling down my right cheek.

"You'd better attend to it."

"Yes, sir."

Warm fingers met mine. It was her silk scarf which she was pressing into my hand. I thrust it in my left breast, then took my own handkerchief and held it to my cheek.

I was chuckling to myself as I fancied the Governor's guards tumbling over each other in their retreat, when Captain Blaise broke in on me. "Aren't you laughing rather soon? You're not over your troubles yet."

"Troubles, sir? Troubles?" It was not at all like him, and his voice, too, was unwontedly harsh. "Troubles?" I almost laughed aloud again. He did not understand—I had only to lean forward to gaze into her eyes. I had only to reach out to clasp her hand. Troubles? Well, possibly so, but I smiled to myself in the dark.

IV

Ere we had fairly boarded the brig they were in chase of us. We could see lights flitting along the lagoon bank and hear the hallooing of native runners—the Governor's, we knew. And for every voice we heard and every light we saw, we knew that hidden back of the trees were a dozen or a score whom we could not hear or see. And on the black surface of the lagoon, paddling between us and the bank, as we worked the ship out, were noiseless men in canoes. We could not see them, but every few minutes a mysterious cry carried across the silent water, and the cry, we knew, was the word of our progress from the Governor's canoe-men to the messengers on the bank.

The lagoon emptied on the south into the Momba River, which twisted and turned like so many S's to the sea; on the north was the passage by which we had come, that which led to the sea by way of the bar. But there was to be no crossing of the bar for us that night. Ten miles inland we had smelled that sea-breeze and knew what it meant; but Captain Blaise, nevertheless, held on with the *Bess* toward the bar. We could hear their crews paddling off and shouting their messages of our progress until they were forced by the breakers to go ashore. Their parting triumphant shouts was their word of our sure intent to attempt the passage of the bar.

When all was quiet from their direction, we put back to the lagoon and headed for the river passage. But one ship of any size had ventured this river passage in a generation, and the planking of that one, the brig *Orion*, for years lay on the bank by way of a warning. "But the *Orion* was no *Dancing Bess*," commented Captain Blaise. Surely not, nor was her master a Captain Blaise.

The top spars of the *Bess* had been slung while we were ashore, and by this time we had also knocked away the ugly and hindering false work on bow and stern, so that with her lifting foreyards which would have done for a sloop-of-war, and on her driving fore and aft sails which could have served the mizzen of a two-thousand-ton bark, the *Bess* was now herself again. And she had need to be for the work before her.

Captain Blaise ordered her foresails brailed in to the mast to windward and her foreyards braced flat, this that she might sail closer to the wind.

Entering the narrow passage, she was held to the edge of the low but steep bank to windward; so close that where the low-lying reeds grew outward we could hear them swishing against her sides as we passed on.

Miss Cunningham, having seen her father comfortably established with Ubbo in the cabin, had come on deck, and Captain Blaise, busy though he was, took time to make her welcome. No need for him to boast of his seamanship—the whole coast could tell her that; but how often had a beautiful girl a chance to see the proof of it?

We followed the curve of the river's bank almost as the running stream itself. When we came to a sharp-jutting point, Captain Blaise himself, or me to the wheel, would let her fall away until her jib-boom lay over the opposite bank; and then, her sails well filled, it was shoot her up into the wind and past the point before us. Twenty times we had to weather a point of land in that fashion. Fill and shoot, fill and shoot, never a foot too soon, never a foot too late—it was a beautiful exhibition, and only a pity it was not light for her to see it better.

James Brendan Connolly

We were clear of the river at last; that is, we were in the river's V-shaped mouth, the delta. The south bank extended westerly, two miles or so farther to the sea, and the other bank north-westerly toward Momba Bar. Now we were able to get a view of the coast line, and northward to beyond the bar it was an almost unbroken line, we could see, of lights flaring from high points along the shore.

Captain Blaise hove her to until he should see a guiding rocket from the men-of-war which he knew were waiting. And presently one came, a blue and gold from due west, and another red and gold from the west-nor'-west, then a red and blue from north-west by west. Presently there was another, from abreast of and close in to the bar. And we knew there were more in waiting than had signalled. It was already a solid line across the mouth of the river.

If those ships guarding the river's mouth were only anchored, our problem would have been simplified; but they were constantly shifting, and as they showed no sailing lights, no telling where, after a signal flashed, they would fetch next up; and always, showing no signal-light whatever, would be the others guarding what they would like to have us mistake for an open passage in the dark.

Their sending up so many signals indicated a bewilderment as to our whereabouts. By this time they must have known ashore that we were not anchored inside the bar; and out to sea they must have known we had not foundered in the surf, and also by this time they had probably discovered that we were not in the lagoon.

"They will puzzle it out soon. Get your floating mines ready," ordered Captain Blaise. That was my work, and in anticipation of it I had knocked together two small rafts loaded with explosives and a large one with explosives and combustible stuff to burn brightly for half an hour or so.

"What does this mean?" Miss Cunningham was at Captain Blaise's elbow. She could not have asked a question more pleasing to him.

"It means that we are like a rat in a hole with half a dozen big cats guarding the exit. It is an acutely angled corner we are in, Miss Shiela, and a string of corvettes and sloops-of-war stretched, no knowing just where, across the narrow way out. So far they do not know we are here, but before long it is bound to occur to some of them that this is the *Dancing Bess* and that she has made the Momba River passage—and then they will crowd in and pounce on us. That is, if we don't get out before that."

"I see. I must go down and tell father. He's not worrying, but he wants to know what's going on."

He let the brigantine now run offshore, parallel with the southern bank, almost to the entrance. Then we doubled back on our course. As we came about he called, "Ready with your mines, Guy?"

"Ready, sir!"

"Let go!"

At the word over went the big raft. We sailed on for a quarter mile or so. "Let go!" Over went the second. A quarter mile farther and the third one went. Each mine had its time-fuse. In a very few minutes—the *Bess* was in by the corner of the delta again—the inshore mine exploded.

Following the noise and flame there was a quiet and a great darkness, and then from the southerly guard-ship a rocket, while from the shore burst forth new lights. If the surf had not been roaring, we knew that we could have heard those joyful yells from the watchers up that way. Everybody on the coast knew that the *Bess* carried two long-toms and no lack of ammunition for them. We could imagine their chuckling over our explosion.

Then came the second explosion, and five minutes later the third, and from her a great flame which continued to burn.

"Captain Blaise, I don't understand. Why that fire-raft?" Miss Shiela had reappeared on deck.

"Why? We are hoping that they will think that we are sailing out to sea in line of the explosions, just the opposite from what we are doing. If they will but think that that burning raft is our burning hold and that we are in distress, why— Look, Miss Shiela!"

Two war-ships were now signalling to each other recklessly, and their signals gave us a chance to reckon pretty nearly the course that they were steering. Both ships were headed straight for the burning raft. As they came on they uncovered their sailing lights, to prevent collision with each other, and watching these two ships' lights we might have picked a way directly between them. But if they happened to have another ship under cover in that apparently open water, we would be lost; and also, in passing between, we would have blocked off the lights of each in turn to the other and then they would have us.

Between the bar and the sailing lights of the inshore ship of the pair now bearing down, we knew there was another ship. We had seen her signal early, and that ship, we knew, would be held as close to the line of surf as her draught and the nerve of her commander would allow. Captain Blaise, reckoning where she should be, laid the *Bess's* course for her. "She's used to having a little loose water on her deck—let her have it again," he said, and at this time we had everything on her, and if I have not made any talk of it before, I'll say it now—the *Bess* could sail.

We were now heading about a point off the edge of the outer line of heavy breakers, and as the *Bess* had the least free-board of any ship of her size sailing the trades, she was soon carrying on her deck her full allowance of loose water. Amidships, when she lay quietly to anchor, a long-armed man could lean over her rail and all but touch his fingers in the sea. Now, with the wind beam, over her lee rail amidships the heavy seas mounted. On the high quarter-deck we had only to hang onto the weather-rail, but the men stationed amidships had to watch sharp to keep from being swept overboard.

She was long and lean. It was her depth, and not her beam, which had held the *Bess* from capsizing in many a blow. Ten years Captain Blaise had had her, and in those ten years, whether in sport or need, he had not spared her. She was long and lean, and as loose forward as an old market basket.

Loose and lean and low, she was wiggling like a black snake through the white-topped seas. We had men in our foretop looking for the guard-ship, and because they knew almost exactly where to look for her, we saw her in time and swung the *Bess* inside her, yet closer to the breakers. Her big bulk piled toward us, her great sails reached up in clouds— shadows of clouds. Past our bow, past our waist, past our quarter. We could pick the painted ports and the protruding black muzzles of her port battery as she passed, a huge shapeless shadow racing one way, and we going the other way like some long, sinuous, black devil of a creature streaking through a white-bedded darkness.

We were by before they were alive to it. A voice, another voice, a hundred voices, and then we saw her green sidelight swing in a great arc; but long before then we were away on the other tack, and so when her broadside belched (and there was metal sufficient to blow us out of water), we were half a mile away and leaping like a black hound to the westward.

A score of rockets followed the broadside. Captain Blaise glanced astern, then ahead, aloft, and from there to the swinging hull beneath him. He started to hum a tune, but broke it off, to recite:

"O the woe of wily Hassan
When they break the tragic news!"

And from that he turned to Miss Cunningham with a joyous, "And what d'y' think of it all?"

She looked her answer, with her head held high and breathing deeply.

"And the *Dancing Bess*, isn't she a little jewel of a ship? Something to love? Aye, she is. And you had no fear?"

"Fear!" Her laughter rang out. "When father went below, he said, 'Fear nothing. If Captain Blaise gets caught, there's no help for it—it's fate.'"

And I knew he was satisfied. She had seen him on the quarter of his own ship and he playing the game at which, the *Bess* under his *feet*, no living man could beat him; and in playing it he had brought her father and herself to freedom. It was for such moments he lived.

The night was fading. We could now see things close by. He took her hand and patted it. "Go below, child, and sleep in peace. You're headed for home. Look at her slipping through the white-topped seas, and when she lays down to her work—there's nothing ever saw the African coast can over-haul us. No, nothing that ever leaped the belted trades can hold her now, not the *Bess*—while her gear's sound and she's all the wind she craves for."

"I believe you, Captain." She looked over the roaring side. Long and loose and lean, she was lengthening out like a quarter-horse, and he was singing, but with a puzzling savageness of tone:

"Roll, you hunted slaver
Roll your battened hatches down—"

"Good-night, Captain." She turned to me. She was pale, but 'twas the pallor of enduring bravery. There was no paling of her dark eyes. Even darker were they now. "Good-night—" She hesitated. "Good-night, Guy."

"Good-night, Miss Shiela," and I handed her down the companion-way. At the foot of the stairs she looked up and whispered, "You must take care of that wound, Guy." And I answered, "No fear," and then her face seemed to melt away in a mist under the cabin lamp.

Astern of us the dawn leaped up. It had been black night; in a moment, almost, it was light again. I remembered what Captain Blaise had said of a sunset in Jamaica; but here it was the other way about—a purple, round-rimmed dish, and from a segment of it the blood-red salad of a sun upleaping. And pictured clouds rolling up above the blood-red. And against the splashes of the sun the tall palm-trees. And in the new light the signal flambeaux paling. And the white spray of the bar tossing high, and across the spray the white-belted squadron tacking and filling futilely.

I grew cold and wondered what was wrong. I dimly saw Captain Blaise come running to me. "Guy! Guy!" he called. I remember also myself saying, "Nothing wrong with me, sir—and no harm if there is. It's sunrise on the Slave Coast and the *Dancing Bess* she's homeward bound!"

# V

The blue-belted Trades! Day and day, week and week, the little curly, white-headed seas, the unspecked blue sky, and the ceaseless caress of the pursuing wind. No yard nor sail, never a bowline, sheet, or halyard to be handled, and the *Bess* bounding ever ahead. Beauty, peace, and a leaping log—could the sea bring greater joy?

Captain Blaise had located the bullet—the second shot it must have been—which had lodged under my right shoulder and cut it out. We were nearing home, and the fever was now gone from me, but I was not yet able to take my part on deck. "Perhaps to-morrow," she had said. And to-morrow was come, and I lay there thinking, and at times trying to write.

She had left me alone for a while. Her father had called her to hear another of the Captain's stories. Through the cabin skylight I could see her, or at least the curve of her chin, and her tanned throat and one shoulder pressing inward under the skylight shutters. Her face was turned toward Captain Blaise, whose head and shoulders, he pacing and turning on the quarter, came regularly within range. But she was not forgetting me; every few minutes she thrust her head beneath the raised skylight hatches and looked down to see that I wanted for nothing, and always she smiled.

I was propped up in an easy chair. Up to two days back I had been on a cot. Mr. Cunningham had improved so rapidly that for more than a week now he had been allowed on deck, and there he was now, as I said, listening with his daughter to the tales of Captain Blaise. His laughter and her breaths of suspense, I could hear the one and feel the other.

I took up my pad of paper and resumed my writing. And reviewing my writing, I had to smile at myself, even as I used to smile at Captain Blaise when he would submit his couplets or quatrains for my judgment. He might marshal off-hand a stanza or two of his vagabond thoughts, but here was I carefully composing with pencil and paper, and had been for a week now.

I had never been ill before, never for five minutes. And this illness had driven me to a strange introspection. There had been time to think. I smiled at Captain Blaise's amateurish rhymings on the veranda of the manor-house. I had condemned him in my own mind for this death or that death of his irregular career; on that last night on the veranda I had even allowed him to read my thoughts of such matters. And now I could not recollect of his having ever killed or maimed except in defence of his life or property; and yet that night in Momba I had shot, caring not whether I killed or no. Self-defence? At the instant of shooting I had thought, had almost spoken it aloud: "There! There's for a channel to let the starlight into your unclean brain." Self-defence? Tish! The Governor's son desired, possibly loved in his way, a girl that I had known no longer than I knew him, and there it was—I loved her, too! Captain Blaise himself had probably never killed on less provocation; and meditating on his emotional side, on his many provocations, his life-long environment, I had to concede that the Captain Blaise I condemned was a less guilty man than I.

This, as I was beginning to see, was but an argument with myself for a final dismissal of my old life. Surely I should be ashamed to admit that in such fashion was my brain trying to fool my soul; but so it was. Remorse? I should have been worn with remorse, I know; but I was not. I tried to grieve for my hasty judgment of Captain Blaise: and I did. But for the Governor's son, not a qualm. I, too, like Captain Blaise, had become the creature of hereditary instincts and overpowering emotion. Never in all my life before had I thought that any sin or shortcoming of mine was ever to be anybody's business but my own. My salvation lay in the future, which, now that my conscience was awakened, I would have only myself to censure if it did not become what I wished.

But these serious thoughts were of previous days. This morning I was to have some little composition ready for her when she came down. I turned to my paper and pencil and began to write. But thoughts, such thoughts as I conceived would please her, came slowly. My new conscience or it may have been the voices of the quarter-deck,—her father's questions, Captain Blaise's muffled answers, her exclamations of delight and wonder,—all these diverted me. In despair I tried to catch, as I usually could, what Captain Blaise was saying, but to-day he spoke in so low a tone that I could not quite.

Ubbo came down for a chart, a particular chart which Captain Blaise has always kept apart from the others. I pointed out to him where he would find it. And my eye followed his figure up the cabin steps. In a sailor's costume Ubbo was proud but perspiring, though devotion shone out in every drop of perspiration.

Through the skylight I saw Captain Blaise take the chart from Ubbo, unroll and scan it. "I was right. Yes, here's the spot." He was addressing Shiela. "In red ink, see, and here's about where we are now—not ten miles from here, north by east."

Shiela was bending over the chart when "Sail-ho!" rang out from the lookout in the foretop. He had a grand voice, that man on watch.

With one hand Captain Blaise held the chart so Shiela still could read it; with the other he reached through the skylight opening for his long glass. After a long look I saw that he did not resume his narrative. By that I knew that the stranger was troubling him.

Shiela came below to see me. The traces of tears were in her eyes.

"It's a large ship to the northward," she said. "From something Captain Blaise whispered to father it may be a man-o'-war, though I hope not. But what have you done since I've been gone? You mustn't feel put out when I have to go on deck. It's an ungrateful girl, you know, who is not courteous to her host, especially when that host is Captain Blaise. Think what father and I owe him! And what a wonderfully interesting man he is! And what adventures he has had!"

"But what made you cry?"

"Captain Blaise was telling of a happening on this very spot almost. It was a ship from Cadiz for Savannah. She had taken fire. He picked up among others three people lashed to some pieces of wreckage—a man, a woman, and their baby. She was dead and he dying. He did die later aboard his ship, the predecessor of the *Bess*. The baby lived. Do you recall the story?"

"No, he never told me that one. And the baby?"

"The father had practically supported the baby in the water for four days—the baby was less than a year old—and the mother had nursed him till she died. For two days, the man said, with nothing to eat herself. She and he, they had practically killed themselves for the baby boy. She was a

Spanish woman—a lady. The father died aboard Captain Blaise's ship. He was an American who had married abroad without consulting his father, and the old gentleman made such a fuss about it that the young man had stayed away— intended to remain away and renounce his heritage; but at last the father had sent for him, and he was then on his way home. But you should have heard Captain Blaise tell it. He made us feel that mother's love for her baby, that mother who was dead before he picked her up, and made us feel, too, what a man the father was. What an actor he is! I tried not to cry, but I did. But let me see—what have you there?"

I showed her some things. She picked up the nearest and read it aloud:

"I was walking down the glen—
O my heart!—on a summer's day.
He passed me by, my gentleman—
Would I had never seen the day!

"True love can neither hate nor scorn,
And ne'er will true love pass away.
And his hair was silk as tasselled corn,
My heart alack—that summer's day!

"Oh, he wore plumes in his broad hat
And jewelled buckles on his shoon,
And O, the sparkle in his eye!
And yet his love could die so soon!"

"H-m. Suggests satin breeches and hair-powder, men who could navigate a ball-room floor more safely than the Trades, doesn't it? Wherever did you get such notions?"

I showed her a volume, one of Captain Blaise's, an anthology of the Elizabethan and Restoration poets. "I was trying to write like one of 'em," I explained. "And I thought it was pretty good."

"I don't—a poor girl believing that Heaven made her kind for the high people's pleasure. No, I don't like that. And 'hair as silk as tasselled corn!' Do you like tasselled corn hair?"

"Why, no—in a man. But my own being black—"

"Hush! Black's best. No, you're not intended for that kind of writing."

"But here—listen:"

> "'True love can neither hate nor scorn,
> And ne'er will true love pass away.'"

"Don't you like that?"

"Something like it's been said so often. Why don't you put it in your own words?" She took up another sheet. "What's this about?"

"That's about a day and night at sea—a fine day in the Trades, such a day as to-day—and last night."

"It *was* a beautiful moon last night, wasn't it?" And she read to herself. Coming to the last stanza, she read aloud, unconsciously I think:

> "The stars gleamed out of a purple light,
> The moon trembled wide on the sea;
> The Western Ocean smiled that night—
> Sweetheart, 'twas a dream of thee!"

She paused. "But the ocean doesn't smile." "But it does.

Smiles and frowns, and roars and coos, and coaxes and threatens, and strikes and caresses, and leaps and rolls—and so many other things. I've seen it. And Captain Blaise will tell you the same."

She looked strangely at me. In the deep sea I had seen, at times, that deep dark blue of her eyes—ultramarine, they call it; but hers softer. I almost told her so, but I was afraid.

She looked away and repeated softly:

"'The Western Ocean smiled that night—Sweetheart,
'twas a dream of thee!'"

It's pretty, but more like what men who cruise for pleasure would write. You're a sailor—have taken a sailor's chances. Why don't you write like a sailor? It is a sad sea, a terrible sea, despite all your beautiful blue Trades. Why don't you write of the tragic sea?"

"I knew that some time you would say something like that. I've seen it in your eyes before."

"You have?"

"Why, many times. And so, here." And from between the pages of Captain Blaise's book of verse I drew another sheet. At that time I would have been ashamed to let anybody else see these things, but I did not mind her. "Here," I said, "is one I felt. One night in the Caribbean we were caught in a tornado, and we thought—Captain Blaise said afterward he thought so too—that we had stood our last watch. And at the height of it—we could do nothing but stand by—one of the crew, a young fellow—I was only sixteen years old myself then—said to me, 'Oh, Master Guy, what will she say when she hears?' He meant his young wife. He'd been married just before we put out, and she'd come down to the ship to see him off. So listen:

> "'The spray, most-like, was in my eyes,
> He waved his hand to me—
> The wind it blew a gale that day
> When he sailed out to sea.'"

"Ah-h!" She leaned closer.

"It *was* a gale the day we put out. We had to get out—in Charleston Harbor it was—and they were hot after us—gale or no gale, Captain Blaise put out. I'm trying to imagine what she would think when she heard.

> "'And now no spray is in my eyes,
> No hand is waved to me—
> But all the gales of time shall blow
> Ere he comes back from sea!'"

"And she a bride! Oh-h, the poor girl!" She had leaned over my shoulder to read it for herself, and her breath was on my cheek.

"That is why, if I had—a wife, I should dread the sea."

"And that is why a woman—But how long have you been writing poetry?"

"Poetry? Or rhyme? Never before the day I saw you."

"But when did such ideas before take hold of you?"

"The other night I was lying here looking up, and after a time the moon shone through onto my cot, and you crossed its path—you had given me my night cup and I had pretended to be asleep; and I thought of you looking out on the moonlit sea and I got to wondering what you were thinking of. And I remembered a thousand such moonlit nights when you were not there. And I thought what a difference it would have made had you been there, and so when I say

"'The Western Ocean smiled that night—Sweetheart, 'twas a dream of thee!'"

"you must not smile. I meant it; for if the ocean smiles and whispers and makes men dream of—"

"Oh-h!" her head had settled and now her cheek was against mine. "Go on," she said softly.

"It made me dream of her that was never more than a dream-woman until I saw you. No longer a dream—not after you stepped out onto the veranda of the Governor's house that night in Momba. I knew it again when, looking out from the shrubbery in the garden, you looked at me and said, 'And who is this?' And I knew it when with you in the long-boat, when I wanted to reach out and take your hand—"

"And why didn't you? I knew you were weak from your wound, and it would have been a charity in me to cheer you up."

"Divine charity—but I was not weak—not from any wound. I had not the courage. A sailor may shape his course by a star, but that does not mean that he ever thinks of reaching up and trying to grasp it."

"And you've heard the sea whisper, too, Guy?"

"Many a time. In the night mostly—in the mid-watch, when it's quietest. I've leant over the rail and heard it whisper up to me. People laugh at that, but they know nothing of the sea. And the day, or the night, comes to some men, when she whispers up to him and beckons with her wide arms and on her deep bosom offers to pillow him, and weary of the wrong-doing, mostly it's wrong-doing, or despair, when men hear it—weary, weary to death, they are glad to—"

"No, no—no, Guy—you must never go like that!"

"But when a man's alone?"

She rested her chin on my shoulder, she reached a hand down to mine. "You will not be alone, dear—never, never again."

A voice from above recalled me. "Guy! O Guy! If you can make shift to come on deck, you would do well. We are in close quarters and like to be yet closer."

I looked up, not in full time, but in time to catch a glint of his eyes. Pain in his voice, suffering in his eyes—never till that moment did it come to me that this whole cruise had been but a wooing of Shiela Cunningham. And I, who owed him everything in life, I had stood in his way. And even with Shiela there my heart ached for him.

# VI

When I made the deck I saw that off each beam was an American frigate, and ahead was the land—the coast of Georgia.

No doubt of what they were after. The *Bess* was a much-desired prize, and known as far as a long glass could shape her lines or pick her rig. "But there is yet time, sir," I suggested, "to put about, run between them, and escape to the open sea."

"There *is* time," he answered curtly. He had not looked fairly at me since I came on deck. "But I am going to land our passengers, and without risk of their capture."

I thought that he had in mind to hold up for the mouth of the Savannah River, and run on up the river to the city. He could do that, though it would mean the final abandonment of the brigantine and, most likely, the identification of Captain Blaise with Mr. Villard of Villard Manor.

Though these were two fast-sailing frigates, we were outrunning them, not rapidly, but sufficiently to make it certain, while yet we were a mile offshore, that we would easily make the river entrance, if such was his intention. But evidently not so, for he now ordered the gig ready for lowering and had Mr. Cunningham's strong-box brought on deck.

"Shall I also take that package you spoke of?" asked Mr. Cunningham.

"Surely. It is ready in my room." And he went below and came up with it, a great beribboned and bewaxed envelope, saying, "Deliver it when the time comes, Gad. Or wait, let Miss Shiela do it," and handed it to her instead.

She blushed vividly and placed it in her portmanteau. "Thank you, sir," she said.

I had difficulty in keeping my eyes off her, even though I was again acting as first officer of the *Bess*, and my first duty just now was to keep an eye on the two ships and render judgment as to their intentions.

"That fellow to the south seems to have decided to bid up for the Savannah River entrance on the next tack, sir," I reported.

"Yes." He was busy with the Cunninghams and spoke absently, though it was also likely that he saw better than I did what the man-o'-war would be at. "That's good. Let him stretch that tack all he pleases."

"Then we are not to stand in yet, sir?"

"Not yet, not till the northerly fellow comes into stays. We'll tack then, but not for the river."

The frigate to the north came into the wind, and as she did we wore ship and stood up; not a great divergence from our old course, but enough to make them think we might yet come about and try for the open sea. The ship to the south of us took notice then and came into the wind, and while they were hanging there we eased off and headed straight for the white beach to the north of the river.

Both ships, after the loss of some minutes in irons, once more filled their sails and made straight for our wake. Now they seemed to say, "Another half-mile on that leg and you won't make either the river or the open water."

As we neared the white shore an inlet opened up before us. "There's something, Gad, no chart will show you," observed Captain Blaise. "There's a channel, carved round an island since the last government chart was plotted. They're doing some puzzling aboard those war-dogs now, I'll warrant. They're thinking we're going to beach and abandon her, I'll wager."

The *Bess* held straight on. It was an inlet which went on for half a mile or so before turning obliquely to the north. It was wide and deep enough for us—plenty; but a frigate's tonnage would have her troubles, if she tried to follow.

We weathered the first bend. Before us was another bend. I remembered now that years before, when I was a little fellow, I had come in and out of this very place. I began to recollect dimly that after a while it came to the open sea again some miles to the north.

We were almost to the other entrance when he ordered the *Bess* hove-to and the gig lowered. Into it went the strong-box and the Cunninghams and Ubbo. "And you, too, Guy." He was looking at me queerly. "Mr. Cunningham is still weak. And Shiela, brave as she is, is only a woman—a girl. Will you see that they are landed safely? That is the main shore. See that their luggage is carried up to the top of that hill. In the creek beyond that hill is an old darky who will take them in his little sharpie by way of a back river to Savannah."

And so I was to have a few more minutes with her. At the gangway he took my hand and held it while he said, "You're weak yet—don't hurry. Those two frigates won't follow us in here." I remember wondering why only Ubbo was in the boat besides ourselves; but I was too excited at the thought of so soon landing her to think logically. As I was about to step into the gig he whispered, "Take good care of her, won't you, Guy?"

"Why, of course, sir."

"That's the boy." He pressed my hand.

We shoved off, Ubbo rowing. In two minutes we were on the beach. I was still too weak to be of much help to Ubbo with the strong-box, and so it took us some time to get it to the top of the hill. We covered it with sand and brush to guard against a possible landing party from the frigates. Shiela's idea that was, and it delayed us another few minutes.

I turned to go. Shiela, she was nervous too, but smiling. "Shiela—"

"You're not going back to the ship?"

"But I must—I must."

"No, you're not—and you must not. Here." She had taken the bewaxed and beribboned package from her little handbag. It was addressed to "Guy Villard, Esq., Villard Manor, Chatham County, Ga."

"But who is he?"

"Who is he? Who are you?"

"Guy Blaise."

"No, you're not. Open it and read. Or wait, let me read it."

And it is true that not till then did I suspect. I thought that I might have been his son, or the son of some wild friend, born of a marriage on the West Coast or other foreign parts. But of this thing I never had a suspicion.

I was the baby boy picked up in the wreckage of the burning ship. There were the marriage certificates of my father and mother, and the title deeds to the Villard estate. It had been a great temptation—he the next of kin, my father's cousin, and no one knowing. And he, too, feared the strange blood. But watching my growth, he had come to love me, and wanted me to love him, and feared my contempt if I should learn. All this was explained in a letter in a small envelope, written recently and hastily. Together, Shiela and I, we finished the reading of it:

> Though I'm not so sure now that you shouldn't thank me for withholding your inheritance until the quality of your manhood was assured. It is true that I imperilled your mortal body a score of times, but through fifty-score weeks I nurtured your immortal soul, Guy.
>
> And now I am going back to that sea wherein I expect to find rest at the last, and let my friends make no mourning over it, Guy. 'Tis a beautiful clean grave, no mould nor crawling worms there. But if it be that the sea will have none of me, and the metalled war-dogs drive me, and spar-shattered and hull-battered I make a run of it to harbor in my old age, I shall come in full confidence of a mooring under your roof, Guy. And who knows that I won't be worth my salt there?
>
> You have won her, Guy. I knew you would from that night in Momba when you sat in the stern sheets and laughed. 'Twas in your laugh that night, though you did not suspect it. But I know. The tides of youth were surging in you. Beauty, wit, and courage—with these in

any man I will measure sword; but the tides of youth are of eternal power.

I should like to dance your children on my knee, Guy, and lull the songs of the sea into their little ears. I've a fine collection by now, Guy—you've no idea—ringing chanties to get a ship under way, and roaring staves of the High Barbaree, ballads of the gale, and lullabies of west winds and summer nights. And your children, Guy, will grow up none the less brave gentlemen and fine ladies for the strengthening salt of the sea in their blood and the clearing whiff of the gale in their brains. So a fair, fair Trade to you and Shiela—the fair warm Trades which kiss even as they bear us on—and do not forget the tides of youth are flooding for you. Take them and let them bear you on to happiness and wisdom.

I felt weak and dizzy, but I rose to my feet and started down the hill. Shiela caught me and held me. "Look!" She was pointing out to sea.

There she was, the *Dancing Bess*, holding a taut bowline to the eastward. And there were the two frigates, but they might as well have been chasing a star.

"Look!" She handed me the glasses. I looked and saw her ensign dipping. I took off my hat and waved it, hoping that with his long glass he could see. He must have seen, for the ensign dipped three times again, and from the long-tom in her waist shot out a puff of smoke. We waited for the sound of it. It came.

Farewell that meant. I watched her till her great foresail was no larger than a toy ship's. Then I sat down and cried, and had no care that the negro slave and servant, Ubbo, saw me.

Mr. Cunningham came and sat beside me. "Guy," he said, "don't worry about him. He'll come through all right. He has great qualities in him."

"He's good, too—too good to me."

"Great and good," exclaimed Shiela. "He could love and was lovable. And what's all your greatness to that?"

It may be that she who knew him least understood him best. She was crying too.

When her great square foresails were no more than a gull's wing on the hazy horizon we waved her a last salute. Then we made our way to the creek and sailed up Back River, past Savannah, and on to Villard Landing. And hand in hand Shiela and I walked up between the row of moss-hung cypress trees to the manor-house and—Home.

# DON QUIXOTE KIERAN, PUMP-MAN

## I

He came into the outer office of the great oil company, and through the half-open door of his private office the new superintendent observed the stimulating style of his entrance. Looking for work, no doubt of that, but not looking like a man who was apologizing for it; and that in itself was a joy to the new official.

No hesitating—"Please, sir, who is the gentleman,"—no timid waiting on any languid understrapper's pleasure for this one. A short pause; his dark eyes swept the room from wall to wall; his black head bent respectfully and not without appreciation toward the pretty stenographer; and then, before the leisurely office boy thought it time to rise and ask what he wanted, he was at the rail-gate. And when the gate did not at once swing open, he stepped lightly over it; and singling out from all the furtively smiling males the head clerk, he charged straight across the floor toward that important person's desk.

And the head clerk, who was also the head wit, took a peek at him coming, and very politely said, "Pray be seated?" And, also very politely, "From whence came you and what willst thou?"

The chuckling heads bobbed above the rows of desks. The head clerk himself had to gaze window-ward to smother his smile.

"Gramercy, kind sir—"

"Gramercy? Eh, what? Gramercy?"

"Gramercy Park—you know where Gramercy Park is? Or didn't you ask me where I came from?"

"Oh-h-Oh-h, yes."

"Of course, and I'm after a berth as pump-man on your oil ship sailing to-day for the Gulf."

"And what, may I ask, do you know of our class of ships?"

"Only what I've heard—most modern oil-tankers afloat, and I'd like to try one out—and sail the Gulf again, if you'll give me the chance."

"M-m—what are your qualifications?"

"Qualifications? For pump-man on an oil-tanker?"

"Pump-man—yes. And on an oil-tanker. I'm not hiring a rough rider, or a policeman, or an aeroplanist—just a pump-man."

Through his open door the new superintendent caught the wink which his head clerk directed at the second clerk. And caught it so easily that the thought came to him that to share in the humor of the head clerk may have been one of the recreations of his predecessor.

"What has been your experience with marine machinery? What were your last three or four places?"

"My last three or four? Well, one was being second-assistant engineer on a government collier from the Philippines with a denaturalized skipper, and for purser a slick up-state New Yorker; and both of 'em at the old game—grafting off the grub allowance. And that's bad."

"Eh—what's bad?"

"Grafting off the grub. Men quit a ship for poor grub quicker than they do for poor pay. For a week after we hit San Francisco I didn't get any further away from the dining-room of the nearest hotel—well, than"—he turned suddenly—"than that fellow there is from here—that fat, knock-kneed chap there who seems to have so much to say about me." The second clerk, who was also the second head wit, yelped like a suddenly squelched concertina and was quiet.

The new-comer, after a grave study of the knock-kneed one's person, resumed his narrative. "Then oiler on a cattle steamer. Ever been on a cattleman?"

"Huh!" The head clerk was scowling tremendously.

"No? You ought to try one sometime. Some are all right, but some are"—he looked sidewise at the stenographer—"well, no matter. One night two sweet-tempered, light-comp-lexioned coal-passers hit me together, one with a shovel, the other with a slice-bar. It was the slice-bar, I think, that got me. I didn't see it coming—or going either—but probably it was the slice-bar." He bent his neck and parted the heavy black hair. A white welt showed through the hair.

The head clerk flashed an enlightening wink toward the

second head clerk; but the second clerk, seeming to be less interested than formerly, the wink was flashed over to the stenographer; but as she, too, seemed preoccupied, the head clerk, rather less buoyantly, inquired, "And what did you do to the two coal-passers?"

"For what I did to them—after I came to—I had to jump into the Mersey and swim ashore. British justice, you know. Inflexible!—especially to a foreigner who cracks a couple of domestic skulls."

"And then?"

"English navy."

The head clerk began to flash again. "And what, may I arsk, was wrong—haw, haw!—wrong with the sair-vice?"

The new-comer almost smiled. "The grub, for one thing. My word, the grub! Blow me for a bleedin' Dutchman, but I couldn't go the grub; y'know. An' a man's a man, with a man's 'eart an' feelin's, even if 'e's nowt but a sailor, ain't he now? You're bloody well right 'e is. But I took a fall out of a submarine before I quit. 'Ave you seen 'em—the little black chaps wot goes down an' comes up like bloomin' little poppusses?"

The head clerk unobtrusively relapsed into his every-day speech. "And weren't they exciting enough for you?"

"The one I was in was. But you see, sir, she sunk one d'y an' all 'ands with 'er."

"Evidently you didn't sink with her. Or maybe you're amphibious?"

"Amphibious? Oh, I s'y now, but that's a good one. My word! But you was jokin', wasn't you, sir? Of course you was. No, hi 'appened to be ashore that d'y, sir. A mistike, sir, you see. But such a turn of wit as you 'ave, sir!"

The head clerk suddenly shed his smile. "Never mind about my wit. What then? You deserted?"

"Not hexactly, sir. I was hofficially dead, sir. Ought to 'ave been at the bottom, sir. O yes, sir. An' when I comes along an' declares myself, they said I was a himposter—himposin' on honest people, sir—mikin' a 'ero o' myself, sir, as bein' the only man to escipe, sir. An' so I comes aw'y—in a 'urry, sir. But if I was married, sir, my widow could 'ave 'ad 'er pension, sir. Yes, sir, 'er pension."

"That's a queer thing."

"Do you think so, sir?"

The head clerk unexpectedly bounced up and down in his chair. "See here, don't imagine you can make fun of me, because you can't."

"Now don't get grouchy. When you pull out a cigar and start to light it, don't blame a man looking on if he thinks you don't object to smoking. Anyhow, after my navy experience I came back home and landed on an East River tug. Said I struck the busy season. Must have struck a busy concern, too. From daylight to ten, eleven at night—once in a while a night lapping over. Nothing doing but work. I don't mind work, but this indulging a lawless passion for it—not for mine. I've had three months of that, and I think I'm due for a change. And don't you think that's enough autobiography to qualify me for pump-man on an oil-tanker?"

The head clerk yawned prodigiously, and hummed, and whistled, looked out of the window, and by and by found time to say, "you can leave your name. And sometime possibly"—and just then the buzzer clicked, and the applicant saw him disappear into the private office.

*     *     *     *     *

It was only the new superintendent's second day, and to the head clerk he still seemed an unaggressive sort, not much to look at, and, so far, not much to say. A clever man ought to be able to handle him. And yet, as the head clerk was crossing the floor of the private office, the eye of the new superintendent never looked away. Yes, he did have a puzzling eye.

"Close the door, Mr. Grump. Why not ship that man for that berth? He seems competent."

"The captain of the *Rapidan* said he had a man in mind for the place, sir."

"M-h-h. And something of a martinet, isn't he, this *Rapidan* captain?"

"Something, sir."

"M-h-h. But even so, he probably won't object to my naming one man of his crew. And I would like it if you would sign this man."

"The captain of the *Rapidan* has always selected all his own crew, sir." The head clerk had rested both hands, with fingers spread, on his chief's desk. His chief making no reply, the head clerk added: "And he rather resents interference from the office."

The superintendent was playing idly with a paper knife. His gaze seemed to be directed to the lower buttons of his head clerk's waistcoat. "Interference?" he repeated. "Interference? Mr. Grump, you have a reputation for humor, or so I judge. I've been listening to you trying to bedevil that man out there, but I'm afraid your humor is a little on the slap-stick order. And so"—the superintendent raised his head—"if I use a club on you, instead of the point of a rapier, I hope you won't think I do it out of natural brutality."

Their eyes met. The head clerk straightened from shoulder to heel. "And now, this is not a request; it is an order: Sign that man."

"Yes, sir."

"And Mr. Grump, why did you ask all those questions of a man you had no notion of shipping?"

"Why, sir, I meant no harm by that, sir. All kinds come here looking for berths on our ships, and some of them are rather queer ones, you know, sir, and we like to have a little fun with them."

"Have fun with that man? I wish I had your intellectual nerve."

"You know him, sir? If I had known—"

"I don't know him. I saw him and listened to him, as you did. But let me tell you something, Mr. Grump. You're paid $5,000 a year here, and presumably you know your business. I get several times that. Presumably I, too, know my business. But when you or I reach a stage where we can have fun with that man out there, then you and I won't have to rest content with our relatively subordinate and unimportant executive positions in the Northern and Southern Oil Company."

"Subordinate positions, sir!"

"Exactly. And Mr. Grump?"

"Yes, sir."

"Why is it that good men don't seem to stay long on some of our ships, especially on the *Rapidan*?"

"I couldn't say, sir."

"No? Too bad you didn't take the trouble to find out during all the years you've been here. Possibly I can find out. I'll take passage on the *Rapidan* this trip. But say nothing about it to anybody, mind. If the captain wishes to know something more of his passenger, say that it is a friend of the third or fourth vice-president, or of one of the directors, or of the office boy's, or the stenographer's, or anybody at all, taking a little sea trip for his health. And his name—" He picked up the telephone directory, inserted the blade of the paper knife, opened the book, and laid the knife across the page. "Noyes. Noyes sounds all right. Tell him the passenger's name is Noyes. And that's all for now, except that you sign that man."

"Yes, sir." The reorganized head clerk clicked his heels, wheeled, marched to his desk, and without delay signed John Kieran as pump-man for the Gulf voyage of the oil ship *Rapidan*.

II

It lacked two minutes to sailing time, and the passenger was in the cabin mess-room, when he heard the exclamation. "Here he comes now."

He looked through the air-port. Out on the deck was a huge fellow gazing up the dock. The passenger, who knew the big man for the boson, gazed up the dock also and saw that it was the pump-man coming; and he was singing cheerily as he came:

"Our ship she was alaborin' in the Gulf o' Mexico,
The skipper on the quarter—"

Usually it is only the drunks who come over the side of an oil-tanker singing, but this was no drunk. Drunks generally make use of all the aids to navigation when they board a ship. Above all, they do not ignore the gang-plank. But this lad wasn't going a hundred feet out of his way for any gang-plank. He hove his suit-case aboard, made a one-handed vault from dock to deck (and from stringpiece to rail was high as his shoulder), and when he landed on deck it was like a cat on his toes; and like a cat he was off and away, suit-case in hand, while those of the crew who had only seen him land were still wondering where he dropped from.

The big man plainly did not like the style of him at all. "Here you!" he bellowed, "who the hell are *you*?"

And the new-comer ripped out, "And who the hell are *you* that wants to know?"

"Who'm I? Who'm I? I'll show yer bloody well soon who I am."

"Well, show me."

"Show yer?"

"Yes, you big sausage, show me."

"Show yer? Show yer?" The big man peered around the ship. Surely it was a mirage.

At the very first whoop from the big man the pump-man had stopped dead, softly set down his suit-case, and waited. Now he stepped swiftly toward the big man. And to the passenger, looking and listening from the cabin mess-room, it looked like the finest kind of a battle; but just then the captain came up the gang-plank calling out, "Cast off those lines. And don't fall asleep over it, either." The deck force scattered to carry out his orders. The pump-man picked up his suit-case and went on to his quarters.

Next morning (the ship by now well down the Jersey coast and the passenger on the bridge by the captain's invitation) again was heard the carolling voice:

"Our ship she was alaborin' in the Gulf o' Mexico,
The skipper on the quarter, with eyes aloft and low.
Says he, 'My bucko boys—'"

that far when the big man's hoarse bass interrupted, "Say you, what about that Number Seven tank?"

"—Says he, 'My bucko boys, it's asurely goin' to blow'"

The pump-man paused, inclined his head, set one hand back of his ear, and asked, "And what about Number Seven tank? And speak up, son, so I can hear you."

"Speak up!" The big man roared to the heavens. "Speak up! Don't tell me to speak up. Did yer clean that tank out?"

"No, I didn't clean it out."

"Yer didn't? And why in hell didn't yer?"

"Because I don't have to. But I put a couple of men to work and saw that they cleaned it out. And it was done before you were out of your warm bunk this morning."

"Who's that big fellow?" The passenger put the question to the captain.

"That's my bosun—and a good one."

"And the other? Know anything of him?"

"The singing one? Nothin', except he's the new pump-man. And I can see right now it won't be many hours afore the bosun'll beat his head off."

"You think he will?"

"I *know* he will. Why, look at him—the size of him, and solid's a rock."

The passenger took another look over the top of the bridge canvas. He was surely a big man; and under his thin sleeveless jersey, surely a solid man. And the pump-man, in his skimpy, badly-fitting dungarees, though of good height, did not look to be much more than half the other's bulk.

"That same bosun's beat up more men than any shipping agency ever kept a record of. That's Big Bill. And if you'd ever travelled on oil-tankers, you'd 'a' heard of him. He's a whale. Take another look at him, Mr. Noyes."

Noyes took another look. The boson surely was a tremendously muscled man. He was knobbed with muscle. But
Noyes had his own opinion about the two men, and he
hazarded it now.

"But he's a wonderfully quick-moving fellow, that pump-
man, captain. And he's surely got his nerve with him. Look
at him leap across that open hatch! If he fell short he'd get a
thirty-foot drop and break his neck."

"And I wish he would break his neck. And so can a kangaroo
hop around, but you wouldn't pick a kangaroo to fight a bull
buffalo. You'll find out the difference, if ever he tackles my
bosun. And no fear my bosun won't get him. He'll get him,
you see. And when they come together I'll take good care
there's no interruption."

"But why does the bosun hound him so? This man was no
sooner aboard than the bosun began to crowd him."

"Did he? And perhaps you think the bosun of an oil-tanker's
goin' to hand a man a type-written letter every time he wants
to have a word with him. He's a good bosun. He knows his
business, and he saves me a lot of trouble."

And what the captain did not say, but what Noyes imagined
he saw in his eye, was: "And I'll be telling you pretty soon to
keep to yourself your opinion of ship's matters."

When Noyes went to his room that night, it was for a stay of
two days. More than a year now since he had been to sea, and
the weather passing Hatteras had been bad. But now it was the
fourth day out, and Hatteras was far astern, and the ship was
plunging easily southward, with the white sandy shore of

Florida abeam. A fine, fair day it was, with the Caribbean breeze pouring in through the air-port. The passenger shaved and washed and got into his clothes. Above him he could hear the captain dressing down somebody. He stepped out on deck.

It was two sailors who had complained of the grub, and he had made short work of their complaint. "I'll give you what grub I please. And that's good grub." That and more, and drove the two sailors, with their dinners on their tin mess-plates, down to the deck.

Noyes, who remembered that the company allowed fifty cents a day per man for grub, took a look and a whiff of the protested rations as the men went by. "Phew!" He ascended to the bridge. The captain turned to him. "Did you see those two? Complaining of the grub, mind you. What do they know of grub? In the hovels they came from they never saw good grub."

Noyes made no answer. He was interested just then in the pump-man, who now came strolling along and presently overtook the protesting sailors. The better to observe proceedings, Noyes took his station on the chart bridge aft. "And did you fellows think that any polite game of conversation up on the bridge was going to get you a shift of rations?" the pump-man was saying. "Don't you know that what he saves out of the ship's allowance goes into his own pocket? What you fellows want to do is to go and scare the cook to death—or half way to it. If it's only for a couple of days, it'll help. Here, let's go back and shake him up. Besides, we might as well start something to make a fellow smile. Most morbid packet ever I was in. You'd think it was a crime to laugh on her. Come on."

The galley was a little house by itself on the after deck of the ship. Noyes saw the pump-man call out the cook, and after a time, their voices rising, he heard, "Now, cookie, no more of that slush. Mind you, I'm wasting no time talking to the captain. I'm talking to you. We know that he slips you a little ten-spot every month for keeping down the grub bills; but even if he does, you'll have to dig out something better."

"I'll be giving you what I please."

"You will, will you?" The cook was a good-sized man, and he held a skillet in his hand, but he was taken by surprise. The pump-man whipped the skillet from him, whirled him about, ran him into his galley, and closed and bolted the door behind him. A stove-pipe projected from the roof of the galley. The pump-man climbed up, stuffed a bunch of wet cotton waste into the stovepipe, and with a valve which he seemed to be taking apart, took his stand by the taffrail.

Every few minutes he got up from his valve, put his ear to the door of the shack, and listened. After twenty minutes or so he opened the door, lifted out the cook, and held him over the rail. He was gulping like a catfish.

Noyes looked to see if the captain had witnessed the little comedy. Evidently he had, for Noyes could hear him swearing.

Noyes, now on the bridge, was still chuckling over the picture of the scared cook when the pump-man came walking forward. He was swinging a pair of Stillson wrenches, one in each hand, as if they were Indian clubs, and singing as he came:

"Our ship she was alaborin' in the Gulf o' Mexico,
The skipper on the quarter, with eyes aloft and low.
Says he, 'My bucko boys, it's asurely goin' to blow—
Take every blessed rag from her, strip her from truck to toe,

James Brendan Connolly

And we'll see what she can make of it.'
And O, my eyes, it blew! And blew and blew,
And blew and blew! My soul, how it did blow!
Aboard the *Flying Walrus* in the Gulf o' Mexico.

"The sea—"

Noyes saw him leap to one side, even as he saw a heavy, triple-sheaved block bound on the steel deck beside him. Noyes looked up. Aloft was the boson, apparently rigging up some sort of a hoisting arrangement.

The pump-man stopped to pull out a handkerchief and wipe his forehead. Then he, too, looked up. "Fine business. But did you think for a minute you—that I didn't have my eye on you?"

It took the boson a minute or two to find his tongue. When he did, it was to say, "Young fella, did you ship for a opera singer or wot?"

"I shipped for what you'll find my name signed against in the articles, and I'm on the job every minute. And I'll go on singing if it pleases me. And if it pleases me, I'll finish that song, too."

"Not on this ship, you won't, 'less you sing it in your sleep and me not in hearin'."

"I'll finish it on this ship, son. And it won't be in my sleep and you'll be within hearing."

A group of deck-hands snickered, and the boson pretended to climb down from the rigging. "You swine! What the—"

They retreated in terror. "It wasn't at you we was

laffin', boson."

"Well, see that yer don't, yer cross-eyed whelps—see that yer don't."

"And do you mean to say, you collection of squashes, that you were laughing at me?" The pump-man, still grasping a wrench in each hand, started across the deck after them. "D'y' mean to—"

Down the gangway they retreated in a body. Noyes looked to the captain, but the captain was looking out over the ship's side.

Noyes went down to luncheon, and after luncheon took his cigar and his book to his room. When next he came out, he felt that something had happened since the little adventure of the falling block. The captain was pacing the bridge by fits and starts. The boson was leaning over the quarter-rail. The pump-man was busy on a small job forward.

The quiet was unnatural. Noyes decided to take his constitutional on the long gangway of the main deck. As he paced aft he saw that some of the crew were laying the hatches on one of the tanks. He paced forward. By the time he was aft again they were overhauling a large tarpaulin. He watched them while they stretched it over the hatch covers. He wondered what they were about, for the tanks of an empty oil ship are usually left open in fine weather.

Presently he heard one of the men say to another as they stamped down the tarpaulined hatch, "There—there's as good a prize ring as a man'd want." And then he began to understand.

He stayed aft, while through the smoke of one long cigar he

James Brendan Connolly

thought it out. When he next went forward he stopped beside the pump-man, who was cutting a thread on a section of deck-piping. "Do you mind my watching how you do that trick?" he asked.

The pump-man looked up. "Surely not," adding after a moment, "though there's nothing much worth watching to it."

Noyes noticed how deftly the tools were handled. Then he said, "So you and the big fellow are going to have it out?"

"Yes, during dinner we agreed to settle it."

"But he's a notorious bruiser—liable to kill you."

"Maybe, but I don't think so. I've trimmed 'em bigger."

"Not bigger, if they could fight at all?"

"Maybe they couldn't, but"—from beneath the grease and soot of his face his teeth and eyes flashed swiftly upward—"they said they could."

Noyes took another turn of the long gangway. The tarpaulin was now clamped tightly to the hatch-combings, rendering it smooth and firm under foot. Camp-stools for the principals were also there, and two buckets of freshly drawn water in opposite corners.

"Mr. Kieran"—Noyes had halted again beside the pump-man—"what is it the captain's got against you?"

"Why"—he hesitated—"I don't think he's got anything against me exactly." His next words came slowly, thoughtfully. "He may have something against my kind, though."

"What do you mean by that?"

"Well, you see, a man of the captain's kind can never get a man of my kind to play his game—and he knows it. What he wants around here is a lot of poor slobs who will take the kicks and curses and poor grub, say thank you, sir, and come again."

"But what game does he want you to play?"

"Well, I'm the pump-man. The ship has big bills for valving and piping and repairing. If ever the office got suspicious and called me in on it, why—" he shrugged his shoulders.

Noyes studied the sea for a while. By and by he faced inboard. "Kieran, I've seen ships before, even if I do get sea-sick sometimes. Was that an accident to-day, that block dropping on you—almost?"

"Accident?" The recurring smile flashed anew. "That's the third I've side-stepped in two days. I was in the bottom of a tank yesterday when a little hammer weighing about ten pounds happened to fall in. In the old clipper-ship days, Mr. Noyes, a great trick was to send a man out on the end of a yard in heavy weather and get the man at the wheel to snap him overboard. On steamers, of course, we have no yards, and so little items like spanners and wrenches and three-sheaved blocks fall from aloft. But that's all right." The pump-man, all the while he was talking, kept fitting his dies and cutting his threads. "I've got no kick coming. I came aboard this ship with my eyes open, and I'm keeping 'em open"—he laughed softly—"so I won't be carried ashore with 'em closed."

Noyes took a close look at the pump-man. The trick of light speech, his casual manner in speaking of serious things, was not unbecoming, but this was a more purposeful sort of person than he had reckoned; a more set man physically, a more serious man morally, than he had thought. There was more beef to him, too, than ever he guessed; and the face was less oval, the jaw more heavily hung. The under teeth, biting upward, were well outside the upper.

"But the bosun—he's altogether too huge," mused Noyes. He threw away his cigar. "Kieran, you're too good a man to be manhandled by that brute. You say so, and I'll stop the fight. I've got influence in the office, and I think I could present the matter to the captain so that he will pull the bosun off."

"Thank you, Mr. Noyes, but you mustn't. I'd rather get beat to a pulp than crawl. All I ask is that nobody reaches over and taps me on the back of the skull with a four-pound hammer or some other useful little article while I'm busy with him."

"And when is it coming off?"

"Soon's we go off watch—eight bells."

"Eight bells? Four o'clock." Noyes drew out his watch. "Why, it's nine minutes to that now."

"So near? Then I'd better begin to knock off, if I'm going to wash off and be ready in time, hadn't I?" He finished his thread, gathered up his stock and dies, and strolled off.

Noyes headed for the bridge. The captain's glance, as he came up the ladder, was not at all encouraging; but Noyes was already weary of the captain's hectoring glances.

"Captain, are you going to let it go on?" he asked, and not too deferentially.

"Let what go on?"

"That fight. They're going to have it out in a few minutes. Aft there—look."

"I'm not looking. And I'll take good care I don't—not in that direction. And what I don't see I can't stop, can I? Besides, I hope he beats that pump-man to a jelly."

"Why, what's wrong with him?"

"Wrong? He's dangerous."

"Dangerous?"

"Dangerous, yes. Why, look at the mop of hair and the eyes of him. He's one of those trouble-hunters, that chap. And if troubles don't turn up naturally, he'll go out and dig them up. He's like one of those kind I read about once—used to live a thousand years ago. All he needs is a horse seventeen hands high, and a wash-boiler on his chest, and a tin kettle on his head, and one of those long lances, and he'd go tilting about the country like that Don Quick-sote—"

"Don what?"

"Quick-sote—Quick-sote. That crazy Spaniard who went butting up against windmills in that book of yours you leave around the cabin. A good name for him—Don John Quick-sote—running around buttin' into things he can't straighten out."

"He could do all that and yet be the best kind of a man. And the bosun—why, before I ever heard the name of this ship, I'd heard of her bosun. He's a notorious brute."

"He's the kind of a brute I want to have around. He will do what I order him."

"Did you order him to bring on this fight?"

"And if I did, what of it? Do I have to account to you for what I do on my ship? That pump-man is dangerous, I tell you. Why, just before we sailed, I was telephoning over to the office to find out how he happened to be shipped, and a clerk—"

"The second clerk, was it?"

"What does it matter who it was? He said to watch out for him, too—that he was the kind who knew it all. Wherever the office got him I don't know. And if you know anybody in the office with a pull, you ought to put it up to them, Mr. Noyes, when you go back. This pump-man, he's the kind recognizes no authority."

"Why, I thought he was very respectful toward your officers. And he seems to do his work on the jump, too, captain."

"He carries out orders, yes; but if he felt like it, he'd tell me to go to hell as quick as he'd tell the bosun. I can see it in his eye."

"Don't you think he only wants to be treated with respect?"

"Treated with respect! Who do you think you're talkin' to— the cook? I don't have to treat one of my crew with respect. I'm captain of my own ship, do you hear?—captain of this ship, and I'll treat the crew as I damn please."

"I guess you will, too; but don't swear at me, captain. I'm not one of your crew."

Noyes descended to the chart-room deck. "I wish," he breathed, "that that pump-man had never seen this ship. They'll kill him before the day's over."

III

The after-rail of the chart-room deck looked almost directly down the hatch whereon the fight was to take place. As Noyes was taking his position by the rail he guessed that the bosun must have just said something which pleased the crew, for most of them were still laughing heartily.

Kieran, on a camp-stool, waited for the laughter to simmer down. He fixed a mocking eye on the bosun. "And so you're a whale, eh? And you'll learn me what a whale can do to little fishes? Well, let me tell you something about a whale, son. A whale is a sure enough big creature, but I never heard he was a fighting fish before. Now, if you knew more about some things, you'd never called yourself a whale, but a thrasher. There's the best fighting fish of them all—the thrasher. The thrasher's the boy with the wallop. He's the boy that chases the whale, and leaps high out of the water, and snaps his long, limber tail, and bam! down he comes on that big slob of a whale and breaks his back. All the wise old whales, they take to deep water when they see a thrasher hunting trouble. It's the foolish young whales that don't know enough to let the thrasher alone."

Noyes noted that the crew laughed more loudly at the bosun's rough jeers than at the more sharply pointed comment of the pump-man. But looking them over, he began to understand; these men were nearer to the bosun's type than the pump-man's. And also, no crew could long remain ignorant of which it was the captain favored. If the pump-man won, they would benefit by it, whether they were with him or no—some selfish instinct in them taught them that; while if the bosun were to win (and who could doubt that, looking at the two men?), why, 'twould be just as well to fly their colors early.

Yet there were those who favored the game-looking pump-man. Two or three had the courage to say so. It was these who cried out to give him fair play when some ten or a dozen were for rushing him off the hatch before the fight had begun at all.

Kieran thanked these with a grateful look. "That's all I want—fair play. Keep off the hatch and give us room to move around in."

And yet it did seem for a moment as if the pump-man was to get no fair play, as if the bosun's adherents would overwhelm him as he stood there on the hatch. And Noyes experienced an unpleasant chill and began to appreciate the nerve of this man who defied a crowd of alien spirits aboard a strange ship. It was more than physical courage, and when they were making ugly demonstrations toward the pump-man it was in pure admiration of his nerve that Noyes called out: "Hold up—fair play! Fair play, I say—he's only one."

Coming from the passenger, it was the psychological act at the psychological moment. They drew back, and Kieran, looking up, put his thanks in his look.

The two men faced each other. Kieran eyed the other critically. Up and down, from toe to crown, he estimated his bulk; and then, taking a step to one side, he eyed him once more, as if to get the exact depth of him.

"Well," said the bosun, and harking to his rising voice, his growling adherents simmered to silence, "now yer've seen me, what d'yer think?"

"I've seen 'em just as big, hulks of full your length and beam and draught, and in a breeze I've seen vessels of less tonnage make 'em shorten sail."

"And so yer've been in the wind-jammin' line, huh?"

"That and a few others," answered Kieran tranquilly.

"Yer'll understand a talk then. An' here's a craft won't take any sail in before you. And yer quite a hulk in the water yourself, now yer've come out where we c'n get a peek at yer."

"You ought to see me when I'm hauled out on the ways," retorted Kieran. "A fair little hulk out of water I may be, but it's below the water-line, like every good ship, I get my real bearings. But shall we get to business? I've been hearing about you for years. And for what you're going to do to me since I've come aboard—" Kieran threw up his hands. "Oh, Lord, they tell me you drove your naked fist through the wall of a saloon up on West Street before the ship put out."

"Yes, an' I can drive it through the side of you to-day."

"Man! and I'm not wall-sided either. You must be a hellion. But"—to Kieran's ears had come the sound of muttering in the crowd—"shall we get at it? We ought to make a good match of it. You may be a bit the bigger, but no matter. Three or four inches in height and sixty or seventy pounds, what's that? What d'you say?"—he turned to the crew—"he's big enough to pull a mast down on deck. Are the two of us to settle it here without interference? In the old days men fought so, the champions in front of the armies, and the winning man allowed to ride back unharmed to his comrades."

That picture, as the wily and eloquent pump-man painted it, impressed them. And he looked so frail beside the bosun! They drew well back now; all but one, the crafty carpenter, crony of the bosun and eager tool of the captain. There was that in the pump-man's eyes—the carpenter stepped to the big man's shoulder. "Listen to me. This man's no innercent. I've seen his picter somewheres."

"An' he'll see something of me in a minute, an' more than a picksher. Go away!" The boson shoved the carpenter aside.

"What I like about you, bosun"—Kieran, having shed his dungaree coat, stood now for a moment with a hand resting easily to either side of his waist—"and it sticks out all over you, is your love of a fight. And"—under his breath this, so only the bosun could hear it—"I'm going to satisfy that love of yours to-day so you'll stop your ears up if ever again you hear a man even whisper fight. Yes"—drawing off his undershirt, cinching his trousers straps above his hips, and resuming his easy speech—"I do love a real fighting man. But your friends"—he waved his hand toward the crew—"they must all stand that side. I want no man between me and the rail this side, no man behind me. 'Tisn't fair." He turned to them. "Play me fair in that. I'm giving your man the slope of the hatch, and he's tall enough in all conscience without. So let no man stand behind me."

The arms and torso of the pump-man, as he stood there naked to the waist, amazed Noyes. It surprised them all. He had seemed only a medium-sized man under the concealing dungarees. Noyes saw now that he was a bigger man by fifteen or twenty pounds than he had had any idea of; and were he padded with twenty pounds more, he would still be in good condition. Not a lump anywhere; not a trace of a bulging muscle, except that when he flexed his arm or worked his shoulders by way of loosening them up he started little ripples that ran like mice from neck to loins under the skin; and when, with this shoulder movement, he combined a rapid leg motion, Noyes fancied he could trace the play of muscle clear to his heels. His skin, too, had the unspotted gleaming whiteness of high vitality.

"He's a reg'lar race horse—a tiger," burst out from one admirer in the crowd.

The bosun, also stripped of his upper garments, looked all of his great size, and, moving about, showed himself not altogether lacking in agility. Lively, indeed, he was for his immense bulk, although, compared to the pump-man in that, he was like a moose beside a panther. "It ain't goin' to be so one-sided after all," whispered some one loudly, and recalled the pump-man's leaping across the hatch that very morning. And now, as he ducked and turned, seeming never to lack breath for easy speech, there were others who were beginning to believe it would not be so one-sided either.

"Speaking of wind-jammers, I remember"—the bosun had rushed past him like a charging elephant—"hearing my old grandfather tell of seeing a three-decker manoeuvring once. She'd come into stays about the middle of the morning watch, he said, and maybe toward three bells in the second dogwatch they'd have her on the other tack. A ship of the old line she was, a terrible fighter, if only fighting was done from moorings; but there were little devils of frigates kept sailing 'round and 'round her. What? Why don't I stand up? Stand up, is it? Why, man, I don't see where I've been hove-down yet. Hove-down, no, nor wet my rail yet. And is it you or I is fighting this end of it? Is it?"—a subtle threat with his left, one cunning feint of his right, one whip-like inboring of the left hand, and up came the bosun all-standing.

"You're easy luffed," jeered Kieran. "A moment ago you were drawing like a square-rigger before a quartering gale, and now you're shaking in the wind—yes, and likely to be aback, if you don't watch out."

The teeth locked in the bosun's head—so hard a jolt for so smoothly delivered a blow! He gazed amazed. Again a deceptive swing or two, a fiddling with one hand and the other, a moment of rapid foot-work, a quick side-step, and biff! Kieran's left went into the ribs—crack! and Kieran's right caught him on the cheek-bone and laid it open as if hit with a cleaver.

"Devil take it!" exploded Kieran, "I meant that for your jaw. It's this slippery tarpaulin." He slid his foot back and forth on the black-tarred canvas. "The cook's been dropping some of his slush on it, and you, bosun, didn't see to it that it was cleaned. You ought to look after those little things or the skipper'll be having you up to the bridge. But, come now, just once more"—he curved his left forearm persuasively— "once more and—"

But having caught the flame in the eye that never once looked away from his, the bosun wanted no more of that long-range work. It must be close quarters thereafter, or he foresaw disgrace. He appealed to the men at his back. "He won't stand up like a man. He leaps around like a bloody monkey."

"That's right, bosun. Stand up to him there, you!" That was the carpenter's voice. And others followed. 'Twasn't so men'd been used to fightin' on oil-tankers. No, sir. "Stand to him breast to breast!" The carpenter led further clamorous voices.

"Aye, breast to breast be it." Kieran was standing at ease. "And yet you all been telling how he drove his fist through a pine plank the other day up on the New York water-front."

"Yes, an' I c'n drive it through you, if yer come close to me."

"Close to you? Is this close enough to you?" No more side-stepping, no more swift shifting—just a straight step in, and they were clinched. With arms wrapped around the body of the other, each an inside and outside hold, and fingers locked in the small of the other's back, they were at it. One tentative tug and haul and the bosun began to see that he would need all his strength for this man. Another long-drawn tug and he began to fear the outcome. Again, and in place of his foe coming to him, it was his own waist he felt drawn forward. Slowly he felt his head falling back, and gradually his shoulders followed. In toward Kieran came the hollow of the big man's back, and the big man knew he had met his master; and, bitterest of all, this man poured galling words into his ear as he bore him back; gibing words, in so low a voice that they reached no further than the ear for which they were intended.

"Your own favorite Cumberland grip—where's the whale strength of you now, Bruiser Bill—your buffalo rush, hah? It's my weakness to make a show of you here on this deck— you, my Bruising Bill, the boastful lump of muscle that you are. Just muscle, no more. And now where are you—where, I say?"

The long, smooth muscles of Kieran's back were gathering and swelling. His waist, contrasted with the splendid development under his shoulders, looked slim as a corseted girl's; and not Noyes alone was noting them. Every muscle in the smooth-skinned body—it seemed as if he drew them from his very toes for service in that hug.

The bosun's breath was coming in labored gasps, yet still that terrible man kept holding him close, drawing his waist to him and increasing his pressure as he drew. "You've the tonnage and engine-room of a battleship," jeered Kieran, "but you've only the steam of an East River tug. And a low-pressure tug at that. And what little steam you had is gone. You've a big engine but no boiler. And you know what use an engine is without a boiler, don't you? Well, that's you, son—your steam's gone."

The swimming head kept falling backward toward the ground. And for Kieran, as he felt his enemy weaken, the purple lights were flashing again. The call of battle was ringing in his ears; came back to him the memory of more careless days, when he lived for this kind of thing. After all, what was life but a means whereby to give one's spirit play? And yet again—and yet—was he no more than a brute himself? What was the use? What good would it all do? And suddenly he loosed his grip, and the inert body of the bosun rolled down the tarpaulined hatch and onto the steel deck.

Noyes found himself gasping, almost as if he were in the fight himself. Then he noted that Kieran had raised his hand and was addressing the crew. "Holdup! You said the fight would settle it. Mind your words now—fair play for one against you all. Fair play, I say," and they might have scattered before this blazing, fighting pump-man in the full lust of his power but for the carpenter, who poised a hammer to throw. "What! you would!" yelled Kieran. A leap, a pass, and his fist smashed into the lowering face. Over keeled the carpenter, a tall man, like a falling spar.

"Put that man in irons!" Noyes jumped at the voice. The captain was leaning over the rail beside him.

# IV

"Irons?" The pump-man's head went into the air. For a moment he stood poised on the hatch like a statue. "Irons?" His face paled and hardened and his arms stiffened; but instantaneously, as half a dozen reached out to seize him, he ducked and twisted and side-stepped, and two, who could not be avoided, he knocked swiftly out of his way. He cracked a fist into one face, then the other. There was no malice in it; they simply barred his way to freedom. He leaped from combing to combing of the open hatches. It was thirty feet to the bottom of any one of these empty tanks, and those who followed did so at creeping speed.

He was clear of the mob. A light bound and he was on the ship's rail beside the after-rigging.

The captain, leaning as far out as the chart deck would allow, shook a raging arm at Kieran. "You'll assault, you'll batter my men right and left, will you, you crazy mutineer?"

"Don't call me a mutineer, captain—I've disobeyed no order."

"You are a mutineer. I declare you one now. And you'll go into irons."

"You'll never put me in irons."

"You'll go into irons or you'll go over the side."

"Well, maybe I'll go over the side. But before I go, if I have to go, I'll have a word to say. You've been trying to break my nerve from the beginning. I know your kind that bully and starve your crew, and won't have a man on your ship that you can't bully and starve. And so you set your bully bosun to do me—do me to death, if he had to. And when he's not clever enough nor able enough, you'd put me in irons—in irons here on the high seas—out here where no law can get you!"

The first officer was now on the deck beneath the pump-man. "You'd better come down, Kieran. It will be the safest way in the end."

"Mr. Brown, you're a good officer, and I don't want to cross you, but you're not going to put me in irons."

The ship was rolling gently. Kieran rested one hand lightly, by way of balance, on a stay, and kicked his shoes overboard. "A step nearer, Mr. Brown, and I go after the shoes."

"But it's five miles to the Florida shore, Kieran, and alive with sharks. You'd never make it. Come on now."

"No. Five miles or fifty, I'll have a try at it."

Noyes now laid a warning hand on the captain's arm. "Are you going to insist on putting that man in irons?"

"I am. And stand clear of me, you."

"If you try to, he'll jump overboard."

"And if he does, what of it?"

"If he does, there'll be a bad time ahead for you."

"There will? There's liable to be a bad time for you right now. Do you know you have no rights on this ship unless I say so? Don't you know I can put you in irons, too—that's marine law—if I feel like it?"

"I know what maritime law is. And that's the devil of it when there's a brute on the bridge. You can put me in irons if you want to, but I don't think you will."

"So?" sneered the captain. "I won't? And why not?"

"Because I'm no friendless seafarer. And also because— here's my card. Read it. It's the card of your boss, the man who can hire or fire you, or any other man or officer of this line. And I don't have to give you a reason unless it pleases me. But I'll give a reason at the right time—in your case. And the reason will leave you where you'll never again set foot on the deck of any ship of this line or of a good many other lines."

The captain had set his back to the rail and bared his teeth. Noyes, thinking he was about to spring, braced his feet and waited. Noyes himself was no angelic-looking creature at the moment. His jaw seemed to shoot forward, his eyes to contract and recede.

"And so that's who you are, is it? And you'd break me?"

"Break you, yes. And perhaps put you in jail before I'm done with you. Now will you put him in irons?"

The captain did not spring. He walked to his room instead. And he gave out no order just then; but soon the mess-boy came out and whispered to the first officer, and the first officer said, "Kieran, you're to return to duty," and pocketed his irons and called off the men.

It was an hour after the fight. Kieran had had time to clean up, and now, with the passenger, he was pacing the long gangway.

"And would you have gone over the side?" the passenger had asked.

"I guess I'd had to, wouldn't I?"

"And would you have reached shore?"

"Why not? Five miles—it's not much in smooth water."

"But the sharks?"

"Sharks? Black boys in West Indian ports will dive all day among them for coppers. Sharks and whales—writers of sea stories certainly ought to pension them. There may have been a shark who once made a meal off a sailor, but let you or me drop over the side, and if there's one anywhere near, he wouldn't stop racing till he was a mile away, and if any harmless slob of a whale ever killed a sailor, be sure he did it through fright. But that's no matter. What does matter, though"—Kieran halted and faced the passenger—"are the men who did go over the side, and not within swimming distance of any pleasant sandy beach either. 'Tisn't every protesting seaman who finds the boss of the line on deck to back him up. And, what's harder, how about the men who never had the choice of going over the side? And think of the poor creatures who got so that in time they didn't even want to go over the side, who might have grown into honest, free men, but who, instead of that, learned only to live for the day when they too would have the power to make their inferiors stand around and cringe and whine."

They paced the length of the deck twice before Kieran spoke again.

"They wonder at the decay of our merchant marine. I wonder did they ever stop to think of what men—seamen—think of the service? In the days of sailing ships a man going to sea met with real danger and hardship, and they developed courage and skill and character of some kind. What training does he get to take the place of that now? He's a hand nowadays, a helper, a lumper—not a sailor—on a great big hulk to which disaster is almost impossible."

"But disasters do happen."

"They do, but what is the truth about them? Nine out of ten of them have a disgraceful cause. But the public doesn't hear of that, because the public doesn't go to sea—except as a saloon passenger. The public gets its story from the steamship company's office—always, and you know what kind of a story they put out—put out through newspapers that carry their advertising. You know what that chief clerk or that second clerk of yours would tell any inquiring outsider in case of a loss of life on one of these ships. He'd lie and lie and lie and lie and think he was serving a good cause at that, and the papers publishing the lie would think they were serving a good cause, too—especially the constructive organization papers, as they call themselves. Our big steamship officers these days—outside of the navy—don't get the kind of work that keeps men up to the mark, and not getting it they grow soft—their bodies and their souls become flabby. Engineer officers nowadays have the work cut out for them and they are doing good work, but the bridge officers are no longer men of the sea—they're clerks, agents in floating hotels. And the crew take their tone from the officers. When the commander's weak, your whole outfit is apt to weaken, especially under a strain."

They resumed their pacing, Kieran with head high in the air, inhaling deep breaths of the fresh salt air.

The passenger came out of a deep meditation. "Kieran, you can do a good work for us. Is there any berth with this line you'd like to have? If there is, say so. You can have it. You can have that head clerk's job if you want it. And I think that after a while I could get you mine, for I'm only there to fill a gap."

Kieran shook his head. "It wouldn't do."

"Why not? You're the man for the job."

"No, I'm not the man. You haven't got me quite right. I can point out errors, but I'm not the man to correct them. I'm not a good executive."

"You certainly were the good executive in the bosun's case."

"N-no, no. You mustn't count him. If he was a John L. Sullivan, say, in his good days, it would prove something. Besides, I don't care for fighting—for beating people up. I do hate though to see a bully or a faker getting the best of it, and maybe having had time to knock around and study people, I can pick out a bully or a faker quicker than most people, and seeing somebody getting too much the best of it, why, sometimes I can't help butting in."

"And because of that faculty of seeing things, once you made up your mind to settle down to it, you'd make good on this job I'm offering you."

"No, you've got me wrong again. I'm not a reformer, and never will be, I hope. Reformers, or most that ever I met, are only men who first tried to play politics and got licked at it. I'm only an observer."

"But you like a fight?"

"M-m-m-n not me. And I never did. Any man, of course, likes the excitement once he's into it, but what man enjoys smashing another man in the face? What fights I've been into I couldn't side-step—not without crawling, I mean. No, no, I wouldn't make good on your job. I'd go along all right in your office back in New York for awhile,—for a month, two months, six months,—who knows, maybe a year, and then one day I'd look out the window, take a look down on the Battery, say at the elevated railroad or the Aquarium Building, and the Coney Island steamer dock with the barkers yelling and gesturing, and the loafers on the benches in between, and from that I'd look down the bay and see the Statue of Liberty—some morning that would be, maybe, when the sun was lighting up New York Bay as it does some mornings, or maybe it would be on a late afternoon, with the sun setting over on the Jersey shore, the dark smoke from a hundred chimneys smooching across the pink and purple of it, and, if 'twas summer, a haze like a bridal veil over it all, and between that and the Battery the life of a hundred craft— ferry-boats, tow-boats, lighters, windjammers, steam-yachts, ocean-liners, harbor, coastwise and foreign bound, a hundred different kinds coming and going, the Lord knows where, but to where no four walls will bound 'em for a time, be sure of that. And if ever I did look and looked long enough, be sure the earth would look like it was rolling by too slow and I'd want to get out and give it a push to speed it up. No, no. That"—he looked up at the serene blue—"for my ceiling. And that"—he pointed to the dimpling green sea—"for my office floor. And that"—he waved a hand to space—"for a window. And let all the bruising bosuns and bucko ship's officers afloat jump on me, but give me that and I'll take a chance. And—"

He stopped short and sighed. "I do get going sometimes, don't I?" He looked around the deck. In a bucket of water by the rail the bosun was bathing his battered features. "The bosun reminds me. To-day I promised him I'd finish my Flying Walrus song."

"Go ahead and finish it—that first verse was pretty good."

"The second's better—or I think so. And"—he grinned at the passenger—"I composed it myself, too, to an air running in my head. And I suppose I ought to finish it. And yet"—the bosun was pouring, very quietly, his bucket of wash water into the scuppers—"that would be sort of rubbing it in, wouldn't it?"

"What of it? It will do them all good."

"I don't know about that. If it"—and just then three bells struck, and three bells on the *Rapidan* meant supper for the watch below.

Kieran left to go to supper, and the passenger noted the deference of the crew toward him. Not one who found himself in his way but hopped swiftly aside to give him gangway.

"How conducive to high judgment, how accelerating to respect is success," mused the passenger. "Two hours ago hardly one of them who did not set him down for a half-crazy, or, at least, an over-sanguine visionary—but now—they bound like stags before him, and none more propitiatingly agile than the former satellites of our deposed bosun. A Don Quixote"—murmured the passenger—"maybe, but a 20th century Don Quixote—with a wallop in each hand. If the Don Quixotes generally had his equipment, it would not be windmills alone which would suffer, and some joy then for honest men to watch the tilting."

# JAN TINGLOFF


## THE LODGING HOUSE


Jan Tingloff, not wishing to get too far away from the dry dock, turned up a side street near the water-front, and there, in a basement window of a narrow four-story brick building, he saw the sign "Furnished Room to Rent."

A second look showed Jan that the basement also afforded an entrance to a not too well lit pool-room and that a not overclean alley ran up one side of the building. Jan, with no prejudices against alleys or pool-rooms, entered the pool-room to inquire. "Yeh," said the man behind the cigar-case— "second floor—a week in advance—ring the front-door bell—a woman will come and show you."

A woman who preceded him like a discouraged shadow showed him the room, but it was to the man in the basement that she told Jan to pay the week's rent when he said he would take the room. "Yes; I take the rent—always," this man said; and his eyes brightened as Jan pushed the money across the cigar-case at him. And he wore finger-rings out of all keeping with the dark little place; but he had a pleasant smile for Jan and Jan smiled back at him; for Jan was one of those friendly natures who prefer to be pleasant, even to men whose looks they do not like.

Jan Tingloff slept in his new quarters that night. He saw nobody connected with the house as he passed out in the morning; but that evening as he entered the front-door he heard a cough. It was a woman's cough and dimly he saw a woman's form—a rather slender form. Jan's senses were the kind which see a thing large at first and then go back for details. He hurried to close the door so that the cold November wind would not endanger the poor creature further. As he closed the door she said:

"Good evening."

Jan hurried to take off his hat.

"Good evening, ma'am."

"You go off early mornings, captain?"

"Yes, ma'am." He peered into the twilight of the hall and saw a hand lighting the suspension lamp. "But I'm not a captain, ma'am. I was a seafaring man one time; but I am a ship-carpenter now in a repairing job on a big coaster in the dry dock, and I have to be over there early to get my gang started."

She was turning the wick of the lamp high and then low, and high again, and Jan was vexed to think he had not offered to light the lamp for her in the first place, especially as he now recognized in her the same sad-eyed woman who had showed him his room the evening before. It was twilight then, too, but she had lit no lamp in the hall or in the room, and Jan guessed why and did not blame her for it. The furnishings here, as in his room, were shabby.

Jan began to feel a pity for her. There was that in the curve of her back which caused him to address her with unwonted gentleness—and ordinarily Jan was gentle enough for anybody's taste. Yes, she was the same woman; but if he had met her anywhere else he would not have known her. She was now all tidied up. Her clothes were fresh, her shoulders had lost their droop. Her face was less pale and a glow was coming into her eyes.

Jan's room was on the second floor and now he ascended the stairs to go there. At the top of the stairs he glanced back; but catching her looking at him he looked quickly away. From the darkness of the second-floor hallway, however, he could peer down and she could not see him. She was still there, standing under the lamp which was now at full blaze. One arm had been raised high in regulation of the wick and now she raised the other to steady the lamp, which was swinging. Her figure was in the shadow from the waist down, but her bust, her neck, face and long, slim hands were in full light.

"I'd never took her for the same woman—never!" thought Jan.

Next evening Jan saw her again, this time in the narrow second-floor hallway near the stairs. She shrank against the stair-rail to let him pass. Jan drew up against the wall. She mutely indicated that he should pass.

"After you, ma'am," said Jan, and resolutely waited.

"Thank you," she said, and passed on. At the head of the flight of stairs she turned her head. Jan was still there.

"Is your room all right?" She asked the question hurriedly, awkwardly.

"All right, ma'am."

"And not too noisy for you here?—the basement noise, I mean."

"A ship-carpenter, ma'am—he soon gets used to noise."

"Of course." She glanced furtively at him. "Good-night." She hurried downstairs.

That night when Jan, who read romantic fiction to relieve his loneliness, laid down his stirring mediaeval tale to go to bed, he did not follow up the intention with immediate action, as usual.

By and by he raised the window-sash, and the cool, damp sea-air feeling good, he leaned out to enjoy it. It was a cloudy night, with a touch of coming snow in the air; but for all that a night to enjoy, only for the racket ascending from the pool-room.

"I don't think much of those people down there," thought Jan as he lowered the sash to all but six or eight inches for fresh air and picked up the alarm clock from the rickety dresser. "I wonder if she's one of that crowd?" And he began to wind the clock. "But sure she ain't—sure not."

Jan had been holding the clock absently in his hand. Suddenly he set it down and scolded himself—"Jan Tingloff, remember you has to be up at six in the morning!"—and undressed, blew out the light and slid into bed, and tried to go to sleep. And he did after a while; but his last thought before he fell into slumber was: "Who'd ever think one day a woman could grow so young-looking the next day?"

Many an evening after that Jan met the landlady on the stairs or in the hall, and always she stopped to ask him how he was coming on with his ship; but never any more than that or a brief word as to the weather and his comfort, though there were times when Jan felt he would like to become better acquainted—times when he even had a feeling that if he had asked her to sit down somewhere for a talk she would be willing. Jan had learned, however, that she was married. It had been a shock to learn that. It had come about by his noticing after three or four days the plain gold ring on the wedding finger. He had kept staring at it until she could not help remarking it; and by and by, in a casual sort of way, she had told him she was married.

"And is your husband living, ma'am?" asked Jan.

"He's living—yes," she answered slowly.

That made a difference. Even though a man didn't know anybody in the city except the men he worked with and it was terribly lonesome of evenings—even so, her being married made all the difference. And she must have been a wonderfully pretty girl once—and was pretty yet, now he had a chance to look good at her. Pretty—yes; but—well, Jan didn't know what it was, except that she was all right. Jan knew he didn't know much about women, especially strange women—and he knew, too, that he never would; but he would never believe she wasn't all right—never!

Yes, it was pretty lonesome at times; and there was the girl who roomed on the top floor. Jan was thrilled by alluring glimpses of her in the half-dark recesses of the back halls, but the glimpses remained only glimpses after he saw her one Sunday by daylight. Only then was Jan convinced that she painted. She was a little too much and he took to dodging her. Yet it was a pity—oh, a pity! and Jan, still thinking what a pity, was going out for a lonesome walk one night, when who should meet him on the front stoop but that same top-floor girl! And no sliding by her this time. She nipped the lapel of his coat with a dexterous thumb and forefinger.

"Why, hello, cap! Where yuh goin'?"

"Nowheres."

"Then you got time, ain't you, to buy a girl a glass o'—" She stopped and winked sportively.

"Glass o' what?"

"Why, ginger ale!" She laughed at his surprise. "You thought I was goin' to say beer, or maybe somethin' stronger, didn't yuh? But I don't drink no hard stuff. No. An' I was dyin' for a drink o' somethin' when yuh pops out that door. An' I know yuh ain't any hinge."

"How do you know I ain't a hinge?"

"Oh, don't I? Leave it to me to pick a sport from a piker."

"But I'm no sport either."

"You could if yuh wanted ter. An' yuh ain't any hinge, even if they do say you're a square-head. Come on an' let's go in back an' have a couple o' bottles o' ginger ale in Hen's place."

And Jan followed her into the private room beyond the pool-room—the room to which, as he had gathered before this, the street girls of that section steered drunken sailors. The ginger ale was brought in by the proprietor himself. Jan threw down a ten-dollar bill. Jan had a good many bills with him that evening—his month's wages; and seeing it was the fashion round there to show your money when you paid for anything, why, he'd show them—even if he was a square-head—that he could carry a wad too.

"Say, cap, but yuh must be drawin' down good coin?"

"Oh, a boss ship-carpenter gets pretty good wages." And with one splendid sweep Jan emptied his glass.

"I should say yes. An' there's tinhorners round here that if they had half your wad Hen'd have to ring in the fire alarm to put 'em out—they'd feel themselves such warm rags. But what d'yuh say to another ginger ale?"

"Sure," said Jan, and called aloud for them. And again Hen brought in the ginger ale in two long glasses, but also with two empty bottles to show Jan by the labels that it was the real imported and no phony stuff; and Jan said, "I know! I know!" as he paid and waved Hen away.

A door led from this back room into the lower back hall of the house, and in the shadow of the back hall Jan thought for an instant that he saw the landlady's figure; but he wasn't sure. Two minutes—or it may have been five minutes—later, a boy whom Jan had noticed round the house came into the room by way of that same door and said to the girl:

"Mrs. Goles wants to see you a minute."

"Tell her I got no minute to spare—not now."

The boy went out and quickly came back.

"Mrs. Goles says for you to come out and see her or she'll have the policeman in off the beat. He's at the corner now."

The girl went out.

"Who's Mrs. Goles?" asked Jan of the boy.

"Why, she's the landlady."

"Oh!" said Jan. So that was her husband, the handsome proprietor with the evil eyes. "Poor woman!" muttered Jan, and absent-mindedly drank his ginger ale.

The boy was still there. "Where is Mrs. Goles now?" asked Jan.

The boy jerked his head. "Out there on the back stairs."

Jan stood up. "Here!" He handed the boy a quarter. "A wonder a boy like you hangs out round here!"

"I run Mrs. Goles's errands. I been runnin' 'em since I was a kid. My mother used to work for her mother. She was a lady."

Jan was heading for the side door, the door which led into the alley.

"Will I tell her you're comin' back, mister?"

"Tell who?"

"Why, that girl you was with."

"Tell her nothing. Nor"—Jan nodded his head toward the pool-room—"him. Better go home. This is no place for a good boy like you."

Jan went out by the alley; and from there, after peeking to see that nobody was looking out of the pool-room windows, he stepped quickly up the front steps of the house.

Cautiously he unlocked the door. He could hear voices, but not distinctly. Quietly he tiptoed toward the head of the back stairs. It was Mrs. Goles who was talking.

"Didn't I warn you again and again never to bother him?" Jan heard.

"An' why not?"

"Why? He's a lodger—that's why."

"Is that why? Say, but ain't you takin' an awful sudden interest in yer lodgers though! Are yuh sure you don't want him for yerself? Are yuh sure he ain't something more than a lodger?"

"You—you—"

"Me—me! Yes, me. D'yuh think I ain't been onto yuh? D'yuh think I ain't seen any o' that billy-dooin'—you an' him upstairs in the entryway—huh? An' d'yuh think Hen ain't wise too? D'yuh think he gave me the top-floor room for nothin'—huh? Oh, yes; we're a couple o' come-ons—Hen an' me—oh, yes! Run along now, Salomey—he's there, waitin' for me. D'yuh hear—waitin' for me! They all fall when yuh play 'em right. All of 'em. Thought yuh had'm to yerself—huh? Well, guess different next time; for he's out there waitin' for me—the soft-headed Dutchman! Beat it! Beat it when yer gettin' the worst of it. An' talk any more about a policeman—an' see what Hen says to it!"

Jan could hear Mrs. Goles ascending the stairs behind him. He hurried up, intending to get to his room and hide away before she knew, but it was the last key of the bunch which fitted the lock, and before he had the door opened she was up with him.

She turned the hall light up to see him better.

"Weren't you downstairs in the back room a minute ago?" she asked at last.

"I was; but—" Jan reached up a heavy hand and rubbed his forehead. "I was—I know I was; but—" somehow he was feeling bewildered.

She drew nearer to him.

"Come nearer the light. Stand where the light will be on your face. Let me see your eyes. There—you can't keep them open. Did you drink that second glass of ginger ale—after it was brought in all opened up? Never mind trying to speak— just bow your head. You did? Oh, you poor innocent boy! Here—go into your room. And wait there. I'll be right back. Light the lamp if you can while you're waiting."

Jan managed to light the lamp.

She was soon back with a bowl of something hot which she held to Jan's lips—a nasty-tasting stuff. While he stopped once to get his breath she stepped to the door, took the key from the outside and set it on the inside. She stepped to Jan's side again. "Finish it!" she ordered. "Every drop. There—but sh-h!—hear'em?"

"Hear what, ma'am?"

"The footsteps—coming upstairs. Creeping up. Hear 'em?" She stepped to the light and blew it out. She stepped to the door and turned the key.

"Oh-h!" Jan had fallen backward on the bed and now was rolling from side to side. His stomach was griping him like a burning hand.

"Hold in for a minute if you can!" she whispered

Nausea uncontrollable, as it seemed to Jan, was taking hold of him when a knock came on the door. "Sh-h!" she warned, and Jan controlled himself. He wanted more than ever to vomit, but there came another knock on the door—and another. And then the knob was turned.

A silence then; and then a voice—a man's voice: "I told you you were crazy. He felt dizzy and went out into the street for some fresh air. You shouldn't 've left him once he got the stuff into him. Take a look round the block. He's probably laying in the gutter somewhere with that load into him."

The voice stopped, footsteps followed, the stairs creaked. And Jan's tortured stomach was allowed its relief. And while he retched in the dark Mrs. Goles held his head and, soaking a towel in the water jar, bathed his forehead and face and neck, and kept wetting the towel and bathing his head with the cold water until at last, with a grateful sigh, Jan stood up and said:

"I think it's all gone now."

"That's good. So I'll be leaving you. And you—" They had been talking in whispers, but at this point her voice broke into a cough. When she spoke again her voice was husky and pitched in a higher key. "But you—listen! You must leave this house!"

"Why must I leave?"

"It's no place for you."

"And is it for you, ma'am?" he asked her.

"For me? No—nor for any woman. But I'm talking about you. To-morrow—don't say a word to him downstairs—but to-morrow, when your week's up, take your grip and walk out."

"The day after to-morrow," amended Jan. "Tomorrow's Saturday and I has to be at the dry dock. But what will become of you?"

"There'll nothing become of me—no more than before."

"He will beat you?"

"Beat me! If he don't any more than beat me!" Jan fancied she was smiling at him in the dark. "But I'd better go. Good-night."

"Good-night," said Jan. "And I'll see you to-morrow to say good-by."

"Yes," she said. "I'll be about. Good-night."

"Good-night," said Jan again, and found himself standing at the door after it had opened and closed behind her.

* * * * *

"I wonder," thought Jan, "if he will beat her!" And he stooped to lock the door. His hand was on the key, but he did not turn it. Who was that? Jan had keen hearing. He jammed his ear against the crack. It was the sound of breathing, heavy breathing, of breathing and tramping, and now—Jan had been listening for perhaps a minute—of suppressed voices.

Jan stepped back to the washstand and poured out a glass of water. He took it at a gulp. He had another. It was cold and bracing to his fevered stomach. He stepped to the door, cautiously turned the knob and slowly drew the door to him. He peeped out.

Under the hall light he saw them—she jammed back against the stair-rail and he with his hands at her throat. His back was to Jan.

"Where is it? Come—give up!" he was saying. Jan could not hear what she said; but the man took a fresh grip and shook her. "Don't tell me anything like that! You gave in at last and got the money off him. Give it up!"

"I did not! I'm not that kind of a woman—not yet. I may be yet if you keep on—but I'm not yet. And he's not that kind of a man."

"You're not? And he's not? And you an hour in his room with the door locked! You got money off him! Give it to me!"

"N-no—no!"

"You lie, you—" He shifted his grip to her hair and started to drag her along the hall.

Jan stepped softly out, reached his arms round Goles's shoulders, drew them tight against his own chest; and then, holding him safe with his elbows, he ran his fingers down until they felt the knuckles of the other's hands. And then he squeezed. With thumb and forefinger of each hand he squeezed. Jan could pick up a keg of copper rivets with one thumb and forefinger and toss it across the deck of a ship. And now he squeezed. Goles hung on. Jan squeezed. The knuckles began to crack. "G-g-g—" snarled the other and loosed his grip.

Jan relaxed the grip of his thumb and forefinger, swung the man round, walked to the head of the stairs, raised his left knee, pressed it against the small of Goles's back, shifted his right hand to behind the man's shoulders and suddenly let knee and arm shoot out together. In one magnificent curve, and without touching a step on the way, Goles fetched up on the lower hall floor.

He stood up after a while and made as if to come back upstairs. As he did so Jan made as if to go down.

Goles glared up at him.

"So it is you!"

"Yes, it's me," said Jan. "Come!"

"Come? No! But you wait there, will you? Just wait there and see what happens to you! Wait!" And even as he called that last "Wait!" he was running for the back stairs.

Jan turned to her. She was sitting on the floor with her back against the stair-rail. Her knees were drawn up, and with elbows on knees she was supporting her head in her hands.

"Where is he gone to?" asked Jan.

"I don't know—to get his revolver probably."

Jan bent over to see her face. A great listlessness was all he could read there.

"Would he shoot? Did he ever shoot anybody?"

"Yes—two. But the police never found out. You'd better get out while there's time."

"And won't he shoot you?"

She raised her head to look at him. "No," she answered presently—"not just now. He will some day—that's sure. He promised me that more than once, and he means it; but I don't think he will to-night."

"Then, if ever he meant it, he will to-night," said Jan. "I don't want to get shot; and I'm going. You better come too." She shook her head. "Yes," He put an arm under her shoulder. "Come."

"No, no. I mustn't."

"But you must." Jan put his other arm under her and lifted her to her feet; but yet she lay heavy, half-resisting. "Come," said Jan. "I'll take you out of here—to my mother."

"Your mother?" she repeated, and straightened up; but almost instantly fell back. "But we can't now!" she whispered.

"Why?" whispered Jan.

"It's too late. Hear him?" Jan heard steps on the landing below; and as he listened and looked the light in the hall below went out. "You can't get out the front door in time now," she said hopelessly.

"There's more ways than front doors to get out of a house. And there's lights to put out up here too." He reached up and turned down the lamp-wick, then blew out the flame. "Come," he whispered, and led her into his room and locked the door.

He groped for the bed, tore off the sheets, twisted them tightly and knotted them together. "There!" he said, and, taking a turn of it under her arms, let her down from the window into the alley. Then he swept into his suit-case a few things from the dresser and snapped it, and dropped it out the window.

He was about to fasten one end of the twisted sheets about the bedpost, to let himself down; but hearing the door-knob slowly turning he did not finish the job. He dropped the sheet, lowered himself by his hands from the window-sill and let go. He landed without damage.

"Come," he said, and led the way to the street. At the first corner he turned. At the next corner he turned. At the third corner a cab was in sight. He helped her in.

"Do you know," Jan whispered to her, "a good hotel I could tell him to drive to?"

"With me looking as I am? Why, no. Tell him any hotel we can get into."

Jan addressed the cabman.

"I want"—he said it very distinctly, so that there could be no mistake—"a good hotel to take a lady to."

"A lady? An' a *good* hotel? Sure thing. Jump in."

Jan got in and sat opposite to her. She was restoring order to her hair.

"Did the cabby laugh?" she asked.

"No. Why should he?"

"Why?" Jan saw that she was staring at him. Suddenly her stare was transformed to a soft smile. "Oh-h—sometimes these cabbies think they're funny."

Presently the cab stopped. Jan looked out. It was a hotel, with a wide door and a narrow one. The narrow door was marked "Ladies' Entrance," and through the transom a red light shone.

"Wait," said Jan.

He went through the wide door to the desk. "I want a room for a lady," he said to the clerk.

"Lady? Sure. Four dollars."

Jan paid the four dollars and registered. The clerk touched a bell. A boy bobbed up.

"I will bring her in by the ladies' entrance," said Jan; but in passing out to the street he caught a glimpse of a room across the hall—a room with tables, and men and women at the tables, and drinks on the tables. He halted for a longer look and went out to the cab finally with a troubled look.

"There's a room for you, but"—he took off his hat and ran his fingers through his hair—"I don't think you ought to stay here." He had put his head inside the cab and was speaking low, so that the cabman should not hear. "I don't think it's a nice place for a lady."

"But"—she almost smiled—"I'm afraid we'll have to put up with it. Look!" She spread wide her rumpled skirt. Her eyes rolled down to indicate her torn bodice. With her fingertips she touched the bruises on her face and the marks on her neck. "And I haven't even a hat on," she concluded with an undoubted smile.

Jan gave in. He paid the cabman, and led her through the ladies' entrance to where the bell-boy was waiting. The boy led the way upstairs, opened a door and turned on the light.

"You wait out in the hall," Jan said to the bell-boy. "The lady may want hot water and things to clean up. You know? The lady"—Jan tapped the boy on the shoulder—"fell out of a buggy and lost her hat." He handed the boy a dollar bill. "You understand now?"

The boy tucked the bill away. "I'm wise! I'm wise!" He winked at Jan and left the room.

Jan turned to her. "I'll have a few things sent up in the morning."

She was standing straight and motionless in the middle of the room.

"You're good," she said, but without looking at him.

"And—oh, my mother! I most forgot her. She lives in Port Rock. To-morrow night I'll put you aboard the boat for Port Rock. And I won't be able to see you till then."

"Not till to-morrow night?"

"I has to be at the dry dock early in the morning or they can't start work. Good-night." He was holding his hat very stiffly in one hand. The other hand he extended to her.

"Good-night," the woman said, and took his hand and clung to it. Suddenly she lifted it to her lips and sobbed.

A woman crying and kissing his hand, and all done so suddenly he couldn't stop it—Jan was shocked at himself. "Sh-h!" said Jan. "Sh-h! You mustn't."

"I will. You're the first man ever came to the house who didn't look at me as if I was a streetwalker. And he tried his best to make me one. And I fought him—and fought him; but not a soul to help me. And a woman can't hold out forever. I'd 'a' killed myself, but I was afraid to die that way. I was beginning to weaken when you came. And if you had been the wrong kind of a man—"

"Sh-h! Don't say things like that."

"But it's so. And you helped me to get over it. Before I was married I used to dream of a man like you. But what chance had I in the dance-halls along the water-front and my people dead? And he was a dance-hall hero, the kind girls used to write notes to. I was never as bad as that—believe me I wasn't,—but I married him just the same—at seventeen, and what does a girl know of life at seventeen? And him! Almost on my wedding-day he began to abuse me."

"No, no!"

"It's true. And when you told me you'd take me to your mother—that was the first message I'd got in five years from a man except what was meant for my harm. But a good mother—I'll tell her so she'll understand."

"She'll understand without you telling her. She's brought up a dozen of us and has grand-children—lots of 'em. Sunday morning you'll be in my mother's house in Port Rock."

She stooped to kiss his hand again.

"Here! Here—you mustn't!"

"I will—I will! And there! And there! And now good-night."

"Good-night," mumbled Jan. He hurried out of the room and all but fell over the bell-boy in the hall. "What you hanging round for?" Jan almost hissed. "Go below."

The bell-boy hurried downstairs and "Say, but that's a new kind of an elopement for this shack!" he exploded to the clerk, and repeated what he had heard.

The clerk took a look at the register and read: "'Mrs. H.G. Goles, City.' Now I didn't notice that before. 'Mrs. Goles' he registered, and not himself. Goles? I wonder if that's Hen's woman? Well, if it is he'll get his good and plenty before Hen's done with him."

"Yes, and the police'll get Hen. And, say, that Swede ain't such a gink when yuh get a second look at him."

"I don't know. I didn't get a second look at him; but the way he pulled out that wad—I charged him four bucks for a dollar-'n'-a-half room. And—"

"S-st!" warned the boy.

It was Jan re-entering the office.

"What's wrong?" demanded the clerk.

"Paper and envelope, please," said Jan.

"Oh!" The clerk looked relieved and passed them over. Jan took out a carpenter's thick-leaded pencil and wrote on the sheet of paper: "You must buy some things for the trip on the boat." He looked at the clerk and then at the boy, and went out into the hall, folded one ten-dollar bill and two twenty-dollar bills inside the sheet, sealed and addressed the envelope, and brought it in to the boy.

"You take this up to the lady. Give it to her and hurry away before she can open it. And if you are back in two minutes—"

The boy was back in less time. Jan gave him half a dollar and passed out into the street.

# THE PORT ROCK BOAT

The Port Rock boat was due *to* leave her dock. The first mate made his way to the upper deck. He found his captain in the pilot-house, studying the barometer.

"Freight all aboard, sir."

"All right," nodded the captain; "but did you hear about the storm flags being up?"

"So I heard, sir."

"M-m! Close that door. It's cold." The mate closed the door; but almost immediately the captain raised a window and gazed down the harbor. "It looks bad to me," he said after a while.

"It is a bad-looking night," assented the mate.

"A wicked night!" barked the captain; and gathering one end of his moustache between his teeth, began to chew on it.

The mate pursed his lips. "What will I do, sir?"

The captain stopped chewing his moustache. "It all comes down to dollars and cents. Use our judgment and stay tied up to the dock here and it's go hunt another berth. Do you want to hunt another job?"

"Not me. I got a family to look after."

"N' me. We'll put out."

"All right, sir." The mate descended to the wharf. "In with

James Brendan Connolly

that freight runway and plank!" he called out to the waiting longshoremen. "And you"—a colored steward was at his elbow—"tell 'em all aboard on the dock and all ashore on the boat that's goin' ashore."

The steward voiced the mate's instructions; the last passenger came aboard and the last friend went ashore. The gangplank was hauled in, the lines cast off and the Port Rock steamer slid out from her slip.

She was well down the harbor before Jan took a piece of paper from his pocket. "Number two hundred and seventy-six," he read. "That's it—two hundred and seventy-six." And seeking out the number he knocked on the door. It opened slightly and Jan saw peeking out at him the lips, chin and half an eye each side of the nose of a pretty and well-dressed girl. Jan looked up at the number over the door again to see if he had made a mistake. Then the door opened more widely—and it was she, smiling out at him; but so rosy and terribly pretty that Jan felt afraid and drew back.

"I thought maybe you would like to get out for some fresh air soon," he stammered.

"I was just trying on the new hat I bought with the money you sent up last night—and a shirtwaist and a lovely long coat. How did you get through the night?"

"Fine! I went over to the dry dock and turned into a bunk on the schooner."

She made a mouth at the mirror. "That was no place to sleep. You should have taken a comfortable room at the hotel."

Jan was silent.

"Yes, you should. I'll be right out."

She came out, but with her face veiled, and clung close to him as they walked the deck. Jan sniffed the air.

"Snow, I think," he said.

"Meaning a storm? I was never in a storm. Are they terrible?"

"A storm is nothing," said Jan, "when you get used to them. But will we go in to supper?"

They went in. The boat was now outside the harbor and pitching slightly.

She did not eat much and at length laid down her knife and fork."

"Sea-sick?" asked Jan.

"No. I must be too frightened to be sea-sick."

"Frightened of what?"

"Of him." She leaned across the table. "I'm sure I saw him. Yes—spying through the window of my room just before I left it just now."

Jan tranquilly went on eating. "He can't hurt you aboard a boat."

"I don't mind that, so he won't hurt you."

Jan shook his head. "He won't because he can't on here without getting caught."

They stepped outside at last. Cozy enough in the dining-room; but outside the snow was now thick enough to show white on deck where the passengers had not tramped it down. They sought the open space in the bow—Jan to see how it looked ahead and Mrs. Goles to feel the fresh gale blowing in her face.

"It's a north-east snow-storm," said Jan, "and coming thicker. But no danger. No—no danger," he repeated quickly, with a glance at her.

"It's not danger of a storm I fear," she said simply. She was peering, not ahead at the darkening, rising sea but at the form and face of every muffled-up passenger who came near them.

Not many passengers were venturing onto the open deck; and those who did were wrapped high and close, with hardly more than their eyes showing out. "If he comes on us he will come like that—coat collar to his ears and hat over his eyes," she thought as one after another so wrapped appeared and passed; and almost with the thought, catching sight of a lurking man's figure in the passageway between the paddle-box and the outside row of state-rooms, she added aloud: "Let us go up on the top deck."

"It will be pretty cold and rough for you up there," suggested Jan.

"Never mind; let us go there." A man could not very well hide on the more open top deck, was what she had in mind.

They could hardly keep their feet on the top deck. An officer in passing warned them sharply to be careful. She looked after him scornfully. "As if you weren't more at home on the sea than any of them!" she said proudly.

The wind on the top deck was blowing a gale. The snow was pouring down. Another officer bumped into them. "This is no place for passengers!" he yelled. "Better go below and inside the house!" And he hurried on.

"Excited, ain't he?" said Jan. "But maybe we better go below too. But let's go round by the lee side—this way."

In passing the pilot-house a window above them was thrown open and a man's face thrust through, and a man's voice said:

"We'll never make Port Rock to-night, not against this gale and snow. And no use trying to see anything ahead."

Jan peered up through the dark and the snow to see who it might be. Against the light in the pilot-house he could distinguish the head and shoulders of the captain.

"Then we'd better put in somewhere for the night, hadn't we?" Jan knew that for the mate's voice.

"Put in where?"

"I don't know—Gloucester, maybe?"

"Gloucester? And how does Gloucester bear now?—tell me that. And how does any port bear now?—tell me that, too. Suppose we did know, would you try to take her into Gloucester harbor on a night like this? Gloucester!"

"Sh-h! There's something," said the other voice.

The voices were hushed. Two long moans came over the sea.

"Wait for them again. And time 'em." The captain's voice that.

James Brendan Connolly

Mrs. Goles stepped closer to Jan. "Does it mean there's danger to the ship?" she asked in a low voice in Jan's ear.

"No, no. But listen!"

One long moan and one short moan came fitfully over the sea.

"Thatcher's Island steam-whistle," said the captain's voice. "An' bearing so." So thick was the night with snow that Jan had to strain his sight to make out the mittened hand and coatsleeve stretching out through the window over his head.

Jan felt the wind whipping him on the other side, and with that there came from the pilot-house: "Well, if that ain't the devil's own luck! Here's the wind makin' into the north-west and the chief whistlin' up half-steam's all he can keep on her!"

"Ain't it always something wrong! I told 'em about them boilers—that they been leakin' right along. What will we do?"

"Only one thing to do now. Run her before it. Besides, she'll be blown offshore soon now. Run her across the bay. South-south-east. She ought to fetch Provincetown."

"Yes, sir. But when we get out from under the lee of the land what'll happen?"

"I don't know; but I do know what'll happen to her bumpin' over the rocks of this shore on a night like this!"

Jan touched Mrs. Goles's arm. "We better go below now, I think. And you better go to your room and wrap up in any warm clothes you have—two pairs of stockings, if you have them, and things like that. To be ready for accidents, you know. And wait for me in the saloon."

"So there is danger?"

"You must not be thinking of that; but it is foolish not to be ready for accidents. And while you are dressing up I will take a look round."

"Oh, suppose he is aboard! Won't you watch out for him?"

"It's him has to watch out for me on a night like this," said Jan—"and maybe watch out for more than me."

\*　\*　\*　\*　\*

Jan went to his room and put on his extra suit of underwear, and over his vest he drew his sweater. From his suit-case he took his mother's photograph and tucked it in his inside pocket. Then he went up again to the top deck and located a life-raft—made the rounds of the boat-deck and located the life-boats.

It was time now to study the storm. The snow was not so thick, but the sea was making and the wind colder and stronger. A gale from the northwest it would be when they were out in the open bay; and, besides the wind getting stronger the sea would be higher. And it was as high now as was good for this old-fashioned side-wheeler with her old-time single engine.

Jan shook his head and, still shaking his head, once more made the rounds of the boat-deck. Eight boats; and each boat might hold twenty-five people—that is, if it was in a mill-pond. But a night like this—how many—even if the running gear were sound? "No, no," said Jan to himself, and reinspected the lone life-raft on the top deck. Two cigar-shaped steel air-cylinders with a thin connecting deck was the life-raft. Jan had seen better ones; but a raft, at least, would not capsize.

He descended to the main deck, to where, in the gangway between house and rail, he could find a little quiet and think things over. While there, amidships, a sea swept up under the paddle-wheel casing. It boomed like a gun. With it went some crackling. Again a booming—again a crackling. The boat broached to. Sea-water was running the length of her deck.

From out of the snow and night another sea came; and this one came straight aboard, roaring as it came. Jan knew what it meant—there is always the first sea by itself. Not long now before there would be another.

And not long before there was another.

And soon there would be a hundred of them, one racing after the other. And a thousand more of them—only this rust-eaten hull, with her scrollwork topsides, would not hold together long enough to see a thousand of them.

Jan tried to figure out how far they were from the Cape Cod shore. Ten, fifteen, twenty miles. Call it twenty. Jan doubted if she would live to get there, even with the gale behind her.

He walked round the house to look into the lighted saloon. She was there—the poor girl—sitting patiently by herself. Long before this the orchestra had given up playing and only a dozen passengers or so were there; but she was the only lone one—in a red plush chair under a cluster of wall-lights. Besides the passengers, there was one steward and a colored maid, both staring together through the lighted window.

Jan's feet were wet. He went down to the bar, where he called for a drink of ginger ale and a pint flask of brandy. "Of your best," he added.

Leaning against the bar he listened to the loungers there. Four of them were at a table under a window which looked out on the open deck. One was struggling in a loud voice with what should have been a funny story. His companions neglected no chance to laugh, but after each laugh they hastily sipped their drinks. At intervals the wind would shriek and at each shriek they would look past each other with exaggerated calmness; but when the sea pounded the hull, and the spray splashed thickly against the window over their heads, they would look up at the window or across at the door. And when the boat would roll down and, rolling, threaten to dump them all on the floor, they would grab the table and yell "Whoa!" or "Wait a second!" with just a suggestion of hysteria in their throats; and somebody would call out, "Go on with the story, Joe!" and the story-teller would hasten to resume.

Jan turned to the bartender, who was filling waiting stewards' hurried orders calmly if not impassively. After every heavy sea he would stop pouring or mixing to glance with unaffected interest at the beams above him or the door opening onto the deck. He was an undersized man with lean, pale cheeks, a hard chin, and a bright, cold eye. Once he looked fairly at Jan and Jan looked fairly at him. It was like an introduction.

"You a sea-going man?" he asked.

"I used to go to sea," admitted Jan.

"I thought so. But those there,"—he lowered his voice and leaned across the bar to Jan,—"they don't know whether this is a real bad gale or just the reg'lar thing. One of 'em says a while ago: 'This is the kind of weather I like!' I bet it's his first trip. But most of the passengers, the stewards tell me, are turned in, trying to forget it."

"Better for 'em," said Jan.

"Maybe so, too; but what do you think of it?"

Jan shook his head. "I will be glad when morning comes."

"Same here. I've seen it as bad as this a couple of times before." He picked up Jan's bill. "But this old shoe box ain't getting any younger. Here's your brandy. It's good stuff—don't be afraid of it. Seventy-five and fifteen—ninety."

"Have a cigar," said Jan, "and finish the dollar."

"Thanks. I will. But I'll smoke it later, when it's quieter, if it's all the same to you." He rang up a dollar on the cash register and turned to a new-comer who had ranged up beside Jan.

"Brandy," said the new-comer.

As Jan thrust his flask in his inside coat-pocket he flashed a sidewise glance at the man drinking. The man was buttoned up to his eyes, but Jan thought he knew the voice. Jan buttoned up his own coat, said "Good-night" to the bartender and went out on deck, from where, through the window, he could view the customer at the bar.

Jan saw him empty his glass and motion for another drink. He drank that, paid, and turned to go. Jan caught a front glimpse of his face. It was Goles. Jan also saw that the bartender was looking curiously after him.

Jan waited for him outside. As he came almost abreast, the ship heaved and the two men fell against each other, while a great splash of sea-water drenched them. Again a roll and jump, and Goles would have fallen had not Jan held him upright. Goles gave him no thanks, but he said huskily: "I heard one of the sailors say she's a goner." With Jan holding on to Goles, the two men were swaying and stumbling to the boat's heavy rolling and heaving.

"I don't know about that," said Jan; "but she's in a bad way. And it's going to be worse, I think."

"That's what the sailor said," muttered Goles.

"So if you want to shoot anybody you better wait till we're safe—to-morrow maybe. And your wife—But watch out!"

The sea washed fairly over them both. With the wave went a broken rail and part of the splintered house. Following the crashing of the wood and glass came the frightened questions and the patter of excited people running out of their rooms. The story-telling group from the barroom came as one man. The glass of the window over their heads had been showered on to their table. The bartender stopped only to empty his cash register, stuff the money in his pocket, and get into a great coat; then he came running out too. Bottles and glasses were breaking behind him as he ran.

"Come," said Jan. Goles followed. Jan went up and looked into the saloon. There she was, still waiting. "You stay here and I will bring her out," said Jan to Goles—"and don't you open your mouth when you see her."

Goles made no sign. He was gripping the house railing and his face was to the sea.

"Thank God for the sight of you!" she said to Jan as he came in. "Is the ship going down?"

"Not yet. But your husband is outside. He won't say anything. Don't you either. And when—Hold hard!"

The deck bounded up under them. She gripped Jan's coat and Jan gripped a chair that was screwed to the floor; and then the deck rolled far down and Jan's chair came loose, and both were thrown across the saloon. "She is breaking up!" thought Jan. A moment later it seemed to Jan as if all the passengers in the ship had suddenly awakened and were trying to crowd into the place. A ship's officer and some stewards also came running in. The stewards had life-preservers, which they were buckling on to themselves. They remained; but the officer, after a look around, ran out again.

The boat rolled back on her keel. Jan led Mrs. Goles to the outer deck. Goles was there. "Come!" ordered Jan, and led the way to an iron ladder. The boat rolled far to one side and again far to the other. Mrs. Goles felt as if she were clinging to the tail of a kite, but still she clung to Jan; and Jan at last made the upper deck with her. He had forgotten her husband; but when he turned to look back the muffled form was there at his heels.

Jan groped his way to where the life-raft was lashed to the deck. He ordered Mrs. Goles to sit down on the raft. Goles sat down beside her. Goles seemed bereft of all volition.

"You wait here till I come back," Jan said to him and turning to go below, bumped into another man.

"Hello! Is this you?" said the other man. "I thought I saw you come up here. 'And there's the man,' I says to myself, 'to tie to to-night!'"

Jan recognized the bartender. "You're just the man I want, too," said Jan. He dove into his pocket and drew out a revolver. "Here, take this."

"A gun!"

"Yes—and loaded. Watch that man on the raft. And if he tries to hurt that woman or not let her on that raft if the boat goes down, shoot him!"

"You mean it?"

"Yes. He's bad! He's the man who was drinking in your place a few minutes ago—after me."

"Oh, him! Yes; he's bad, all right. He's been drinking raw brandy since seven o'clock. I was noticin' him."

"Don't shoot him unless you have to. And don't let him see me passing it to you. I'm going to get a few more people up to the raft."

"All right—but—Wow! I never shot a man in my life."

Jan had hardly reached the saloon when the great crash came. He was swept away before it. Boom! it was—and again, crash! Now he heard the smothered appeals of people being swept overboard! Crackling wood was following the crash of every sea, and each sea receded only to let the next one strike even more heavily. It was now nothing but solid water that was coming aboard.

Her buoyancy had left her. Her roll had become a wallow. She was settling. "The water's in her hold!" thought Jan, and took a quick look about. All kinds and all ages—but there was one girl with an expression on her face that startled him.

In fine but sodden clothes she was sitting, heedless of every person but the young man standing dumbly beside her. "And I told them I was going to stay with a girl friend out of town over Sunday," she was saying. "And now they'll know. Whether we're drowned or not they'll know. Everybody will know and what will they say?"

Near the girl were a young man and a woman locked in each other's arms. Jan judged them to be a bridal couple. They were saying nothing—just holding each other and waiting. He hesitated an instant and then he saw a woman with a baby. She was leaning heavily against a stanchion crooning to the baby. He now saw that she was almost a middle-aged woman, a poorly dressed and toil-worn woman—a Finnish woman probably. Jan's doubt was gone. He jumped to her side. "Want to save your baby?" The woman looked up at him and down at the baby. "Baby!" she said, and held it toward Jan. "Yes, save baby," she said. "Come!" said Jan, and grasped her hand. Then the lights went out.

Jan had marked the ladder in his mind, and in the dark he made his way toward it; but before he could get to it there were many adventures. He went floundering this way and that, but holding the baby in one arm and dragging the mother with the other, he held on until he bumped into a stanchion in the dark. "It's near here," he thought; and, reaching out with his feet, he found the bottom step of the ladder.

He had two decks to surmount. On the boat-deck, as he passed up, he could hear the ship's men shouting wildly and foolishly to each other. On the top deck he found the three just as he had left them. He gave the woman and baby into the care of the bartender and felt about until he found a coil of rope. He cut it loose and, carrying it back to the raft, lashed Mrs. Goles to a ring. Then, taking off his ulster, he wrapped it round the mother and baby, and lashed her. Then he lashed the bartender and Goles, and took a loose turn about a ring for himself. Then he waited.

It came soon enough. A large section of the top deck floated clear of the upper works. Jan stayed by the floating deck until he felt that the steamer was surely sunk beneath them. Then he cut the raft clear of everything and let her drift.

The raft was swirled from wave to wave. The spray broke over them. "We'll get wet," said Jan; "but one thing—she won't capsize!"

The seas curled and boomed about them; but no solid seas rolled over them. The raft mounted every roaring white crest as if it were swinging from an aeroplane. The spray never failed to drench them and with every heaving sea came bits of wreckage that threatened them; but at least they were living, and not a living soul besides themselves had come away.

# THE RAFT

The clouds raced low above them; but by and by the clouds passed away and clear and cold shone a moon on a terrifying sea. And so for hours—until the moon had gone and the struggling daylight revealed a surf breaking high on a sandy shore. They could not land there; so Jan took the long oar and wielded it over one end of the raft and held her parallel to the beach until he descried a point reaching out into the bay. On the other side of that point would be a lee and safety; but he said nothing of that to his companions yet.

In the middle of the raft lay Goles, huddled and silent as ever. Mrs. Goles, at the farther end of the raft, was mostly watching Jan as he heaved on the oar; but sometimes she seemed to be studying her husband. The Finn woman, nearest to Jan, was hugging her baby to her under Jan's great coat. She, too, when she was not watching her baby, was looking at Jan. The bartender, between Jan and Goles, was looking out for marks ashore.

The bartender was also thinking that the two other men were about the same age, and yet the man in the middle of the raft, when he let his face be seen, looked the older by ten years. All night long he had not spoken and he seldom raised his head—when he did it was to gaze at the land. He seemed to be taking but small notice of anybody. Toward the bartender, who was behind him, he had not once turned his head.

Jan worked on the long oar. The point of land was coming nearer. "A hard drag yet; but we'll be there by sunrise!" said Jan in a low voice to the bartender; at which Goles looked round suddenly—but said nothing.

At last they were under the lee of the point. The sea was

beautifully smooth. Jan stopped sculling and went forward to Mrs. Goles. "The tide has her," he said. "Soon she will be in and we will all be safe!" She looked back at her husband.

The bartender stood up and shouted aloud. "Safe—hah! Say, but ain't it like looking at something in a moving picture though?" He stuck a hand into his coat pocket and pulled out Jan's revolver. He stared at it; then, with a low whistle and a glance at Goles's back, he returned it to his pocket. Only the Finn woman had seen the action.

The bartender shoved a hand into his trousers pocket. He pulled out a handful of bills and silver. "Well, what do you know? And I came near putting that into the safe last night!" He unbuttoned his coat and from his vest pocket he pulled out a cigar. "Well, what do you know?" He next drew out a metallic match-case. "Well, well—dry too!" He lit his cigar, took three or four puffs, contentedly sat down, and began smoothing out and counting the damp bills. "Well, well!— forty-five, fifty-five, sixty, seventy—the only time in my life I ever beat a cash register! Seventy-two—four—and on a good night there'd a been three times the business—eight-four—six—eight. Eighty-eight dollars."

Goles looked over his shoulder at the bartender. He wet his lips and stood up. After a time he threw off his overcoat. "How about a drink from that flask?" he asked suddenly.

Jan, without looking around, drew the flask from his pocket and handed it to him. He had already given the two men a drink each—and the Finn woman and Mrs. Goles two swallows of it during the night; and almost half the brandy was now gone. Goles put the flask to his lips. The bartender stopped counting his silver to watch him; and, seeing it go, he called out: "Say there, Bill, just leave a taste of that, will you?" Goles drank it to the last drop. When he had finished he threw the empty flask overboard. "Well, if you ain't one fine gentleman!" exploded the bartender.

Goles paid no attention to him. "How long before we'll be ashore now?" he asked.

"Only a few minutes now," said Jan. He was still standing with his back to Goles.

"A few minutes?" repeated Goles. At the words his wife turned sharply. Husband and wife stared at each other.

"There's the sun coming over the sand-hill now," said Jan. She turned to look shoreward.

The bartender, counting and chuckling over his money, felt a hand shaking the tip of his sleeve. It was the Finn woman. She pointed a finger toward Goles. The bartender saw Goles's hand come out of his bosom with a revolver.

"So long as we're safe," said Goles slowly, "you're going to get yours—and get it now, you—"

Jan was looking at the shore, but Mrs. Goles had turned with the first word and thrown herself toward Goles as he fired. Mrs. Goles fell before the bullet. "I was going to get her anyway," said Goles evenly, and leveled his revolver at Jan, who had jumped to save her from falling overboard and was now holding her away from Goles.

"I got you where there's no comeback!" gritted Goles, and took careful aim at Jan!—but did not fire. He felt a ring of cold metal pressed against his neck and half turned to see what it was. "Don't shoot! Don't!" he begged.

"You—" The word the bartender gritted out could not be

heard, because he pulled the trigger as he said it.

Goles sagged down until his knees rested on the deck. Then he fell forward and over the side of the raft. There was the gentlest of splashes, a patch of red—a cluster of bubbles which burst like sighs.

"Well!" said the bartender, and held up the revolver in wonder. "I never thought I'd live to kill a man!" He looked to see how the others had taken it, but they were paying no attention to him. He saw Jan holding the baby and trying to hush its little cries for its mother, while the baby's mother was pressing the tips of her fingers gently against the upper part of the injured woman's right breast.

"You mustn't die! You mustn't die!" Jan said when the baby would let him.

"I don't want to die—not now!" she answered.

The Finn woman looked up and smiled at Jan. "Not die. No, no—not die."

The raft grounded gently on the beach. Jan took the wounded girl and set out for the top of the sand-hill with her. The bartender took the baby and toiled behind with its mother.

"Say," said the bartender, "you're all right! How many more children to home?"

"Home?" She held up seven fingers. "And him," pointing to the baby.

"Great Stork! Here!" He set down the baby, drew out the bar-money and offered it to her. "When a ship goes down, I heard a sea-lawyer say once, all debts go with her. And that

James Brendan Connolly

must mean all credits go too. Anyhow we'll make it so now. Here—for you."

"Me? No, no. I have husband. Fine job—dollar-half day."

"Dollar an' a half! It's too much for the father of eight children for one day! But this—see. For baby. And the Lord knows a baby who came through last night and never a yip out of him, he oughter get a million. Here—put in bank—for baby."

"Ah-h! For baby. Tenk you." She beamed and took the money. "You brave man! Him"—pointing to Jan's back— "brave man too."

"Him, brave—yes. But me? No, no. Me scared blue. He'd 'a' shot me next only I beat him to it."

"Kill baby too." She kissed the baby.

\* \* \* \* \*

The sun was well up when they reached the top of the hill—a pale, frightened-looking sun, but nevertheless a sun. The bartender took off his cap and saluted it gravely. Below them lay the town.

"We'll go down there," said Jan to Mrs. Goles, "and from there, when you're well, we'll go home—to my mother. But," he added gravely, "we will go by train."

She smiled weakly at him. "I could go without a train—on my hands and knees I could crawl to the mother of you! You don't know it, but when I was growing up it was a man like you I always used to dream about. And I'm not sure I'm not dreaming now!"

"Don't worry," said the bartender. "We're all awake—and alive. And you bet it's great to be alive again! Ain't it,"—he turned to the Finn woman,—"you mother of eight?"

The Finn woman made no answer. She was nursing her baby.

## COGAN CAPEADOR

I

Eight bells had gone, the morning watch was done, it was almost time to eat, and so Kieran, the pump-man, laid aside the tools of his berth and came strolling aft; and swinging down the long gangway he sang:

"There was a girl,—I knew her well,—a girl in Zanzibar—
A bulgeous man of science said you bet her avatar
Was Egypt's Cleopatra—and from off a man-o'-war
I met her first—and O, her eyes! A blazing polar star!
From which you couldn't head away no more than you could fly—
Gypsy one of Zanzy! For you who wouldn't die!"

It was one of those fine days in the Gulf of Mexico. Abreast of the ship the Florida reefs, low-crested, ragged, and white, loomed above the smooth sea.

Kieran contemplated the line of reefs; presently he leaned over the taffrail and stared down at the whirling propeller; from the screws his gaze shifted to the whirling water above and about them, and thence to the tow in their wake. He put his head to one side, studied the spectacle of the straining hawser and the wallowing barge on the end of it, as if it were a mysterious problem.

"Oh-h, shucks!" He sighed and came suddenly out of his reverie, looked up at the sky, turned wearily inboard, and sat himself on one of the towing bitts.

The passenger, from the other towing bitt, asked what it was.

"I was just thinking that some of us are tied to the end of a string, just like that barge, and we don't know it any more than she does, and no more able to help ourselves than she can—sometimes."

"I never looked at a towing barge in that light before," said the passenger, and lit a cigar. He made no offer of one to Kieran, because he had before this learned that Kieran never smoked.

The ship rolled, the barge yawed, the reefs kept sliding by. The passenger stole a look at the pump-man, and ventured: "Kieran, there used to be, a few years ago, a sprinter, pole-vaulter, and jumper, competing under the name of Campbell in the Hibernian and Caledonian games up north, and you're a ringer for him."

Kieran glanced sidewise at the passenger. "You must have been in athletics yourself—seems to me I've seen you somewhere too."

"Maybe. My name's Benson."

"I remember—a sprinter. And a good one, too."

"Good enough—with no Wefers or Duffey, or somebody like

yourself around," protested the passenger, but immensely pleased nevertheless to be identified after so many years. And they were both pleased and exchanged rapid comment on a dozen incidents of athletic days; and when two ex-athletes get together they run on interminably.

By and by, but not prematurely, the passenger asked, "But *was* there a girl at Zanzibar?"

Kieran made no reply. He seemed to be considering the matter of the barge. After a time he went to the quarter-rail and gazed forward. He came back to his bitt. "I thought so. There's one of those wreckers up ahead. They're always along here—standing by or cruising for any loose wreckage." He waved his hand toward the reefs. "Look. Where their crests don't pierce the surface you know they're there by the surf playing over 'em. Where they lie a little deeper the paler green of the sea shows 'em up. In the deep pockets in between—see?—the sea's of a beautiful deep blue. That's all easy enough, isn't it, but where the drifting clouds shut out the sunlight, where the shadows fall it's all of a color, isn't it? No saying then where it's deep water and where it is shoal. It's the clouds. If the light was always good, there'd be few wrecks along here. And"—he waved toward the barge astern—"there she is tied to us. If this ship piles up on the reefs, she piles up behind us."

"Couldn't they cut her adrift?"

"H-m-m—a drifting barge and the Florida Keys tide-water, where would she fetch up?" And, after a pause, "no fault of hers either, and that seems hard, too. But there's that wrecker—listen."

A hailing voice came floating aft to them. "Ain't seen nothing 'long de way—nothin' to th' east'ard, has you, capt'n?"

"No, I didn't see nothin'. And if I did, d'y' s'pose I'd tell you, you green-sided, patch-sailed whelp's loafer of a black pirate, do you?"

Without turning their heads Kieran and the passenger could hear their captain's voice from the bridge, and also without turning their heads they shortly saw the wrecking schooner slide past their quarter. She *was* green-painted and her sails *were* a scandal, and it *was* a very black and big negro who was standing in her waist to catch the reply, and it was very like their captain to answer as he did.

The big negro only flashed his teeth and waved his arm. His little vessel went drifting astern.

"Pirates and wreckers—look pretty much like honest people, don't they?" commented Kieran. "And they are mostly. At least I've bunked with 'em—white ones, though—and I found 'em pretty much like you and me—except for their ideas in that and maybe one or two other lines. And most people, when you come to know them, aren't so different, except in one way—or maybe two or three ways in some cases. Don't you think so?"

The passenger countered with another question. "You've met a good many different kinds of people in your time, haven't you?"

The pump-man nodded. After a pause he added, "A few," in an absent manner.

The low-lying reefs sank out of sight, and far astern the green-painted schooner merged into the mists. It was a warm, pleasant day.

Kieran roused himself. "No, there wasn't any girl in

Zanzibar. If there had been, a fellow couldn't be advertising her to the crew of an oil-tanker at high-noon, could he? No! But there *was* a girl, and there was a friend of mine—call him Cogan. Oh, not a bad fellow—no worse, maybe no better, than you or I, or most any of the old crowd we used to know, and he happened to drift down the Isthmus way—into Colon—during the Revolution. Ever there?"

"Once, just after the Revolution."

"And what did you think of it—the Revolution?"

"M-m—it surely did happen most opportunely for our interests."

"Didn't it, though? And did you ever notice that quite a few of the revolutions in those Central American latitudes happen most opportunely for some northern interest or other? Well, Cogan was there during the Revolution. He told me of a saloon there, about a minute's walk up from the big steamship dock on the street next the water-side—remember that street?"

"Where the railroad starts to cross the Isthmus to Panama?"

"That's it. And this saloon was on that street—it may be there yet—the Fourth of July saloon with its big American ensign painted on the wall opposite the bar. Remember it?"

"M-m-h-h."

"Well, it was run by a Brooklyn Irishman named Martin Jackson, and Cogan said he remembered the shock he got when he first heard him talk. His Irish brogue had a Spanish accent—do you get that? Well, he has nothing to do with the story, only this—Cogan used to have great ideas about revolutions, and Martin, he knocked most of them out of him. He'd seen twenty of them in his time, Martin had, and when he saw one of them coming now, he just ran up his iron shutters and let it roll by. Business was generally pretty good after a revolution. An easy-going sort of a man, Martin. He didn't even get mad with Cogan when he'd used up hours of his time and then only order ginger ale.

"Cogan saw the Panamanian army at dress parade one day—after the Revolution that was. About two hundred darkies, mostly boys of thirteen or fourteen, barefooted with high-water pants on. Cogan's notion of it was that a dozen good huskies with baseball bats could've landed on their peninsula any fine, sunny afternoon and in ten minutes rushed the whole Panamanian army into the Pacific Ocean—that is, if our warships would let them. If we'd only let the Colombians alone they'd soon've wound up the Revolution—so Cogan thought, and told Martin so. 'But I s'pose they've had hundreds of revolutions in South America?' he says to Martin.

"'Hundreds,' says Martin, and blows more smoke toward the sky. Out in front of the saloon they were sitting, both of 'em balancing between the sidewalk and the wall on the hind legs of their chairs."

"'Anybody ever killed?'"

"'Oh, not more than maybe a few hundred to a time—sometimes a few thousand—'"

"'Hundreds? Thousands?' says Cogan. 'We hadn't any more than three hundred killed—that is, killed fighting—in the whole Santiago campaign.' Cogan had been there."

"'And you have written a library of books about it,' says

Martin. 'But of course when a few hundred are killed down this way—'tis a great joke. And those little black and tan lads of thirteen or fourteen having to go off shouldering a rifle and kill or get killed—they're jokes, too. But if a grown man up in your country does it—the band plays when he goes and comes, and he makes speeches about it at banquets—and sometimes he will draw a pension for the next sixty years after it—' says Martin and said it in his easy way, as if he didn't care much about it one way or the other; and maybe he didn't."

"Cogan didn't find much doing on the streets of Colon after the Revolution was over, so he got in the way of dropping into a place just around the corner from Martin's, a joint where they sold you drinks to tables in the front room and ran faro layouts in two rooms in back—one for whites and one for blacks."

"Cogan drifted in there with a man who looked like the pictures of grand dukes he'd seen—tall, fine broad shoulders, and dressed in white ducks, and wore a long, well-trimmed dark beard, and swung a gold-headed cane, and had a big ring on one finger. Cogan heard him on the wharf that day— he talked pretty good English—helping out a Chinese merchant who was kicking about the freight charges on some cases he wanted to ship across the peninsula. The American gang running the railroad down there used to charge what they pleased in those days, and Cogan had a sympathy for anybody that bucked them—he'd had to pay eight dollars gold for a run to Panama and back himself—and he and the grand duke got chummy and looked the town over together; but not much to look at, and this evening they drifted into this place—the Russian taking a high-ball and Cogan another ginger ale—to have an excuse to hang around and see what was doing.

"There wasn't much doing. Half a dozen discouraged looking girls were sitting to tables in the place. From California, Mexico, Jamaica they were, and had come on just as soon as they could when they heard about the Revolution, thinking that with the crowd of Americans who were sure to rush down to the peninsula, there ought to be a living for a few clever ladies like themselves. But up to this time the rush hadn't got beyond war correspondents and navy people, and now the poor things were sitting to tables and looking as if they wished somebody would loosen up and buy a drink—even if it was no more than a glass of moxie.

"Cogan's grand duke turned out to be a Peruvian, a dealer in Panama hats from Lima, and he told Cogan a lot about Panama hats, which weren't Panama hats at all, and other interesting things—South America politics and bull fighting especially. He had a brother Juan, who was a famous mounted capeador, he said—that's the man who sits with a red cloak on a horse in the first part of the bull fight and Cogan could see that he was very proud of him.

"Cogan and his Peruvian friend were getting on fine, when a tremendous old Indian woman filled up the doorway, and said something in Spanish to the Peruvian, and he got up, explaining to Cogan that his daughter Valera, who had come with him on this trip to see the strange peoples, had sent to say that he must not forget his good-night before she fell asleep. 'She never allows me to forget that,' said the Peruvian. 'Also possibly she knows,' he smiled, 'that if I am at home I shall not be in mis-cheef,' and he said he hoped they'd meet again next day and bowed himself out.

"Cogan went off later to his hotel. That's the same hotel which had been the George Washington Hotel, later the Cleveland House, and at this time was the Hotel McKinley, but with an intention soon to call it the Roosevelt House. If it's there now, it must be the Hotel Taft.

"Cogan had the end room of the lower floor of the hotel wing which ran down toward the beach. The ocean rolled almost up to the window of his room. It was a calm night with no sea on, and lying there, listening, Cogan could just catch the low swish of the surf.

"It was a hot, close night, and Cogan's bed no cooler for being wrapped four times around with mosquito netting, so after he had tossed around an hour or two, he guessed he might as well get up and have a swim. He had only to step through a window, take a hop, step, and jump, and he would be at the edge of the surf; but as he opened up his shutters softly, so as not to disturb anybody else in that wing of the house, he saw that it was already near dawn, and then wh-s-s-t, quick as that, the top edge of the sun popped up.

"Cogan looking out saw a young girl of maybe fourteen years with long black hair hanging loose behind her. It was a smooth, silver-like sea, with hardly surf enough to raise a white edge on the beach, and the girl, ankle deep in the water, was kicking her feet ahead of her, making a great splashing as she marched along. Her legs below her knees were bare, and she was gurgling with joy. By the time she was abreast of Cogan's window, it was full dawn.

"Suddenly she turned, ran in waist deep, and plunged seaward. Cogan, seeing her over her head and alone, began to worry; but he might have saved himself the worry—she came tumbling back like a young dolphin, found her feet on the beach, and flew to where was a cloak and a pair of Chinese slippers piled on the sand. The long rays of the just rising sun were now flashing level atop of the sea, and the sea-water clinging to her in a million twinkling drops as she ran. Cogan remembered a marble nymph he had once seen under a fountain in a square on a sunny morning in Rome, only the figure in Rome was a couple of hundred, or perhaps a couple of thousand, years old and needed washing, and being marble the water didn't cling so lingeringly.

"Her bare young legs, as they twinkled on the beach, were like a pair of moving poems to Cogan, and then the long cloak enveloped her. An instant later the little feet slipped out from beneath the cloak and into the sandals, and then a big woman came running down the beach. Cogan recognized her—the same big Indian who had come after his Peruvian friend the night before. He decided she must be a descendant of the old Incas that Pizarro conquered, and of course that didn't make it any less interesting. She began to scold the girl, peering distressfully around while she was talking as if to see if any early hotel riser had seen them. But the girl only made a face up at her, and that gave Cogan his first sight of her teeth. He thought her the most delightful looking creature he had ever seen. They disappeared between a row of trees further up the beach—a row of palms which guarded a line of cottages from the wash of the surf.

"'That,' said Cogan to himself, when his eyes couldn't make out the fluttering of her cloak any more—'that must be Valera.' And he sat down to the hotel breakfast with a great appetite, thinking happily that by and by he would see her father again."

"But Cogan, who was off a cruiser in Colon harbor, had to be back aboard for quarters that morning; and after quarters it was up the coast to Chiriqui Lagoon to coal ship, and it was three days more before he was back in Colon. His Peruvian friend he could not find, but he looked up the Chinese trader that he'd first seen him with and who had a shop on the corner between Martin Jackson's and the faro joint.

"The Chinaman could tell him. Senor Roca had taken the choo-choo back to Callao—si, si—Oh, yes, for Lima."

"Cogan asked for the name and address and got it. 'Senor Luis Roca,' he repeated. 'I'll remember that—and the street and number. And some day I'll take a run down to Peru—to Lima.'"

"'Si, si—fine cit-ee. And bull fight—granda, senor,' said the Chinaman, who, like Martin Jackson, had also a Spanish accent."

*　　*　　*　　*　　*

The pump-man had come to a full stop. The third officer was standing near. A regurgitating and ruminating little animal was the third officer, who always after a meal came up on deck to lean over the after-rail, and spend a few enjoyable minutes in picking his teeth, and rechewing the lumps of food as they welled regularly into his throat; but otherwise a polite little man, plainly waiting for a chance to say a word to Kieran, but too well-bred to break in on any intimate conversation. However, Kieran remained silent so very long that the third officer turned and ventured: "'Adn't you better go below and have your bit o' dinner afore it's gone, mate?" And Kieran came out of his dream and said perhaps he'd better and stood up to go below; but on the top step of the ladder he paused and over his shoulder threw back to the passenger: "It was a long time, though, before Cogan saw Peru."

When Kieran came on deck again the third officer had gone forward, but the passenger was still on one of the towing bitts and still smoking. Kieran, strolling to the taffrail, resumed his study of the tossing ship's wake and the cavorting barge in tow. When he seemed to have settled the matter to his satisfaction, he seated himself on the other towing bitt.

"You can get an idea into your head and sometimes it'll swing you around like that barge on the end of that hawser, won't it? Or perhaps your mind don't run that way?"

"I don't see," retorted the passenger, "that that barge has to stick there forever. What's to prevent her from making a leap and fetching up suddenly, and if she did she'd part that hawser like a piece of twine."

"Yes, but she won't make the leap—not till something outside of herself drives her to it. If a sea should rise, or a gale of wind, she might. But it would take something like that. In the meantime she points this way and that, slewing now to this side—see—and now to the other—but never getting away from this ship which has her in tow. Our course must be her course."

"Yes, I suppose that is so."

"Well, then, Cogan that I've been telling you about was nearly always in tow of a force that seemed to be outside of himself. A storm, a high sea, or a gale of wind in his case would be an upheaval of his soul like. But in those days he hadn't come to that. Maybe he was still only half awake. Martin Jackson, sitting out on the sidewalk of his Fourth of

July saloon, came nearer to making him think than all of the school teachers he'd ever seen. Maybe, too, life was too smooth in those days. However, he was always in tow of some fancy or other. And one day, being free of the navy, he went to Peru."

"'Twas love at first sight then with that young Peruvian girl on the beach?"

"No, I don't think so—not quite that. Even at that age Cogan could not fall in love with curves and color alone. At any rate, he put out to sea; and the beauty of the little Peruvian girl was with him in many a night-watch. Under the stars he could shut his eyes and see her—the flashing teeth as she grimaced up at the horrified nurse, and the eyes still rioting after the curved lips were closed. And yet it was not her beauty. A hundred rosy-marbled nymphs could have paraded the beach in a thousand silvery dawns and, once out of sight, his heart never quicken whatever it was—the innocence, the breathing innocence of her, it may have been that. And yet there was something more. There must have been. He gave it up, but he knew that if he had been born a girl he, too, would want to paddle in the sea at dawn."

"A sort of poet?" suggested the passenger.

Kieran shot a side glance at the passenger. "H-m-m—a good thing he didn't know it if he was. He was irresponsible enough without having that excuse. If he thought then that it was poetry in him which kept him hopping about the world, he'd have been no good at all. He did enough dreaming as it was. It was probably only the discipline of a warship, of having to do a daily stint, that kept him from loafing all his time away, for, as maybe I've said, a power used to take hold of him at times and swing him. An idea would come to him and he'd follow it like a guide to heaven.

"He wondered what had become of her, and one day, being now free of the navy, he took a bald-headed schooner out of Portland, Oregon, with a load of lumber for Callao. Between watches he studied a Spanish-Without-A-Master for one dollar. The lumber schooner never reached Callao, but she did make one of those volcanic islands to the south side of the harbor—piled up there and began to fill, which forced the crew to leave in a hurry and row into Callao harbor in their quarter-boat. From Callao the crew took a trolley to Lima to see the American consul. In Lima they became scattered, and Cogan and an old fellow named Tommie Jones found themselves together. Cogan had met Tommie in a restaurant in Portland at about the time Tommie was taking notice of a tall, well-nourished, red-headed lass waiting on table there. Tommie was a hearty lad of fifty-four or so, and Cogan had helped the little romance along, and because of his interest in the case was how Cogan and Tommie came to ship together. Well, here was Tommie adrift in Lima after five weeks to sea, and in all that time he hadn't had a drink, and he wanted one now. He had no money, but Cogan had a half-dollar, and American silver is good money in Peru; so Cogan bought Tommie three drinks of some kind of Spanish wine and himself one lemonade for the half-dollar.

"It couldn't have been the wine—he hadn't had enough of that. Maybe it was the reaction from the excitement of the wreck that made Tommie sleepy. He wanted to turn in, and it being now night-time they went into a park where a fine band was playing. It was a beautiful night, with a moon; and under the moon, while the music rolled out, dark-eyed senoritas with their mothers strolled up and down, and the young fellows hung around and got in a word when they could. On the edges the police kept an eye on the loafers.

"The night breeze which made the trees almost talk, the water of the fountain arching under the colored lights, the scent of the flowering bushes—Tommie and Cogan after their five weeks at sea just sat there till long after the music had stopped and everybody gone home. Then Tommie fell asleep, full length under a tree. Cogan tried to stand watch but he was tired, too, and after a while, with his back against the same tree, and the water-play of the fountain still tinkling in his ears, he fell asleep alongside Tommie.

"Cogan had a dream of somebody trying to pull his leg off and it woke him. He looked down and saw that the lace of one of his shoes was untied. He retied it and looked at his chum. He was still asleep, snoring, but there was something missing. In half a minute, his brain clearing, he saw that Tommie's shoes were gone, and also his hat, and his pockets turned inside out. Cogan then noticed that his own trousers pockets were turned inside out. He stood up and caught sight of two fellows just dropping over the tall iron fence surrounding the park. The gates of the park were closed, and locked, too, or so Cogan guessed, and wasted no time in trying them. The fence was pretty high and had iron spikes on top, and he felt somewhat stiff in his joints, but a hot temper is good as a bath and a rub-down any time—Cogan vaulted the fence, and the two natives just then turned and saw him. He was coming on pretty fast and they threw up their hands, dropped the shoes and hat, and went tearing away. Cogan had only to stoop down and pick up the stuff, but it wasn't property he was after. To steal the shoes off of a shipwrecked sailor! Even if they weren't told he was shipwrecked, they ought to have guessed, or so he thought, and he held on after them, and Cogan could run pretty well in those days. But so could one of those fellows. Cogan could soon have caught the slow one, but he kept always after the fast fellow and was feeling sure of his man when he took to turning corners. They had come to a part of the city where the streets were narrow and the blocks short. It seemed to Cogan there was a corner every twenty feet, and it was up hill. His man turned one corner and four seconds later Cogan turned it, and, his man not being in sight, Cogan kept on and turned the next corner. Another twenty yards and he ran up against a high wall. 'Wow,' says Cogan, but with a running high jump, he got his fingers on top of the wall and hauled himself up. There was nobody in sight on the other side. 'Trimmed!' says Cogan, and, sitting on the wall, began to fan himself.

"It was bright light now and the city beginning to come awake. People came out and took down the shutters of shops. Indian women went by with loaded baskets of fruit, and other people drove little burros in carts filled with eggs, chickens, and green stuff; and men and women, with fish to sell in big dishes on their heads, came sliding by, and all yelled loud enough to wake a watch below. Girls with baskets of flowers went by, and one, looking up, spied Cogan and stopped and held her basket up and made a motion for him to buy. He turned his pockets inside out and threw his hands apart. That made her laugh, and she took a flower from the basket, touched her lips to it and threw it up to him. She was a pretty girl,—all the girls were pretty this morning,—but she was prettiest of all, and the flower was of a big blue kind which Cogan had never seen before. He blew a kiss after her and she went singing on her way. Cogan sang a little himself. He was beginning to feel pretty good.

"Boys came and gazed up at Cogan, and sometimes men, and some of them laughed, but mostly they paid no attention to him. He heard a bell tolling and he saw people below him filing toward a gate. They all carried tin cups. He looked further and saw that it was a monastery they were heading for, and that at the gate of the monastery two monks in brown habits were passing out bread and filling the tin cups with coffee. Cogan dropped over the wall, and when he saw that one man had finished with his tin cup he asked him for it. He knew Spanish enough for that. The man smiled and handed it over. Cogan went up to the grating and a monk filled his tin cup with coffee. Another handed him three slices of dark bread. Cogan thanked them, but the monks seemed not to hear. He thanked them again, at which one monk, looking up, set a finger to his lips and motioned him to step aside for the next.

"Cogan finished his breakfast, thanked the native for the loan of the cup, and started to look around. He first tried to find the park where he had left Tommie, but there were so many parks with trees and flowers and fountains in them! He crossed a bridge over a river that must have come tumbling all the way from the top of the Andes, it had such a head of speed on. He patrolled he did not know how many streets, and at last gave up hunting for Tommie, on whose account, anyway, he wasn't worrying, for he knew that Tommie, an experienced old sailor man, had by this time laid his course for the Consul's and been taken care of. He sat on a bench at the curbstone in front of a fruit store to think things over. It was a comfortable seat, except that every time a trolley passed he had to lift his feet high so he wouldn't be swept off his perch.

"As he sat there, a group of well-muscled, well-set-up young fellows passed him. It was a cool, cheerful morning, and they appeared to be full of play. Everybody did that morning in Lima. Cogan knew these at once for some sort of athletes. They seemed to be well known to the store-keepers and the small boys along the street. Their hair, or what he could see of it, was clipped close. Not handsome men all, but all in high favor. Girls flung back light words at them, or tapped them on the arm in passing. Two girls pinned roses on the coats of two of them, who took it all as though they were used to it. 'Big leaguers of some kind,' thinks Cogan, and asked the fruit-stand keeper who they were, and the fruit-seller said 'Torero.'"

"'Torero? Torero?—Ah-h-h'—Cogan recalled his 'Spanish Without A Master'—'Ah-h-h, of course, Toreros—Toreadors' —he remembered the opera 'Carmen'—bull-fighters. Cogan got up and followed them."

"If Cogan had never seen a bull-ring, he would right away have known this in Lima for one. It was a perfect circle, about two hundred feet across, packed with what looked like hard sand and surrounded by a stout stockade, and with seats enough for eight or ten thousand people. The bull-fighters had not minded when he followed them in, and now he took a seat on the empty benches and watched them at practice. They had a bull, a lively one, but a well trained one, too, for when he knocked one of them over he would stand still and not try to trample anybody. He would reach down and prod with his horns, but, as he had a brass knob on each horn, he couldn't hurt them much that way. The fellows with the red capes practised all their tricks, the men with wooden stakes all covered with paper streamers practised theirs, and Cogan's blood was racing in his veins before they were through. These were great athletes—he saw that at once— and with a savage bull with sharp-pointed hoofs and horns in place of that trained manicured one—well, these men would be taking chances which no athlete at home ever had to take, unless they were aerial-bar men in the circus or loop-the-loopers or something like that.

"A few of these men, as Cogan looked on, stood out from the others; and after a time from among those few stood one by himself. From the first Cogan had noticed that he was very fast and clever—and strong, yes. It was his quickness and skill, even more than his strength, which counted. He used the bull's strength against the bull himself. He wasn't much more than medium height or weight, but beautifully developed—they were all finely developed men—and behind his muscular power was all kinds of nervous energy. And a great way of doing things, not an extra motion of any kind—no wasteful flourishes or posings. Not that he didn't have style. Style!—he had so much of it that he didn't seem to be half trying. Everything and everybody seemed to be playing into his hands—even the bull. And he was such a human kind, laughing and joking as he bounded and ran about! And he must have said many funny things, they all laughed so; and he took a lot of trouble to coach some of them in their practice.

"Cogan later saw him in the dressing-room. He came off the field before the others, and while they were yet practising he had had his bath. He was now dressing and Cogan saw that he wore fine linen and fashionably-cut clothes. He had a room to himself off the main dressing-room, and two attendants jumped to serve him. From time to time, standing at the door of his dressing-room putting on a collar or adjusting his tie, he would sweep a glance at Cogan. His eyes were friendly. They were also of good size and deep-set, Cogan now had a chance to see; but they had also an absent, wistful expression which made Cogan wonder, for at this young fellow's age, and he the star of the troupe, it's little in life should have been bothering him.

"By and by the others came in, and with their coming Cogan's favorite was again lively and laughing. Soon he was ready for the street. And all dressed up he was a great swell. As he passed out those in his way skipped to one side, while those in the corners ran forward to catch his eye and smile at him. 'Torellas, Torellas,' Cogan heard again and again in the most admiring and affectionate tones.

"After he had gone out the door, Cogan asked one of the bull-fighters who he was. But his 'Spanish Without A Master' didn't seem to be working very well, and the man he questioned called out 'Ferrero—Oh, Ferrero!' saying to Cogan 'Ferrero spik the Ingliss—O fine-a—good-a Ingliss.'"

"A man that Cogan recognized as one of the liveliest performers in the ring, though somewhat older than the others, came over and bowed politely."

"'Senor, if you will tell me—who is Torellas?' asked Cogan in English."

"'Torellas'—Ferrero pointed toward the door—'he departed only one moment ago.'"

"'Senor, I saw, and thank you. But who is he?'"

"'Torellas? Who ees Torellas?' Not only Ferrero, but every bull-fighter in the place took a peek at Cogan. Ferrero looked around the room to make sure the others had heard. 'He asks me'—or so Cogan guessed he said, for now he was speaking Spanish—'he asks me who is Torellas!' at which they all craned their necks to get another peek at Cogan, and there was a lot of sputtering talk among them. Cogan guessed that they were saying many very funny things about the man who did not know who Torellas was. Ferrero turned to Cogan, now in English, 'Sir, a stranger?' And Cogan said, 'Si, senor, a stranger—from the United States.'"

"And Ferrero said, 'Ah-h—Americano—cer-tain-ly,' in the most charitable tone. 'Senor, I speak your language a leetla bit. It is true I lived one time in your contry—a fine contry is U-ni-ted Stat-es—two years—yes, sir, surely. Listen, please. Torellas, sir, he ees born here, in thees very city, a Peruvian. We are proud of him. The prodeegious skill, the strength, the light foot, the stroke of the espada, the sword of Torellas—a descending thunderbolt it ees—but oh, he ees not to be descripsheeoned. Some day you shall see—you shall not depart until you have seen. Even now he ees in Peru—yes, sir—in all South America the supreme matador. Soon—we have the assurance of it, senor—he shall go to Spain, to Madrid, and in the great bull-ring there he shall kill his bulls before the king and queen, and, have no fear, senor, Spain shall also proclaim his superiority. Already, if he so desires, fifty, seventy-five thousand—truly, sir—dollars gold in the year—shall be his for his splendid genius. Yes, sir—and renown without death. We are proud of him. Even now he ees with us—how shall I say it?—ah, senor, even now, but at twenty years of age he ees with us as the great John L. Sullivano was in United Stat-es when I lived there a leetle boy—in New Yorrik—twenty years ago.'"

"And Cogan said to himself—'This Torellas person must surely be some class.'"

"'And, senor—surely'—Ferrero had only stopped to get his breath—'it would be criminal not to view Torellas in all his splendor—not as you have viewed him this mor-rn-ing—that was play—but in the full strength of his science, his art—deliverin-g, senor, the final stroke to the ferocious bull.'"

"Cogan also began to see that it would be a crime not to view the great man in action, and he was also told that even more than Torellas the matador they loved Torellas the man, the good comrade."

"Cogan became quite friendly with the bull-fighters. He inquired further of Ferrero, who in the ring was a banderillo—that is, one of the people who stick the decorated stakes in the bull's neck—possibly Senor Ferrero knew of a mounted capeador by the name of Juan Roca."

"'Juan? Who does not? Yes, sir. Very much, sir,' and went on to tell Cogan that Juan, the best mounted capeador in all South America, was that very morning breaking in a new horse on the ranch of Don Vicente Guillen outside the city."

"Ferrero was a most friendly person, and invited Cogan to eat with him, and Cogan went. Ten or a dozen bull-fighters boarded in one place near the bull-ring—a large, square, two-story adobe house; a grand house, with walls painted in colors and splendid high rooms arranged around a patio inside."

"It was now high noon, and warm enough in the sunny streets outside, but in the patio it was cool, with a breeze from the Pacific, and after lunch the bull-fighters sat around there and smoked cigarettes and played stringed instruments, all but a few wild ones who went leaping and springing about the garden walks. Cogan could not hide his interest in this jumping exercise, and Ferrero, seeing it, invited him to join in, which Cogan did, and beat everybody there jumping. He did so well that Ferrero asked him if he could jump over a horse, and he said he'd try it. So they went out and got a horse, and Cogan jumped over it. And then they brought in another and placed the two side by side, and Cogan jumped over the pair of them, at which they all shouted 'Bueno, bueno, Americano!' and Ferrero slapped him on the back and told him he must stay with them and practice bull-fighting.

"Cogan had another question. Was not the mounted capeador Juan Roca a brother of Luis Roca, the hat dealer? And he was told that he was, and that Luis Roca was now engaged in an enormous hat business with the United States, and had grown very wealthy, thanks to the increase of trade since the American occupation of the Isthmus. And Cogan inquired further—was there a daughter who would be now about eighteen? 'A daughter? Blood of a bull—surely.' And beautiful? Beautee-full! the Senorita Roca beautee-full?

Mother of God!' If he wished, he could post himself on the Pasada that very afternoon—any afternoon—and see her driving with her jolly good father or her proud mother, or it might be with Senor Lorenzo de Guavera. 'And,' added Ferrero, 'you will meet Juan there also—if he ees returned from the ranch.'

"In the cool of the afternoon they went to the Pasada, which is where everybody in Lima who has a pair of horses and a coachman goes driving of an afternoon. They pace up one side and down the other. Cogan never saw so many fine horses and beautiful women in such a short time. And he saw the hat dealer—the same lively, good-humored Grand Duke man to look at, dressed in the same style of white ducks and big Panama hat, with the same great beard down on his chest. Beside him was a stately, beautiful girl. Cogan stared. He could see the resemblance right away. 'That must be an elder sister,' he thought, 'and that must be her mother.' The mother was beautiful, too; but also she knew it. There was also a well-set-up, well-dressed, well-groomed, distinguished looking man.

"Cogan was staring after the carriage, when he heard a voice in his ear. Ferrero was speaking to him. 'Ah-h, you know heem, Luis, Juan's brother, yes? And the senora?—and the Senorita Valera?'"

"'Valera? But that is not the little girl—'"

"'Leetle girl?'"

"'Has she not—the senorita—a younger sister?'"

"'Sister? There ees no sister—only herself.'"

"And so his little Valera had grown into that stately, self-possessed young lady. Cogan felt sad."

"'And some say he ees to be betrothed to her, yes. Senor—
Mister Guavera, yes—that ees heem. A splendid man. Poor
Torellas. Ah-h, but here ees Juan coming. He speaks the
most beautee-full English. Behold—Juan!'"

"Ferrero was pointing out a square-shouldered, compactly
built, bronzed man of five feet seven or so, who was carving
curved shapes out of the air with his hands and pointing to
one horse and then another in the parade to illustrate his
words. To further illustrate, he carved beautiful figures with
his cane and raised one knee after the other violently to
depict the animal's action. A man full of gimp, Juan seemed
to be. 'It is his new horse,' explained Ferrero. 'He will tell us
of it, too.' And he did—went over it all again after he had
been introduced to Cogan. 'Oh, a marvel of a horse,' he
wound up, 'and I shall ride him in the next fiesta.'"

"Ferrero reintroduced Cogan to Juan as one who knew his
brother Luis."

"'But I met him only once,' added Cogan."

"'Once? It is sufficient,' assured Juan. 'Fully sufficient. To
meet Luis once is to meet him forever. He is always the
same. But some others—not so. You have been shipwrecked,
yes? You lost everything? Ah-h, that is most hard luck, but
do not despair. I, too, was a sailor—one time. One time only,
gracias a Dios! My ancestors, I think, were of the land
entirely. The sea-sickness—pir-r-h—no, no, not for me. But
do not mind. But pardon, senor'—he turned to Ferrero—
'attend to me, Ferrero. I am grieved to-day. It is the senora
again. What matters it whether a man is a muletero, gaucho,
toreador, or what? Torellas, now, has been all—so have I,
her brother-in-law—or a seller of hats or a member of the

cabinet? What, I ask you'—he turned to Cogan—'are we senor? We are men or we are not? So? Very well, let us say no more, but find a cafe and have our coffee. It has been very dusty to-day—very.'"

"Two cups of coffee, and Juan was talking to Cogan like a brother. And he could talk like a highspeed dynamo. 'A man—can he be no greater than a man, I ask you, sir? Luis, he will be glad to see you, if you came in rags—no matter— he is always the same, always. But the senora—pir-r-h. That is it—you have it—Proud! A good woman, mind'—Juan leaned over and tapped Cogan's arm to let him know there must be no mistake on that point—'the best of women, but'— he sighed—'Luis, he is from home six months in the year, and she it is who has the training of Valera. And once she was as like her father as—oh, and such a heart! But she will become—I fear it now—like her mother. And her mother does not want Torellas."

"'And Torellas! A torero, yes. But whether a man is muletero, vaquero, or torero, what matters it? Torellas has been all three, and I, too—I, her brother-in-law, but what matters it? Luis, my brother, was, oh, so poor when they married, but, my friend, I who say it—I, his brother—a scamp possibly, yes, but we had family. A handsome boy was Luis, and she—I admit it—very beautiful and good. But Luis—Luis becomes wealthy. At once the senora must have a grand son-in-law. Torellas is a toreador,—yes,—but also Torellas is something more than that. The strong arm, the quick eye, the'—Juan slapped himself on the left breast—'the brave heart, yes. But more than that. I know, senor, I who have been'—he touched them off on succeeding finger-tips— 'gaucho in Argentina, cowboy in your country, a soldier in the Chilean war, horse-breaker—but I have not fingers sufficient—I who have roamed far, I know men. And Torellas—but you have seen him, senor? Ah-h—then you, too, know. Is he not a man? Ah-h—and surely a man can be but a man. And Torellas,'—Juan pounded the table,—'he is a man—Pir-r'—Juan whirled in his chair—'*Pedro, cafe—al instante. Tres, si, si—tres.*'"

"'But, Juan,' asks Ferrero when the coffee came, 'a few months ago we thought—'"

"'Exactly—we all thought. It is the senora. Listen, Mr. Cogan. You have the warm heart, the friendly eye, you, too, shall know. Torellas and my niece they have regard for each other, and she, the senora, sees no harm until this Guavera, the politician, comes. Oh, a great man—he is to be in the next cabinet—possibly. I repeat—possibly. The senora waits for a chance to terminate with Torellas. Very well. Torellas receives many letters from foolish girls. So do I, and Ferrero. Pir-r-h—what torero of fame does not? And the senora, she points to me—as an example. It is true that I am a weak man and I have no wife—no family—'"

"Ferrero began to laugh. 'Mr. Cogan, there was a lady'— begins Ferrero."

"'T-t-t, Ferrero allow me. If we shall have old woman's gossip, allow it also to be the truth. I was riding, senor, one fine, splendid Argentine horse—such a horse!—when a carriage approached and a lady—such a lady!—veiled, you understand, stands before me and a voice says—"Is this not Senor Juan Roca?" It is true that I had received a note that day—and why not, senor? What heart would not beat—but that is nothing. I had no more than kissed the tips of her fingers this beautiful evening, when a giant of a man leaps out. I did not even know that she had a husband. I do not know yet that he is her husband. I did not even know who she was, and he—he was as one sweeping down from a balloon, an aeroplane; but, senor, I who can be gentle, as you can without doubt understand, I can also be as the sea storm which wrecks great ships. I beat this interloper—ah-h—beau-tifully—'"

"'The whole city knew of it—such a scandal'—concluded Ferrero for him."

"'Ferrero, enough. I am no destroyer of homes. But the senora, Mr. Cogan, takes occasion to point the finger at me. "There is your mounted capeador, your brave toreador," she says to Luis, "and they are all alike." But Torellas is not so. My heart withers for him. You must understand, senor'—Juan turned anew to Cogan—'that Torellas is as my own son. He tells me all. I have seen him burn in one day ten letters—yes, his own heart burning for love, you understand. Such a boy! He should be a Seminarian. But her mother, she says it is scandalous! As if he could stop them from writing! He must give up bull-fighting! Torellas give up bull-fighting! Our matador, the nation's hero, give up—pir-r-h—if I were Torellas—No matter, I tell him to come to the house as before. Luis favors him. I favor him. Old Tina favors him, and, I think—I think—Valera herself—but she is too proud to say. She, also, considers it—beseeched him to give up bull-fighting! That was the senora's influence. If he were an ordinary matador—but the great Torellas! Pir-r-h—but a moment.' Juan whirled to the waiter, '*Pedro, mas cafe!*'"

"Juan downed his coffee in a gulp. 'And you shall come with us to see Luis,' he goes on. 'Come in your shipwreck clothes, it shall not matter to Luis. I recollect now, sir, you are the American sailor he saw one time in Colon. He has conversed many times of you. The senora will not like it, you understand, you a sailor, but with the senorita, it is but to charm the more. She loves me, her hard dog of an uncle, because I, who have adventured, can tell her a thousand tales. You have adventured also and she is yet her father's child. Do not mind that I speak frankly, but come. If I speak thus to you, it is because I know that you, senor, are one to understand and to trust. We shall be glad to see you. You go with Ferrero now? Ver-ry good.' Juan stood up and with his cane he saluted profoundly. 'Good-by, sir. Ferrero, a Dios.' He went as he came, with a rush.

"Stirred up by Juan, Cogan thought of calling that very night on Luis Roca and his family. But he did not go, nor next day, nor that week. He saw Juan regularly in the bull-ring, and always Juan urged him afresh, but Cogan did not go to see the Rocas. 'Later,' perhaps, he said to Juan, who stared wonderingly at him but did not ask why.

"And so things went for several weeks, until that morning when the American battle fleet came steaming into Callao harbor. Cogan was one of twenty or thirty thousand who crowded to the stone pier that day, and when the beautiful white ships came rounding in, he felt very proud. And the yellow tongues of flame flashing and the white sides of the great war-ships gleaming through the smoke—it made a tremendous impression on everybody; but to Cogan's eyes the tears came. People near him said, 'Americano?' inquiringly, to which Cogan's bull-fighting friends replied— 'Si, si, Americano,' and added a 'Heep, heep, hoo-raw!' to make Cogan feel more at home.

"That was the morning that Torellas told Cogan that if he wished he could go into the ring on the occasion of the festival which Peru was to hold in honor of the American fleet. And such an occasion it was to be! A welcome from a younger to the older republic. There was to be a great bull-fight, at which Torellas was to make his last appearance before going to Spain.

"Spain! Madrid! The highest of honors! Cogan looked at

Torellas, but the matador didn't seem to be so very glad."

The pump-man seemed to be listening to something. "Hear 'em?" he asked.

The passenger cocked up his ears, and heard them—several voices from the depths of one of the tanks.

"It's No. 11," explained the pump-man, and hurried away. The passenger saw him disappear into a hatchway. Almost immediately the voices ceased and shortly four deck-hands hurriedly emerged. Kieran followed. "Beat it!" he ordered, and they somewhat sheepishly went forward.

Kieran came aft. "What was the trouble?" asked the passenger.

"That bunch of bone-heads,"—Kieran was talking. He was also pinching the crust from the wick of a candle he held— "they sneaked down there to have a little game. And brought this candle with them—for light. Three weeks ago, up to the dock in Bayonne, a bunch lit a candle to look for something in the corner of an oil ship's tank, and the coroner couldn't tell the buttons of one from the other. Gas, yes. Another half minute and these chaps would've got the surprise of their lives. But maybe I'd better go for'ard and give 'em a few chemical explanations, or some day, meaning no harm, they'll be blowing out the side of the ship. So long."

## III

The pump-man roomed with Jenkins, the third officer, in the superstructure, amidships. The passenger sometimes, as on this night, looked in there.

Jenkins was an Englishman, and of him they told the story that when he first came to the country half the space in his yellow tin trunk was taken up with cakes of Pears' soap. Somebody had told him that he couldn't buy any in the United States. He still had some of his original load of soap, and now hauled the tin trunk out from under his bunk, took out a cake and made a lather, with which he slicked down his thin, sandy hair, smoothing it, the while he gossiped cheerfully with Kieran and the passenger, on each side of the middle parting until it made a straight line between the bottom of his ears to his eyebrows. His ears were stuck high up on the side of his head—a sign of high intelligence, he used to say.

Jenkins had to go on watch at midnight, and so now he was getting ready to turn in. The third officer had a minute way of telling his little experiences, to which Kieran always listened patiently. If Kieran had not, Jenkins would have had no audience at all, for the second officer, a Norwegian, and the first officer, a Vermont Yankee, had no use for any Englishman whatever; and besides that he was only the third officer.

The pump-man had sympathy for Jenkins, but not so much that he would sit and listen while Jenkins talked himself to sleep; so, once he saw Jenkins into his bunk, Kieran used to fly for the open deck.

And here it was the passenger joined him, pacing the long

gangway. The passenger turned and they paced together.

The sound of the captain's voice floated down from the bridge. The passenger, who had small use for the captain, suggested that they go forward; and so they made for the bow of the ship and ascended the ladder to the forec's'le head, and here, after a decent interval, to allow Kieran to absorb the beauty of the tropic night, the passenger said, "How about that bull-fight in Peru?"

"Oh-h—" said Kieran, and after a silence went on to say:

"Well, the day of the bull-fight came, and that afternoon the bull-fighters marched into the ring; and in their smooth-fitting tights—black, white, green, pink, blue, purple, all colors—their short jackets, puffed-out shirts, with the queer little hats and the neat black slippers, well-built fellows, all of them—they made a great showing.

"They marched once around the ring, and then Torellas, who was leading them, halted in front of the Mayor's box and asked permission to kill the bull, and the Mayor, of course, said yes. Then, marching to the opposite side of the ring, to where was the President of Peru in the biggest box of all, with hangings of red and gold, and two American rear-admirals of the fleet on either side of him, Torellas saluted, and tossed up his hat, then his cloak, to the President. And as he did so, around the ring the less famous bull-fighters were picking out friends or great people and to them tossing their hats, by way of doing them honor. Cogan tossed his up among the American blue-jackets, and they, not knowing he wasn't a Peruvian, didn't know what to make of it, but they scuffled for it just the same.

"Torellas was in white tights with black slippers. A small gold cross was pinned to the breast of his fine white shirt. As he stepped back from the President's box he touched a white silk handkerchief to his lips, almost like a woman, but those graceful little movements were as much a part of him as were his strength and nerve. Cogan could hear women in the seats behind him whispering of the beauty of him. Until then it had never occurred to Cogan that the matador was any professional beauty. He surely was a finely developed fellow, a good deal of a man to look at, but for the beauty! No, he wasn't handsome—Cogan took another look—but any man would say a great looking one.

"The ring was now clear, with the bull-fighters hidden behind the stockade, or tucked away in the little places of refuge built against the inside of the stockade. These places of refuge were for the bull-fighters to run into when chased by a bull; and there were half a dozen of them, of heavy planking and about as high as a man's chest, with an entrance wide enough for a man, but not for a bull's horns. Cogan picked out his particular refuge because just above it, in front seats, were the Rocas and Guavera.

"It was now time for the bull-fight to begin, but this was such an extraordinary occasion that a compliment had first to be paid to the visiting fleet, so the Peruvian band played our national hymn, and at the first note every American blue-jacket there stood to attention. Cogan felt as proud as could be of them, in their fresh-washed suits of muster white with the beautiful blue collars and cuffs. Section after section was piled solid with them, and here and there Cogan saw an old shipmate. Just to look at them made Cogan homesick. Four thousand strong they stood stiff as statues to attention, right arms across body and caps held to their left breasts, while the 'Star-Spangled Banner' was played.

"It was all fine; and the 'Star-Spangled Banner' made such a hit that the Peruvian band played it again. And fine musicians they were, too, only as they played it, trying to be terribly respectful, it sounded like a funeral march. But, through it all, our blue-jackets, four thousand strong, stood frozen to attention in their beautiful suits of white with the blue trimmings and their caps held respectfully to their breasts.

"Great! Cogan could hear them all about him saying how noble and affecting. And it was—believe me, it was. And again that fine band arose to play the 'Star-Spangled Banner,' but this time our brave blue-jackets also arose, four thousand strong, in the beautiful muster white suits, and yelled as one—'Oh, cut it out, cut out any more music and bring on the bull.' And they brought on the bull.

"But first a bugle call rang out, and into the ring came the mounted capeador. And it was Juan, and he was riding his Argentine roan. And he took his station in the middle of the ring, and there he waited, in his left hand the reins, and in his right, drooping below his stirrup, a scarlet cape. Great cheers greeted him; and all around the ring Cogan could hear the residents from the high one in the box with the American admirals, from the President down, explaining that this was their famous mounted capeador, Juan Roca, and to have an eye out for Juan's unparalleled skill and his bravery—and did they notice that Juan wore no iron, nor even leather protection to his legs? Everyone called him Juan, as though he was an old friend. Cogan remembered how, on that night in Colon, the hat dealer was as proud as could be of his brother; but no more proud, he now saw, than was everybody here in Lima.

"A barrier of light boarding was raised, and there was the bull, a big, chocolate colored fellow, with heavy shoulders and horns that must have spread three feet. Again Cogan could hear the residents explaining to their American guests that this was one of a famous lot of bulls bred especially for the ring, from the ranch of Don Vicente Guillen, and for this afternoon's sport the government had provided six of these bulls, paying fifteen hundred pesos—about fifteen hundred dollars—in gold for them, and also that the bulls had been fed on half rations for the past forty-eight hours to make them of a high eagerness for this most widely advertised combat.

"Back there in the half light under the shed, Cogan could see the big bull weaving his head from side to side and swaying on his forelegs as he looked out on the ring. The sudden light probably blinded him, for he didn't seem to see, not for a few seconds at least, the scarlet cape Juan was holding up. But when he did! Out he came, head on, for Juan. And Juan stayed there with not a move, until Cogan thought the bull surely had him hooked. But no. At arm's length, and in front of the flaming eyes, Juan flirted the cape, and still in front of the blazing eyes he held it, and behind him, past his horse's withers, he whipped it, and with that, with but a single word, and drawing in on his reins, he seemed to lift his horse off the ground, to whirl him on his hind heels, almost without moving from his tracks; and the bull rushed on by.

"Juan spurred his horse, waved the scarlet cape aloft, took up a new position, and the people cheered. And again cheered as the bull charged, for once more Juan was safe away. Oh, Juan was the brave one! And Juan looked toward the other bull-fighters, as if to say: 'And now is not this Argentine a horse to talk about?' And that horse Juan patted and whispered to, and laughed and sang to him; and with the reins taut in the left hand and the flaming cape always in his right, he did as he pleased with that bull. He talked to the bull, too, but differently—he knew how—to make him angry, and the bull frothed and tore up the sand to get at him, and a dozen times it looked as if the bull would bowl over and gore both the horse and Juan, but always just in time Juan flashed the red cape, and always he and the wonderful horse would come safe away. Juan was certainly the champion horseman of all that Cogan had ever seen. And when Juan rode out of the ring and the bull stood there and looked after him, bewildered like, Cogan didn't half blame him, for the pair of them, Juan and his horse, certainly made a tough combination.

"And then into the ring came the capeadors on foot. Cogan took part with these. They were to play the bull on foot as Juan had been playing him on horseback, but instead of one there were eight of them in the ring together. And one after the other, five, ten, or a dozen paces away, they waved a red cape in front of the bull, at which he glared and lowered his head and charged; but always he charged in one way, head down and eyes only for the red cape, and there was the way the man beat the brute. The bull had his speed, strength, endurance, but nothing else. Once he put his head down he had eyes only for the red cape, and so long as the capeador handled his cape and himself with speed and skill, and no accident happened, he might count on getting safe away.

"Cogan only tried to repeat in the ring this day what he had been doing for weeks in practice. As the bull came charging, he used the cape to lead him to one side, allowing just room enough for the horns to pass. If he waited too long before he turned the bull, of course it would mean trouble; but if he turned the bull too soon, it would be clumsy. Whatever else he did the bull-fighter must not be clumsy. The first time he tried it, Cogan didn't do a good job—the bull was faster than he realized, and he had to run for one of the little places of refuge with the bull after him. Then the crowd roared, or they yelled 'Malo, malo,' which is the same as if a crowd of baseball fans yelled 'Rotten, rotten!' Next time Cogan did better, and then it was 'Bueno, bueno!' from everybody.

Possibly the applause was all the louder because by this time the rumor had spread that he was not only a new-comer, a stranger, an American, but also a sailor, and these four thousand American sailors were this day the guests of the nation. Cogan could not help looking up to Valera and her father after he had done his good turn, and was thrilled to see them both cheering and smiling at him.

"So far it was clever, neat work on the part of the capeadors, but nothing wonderful, nothing to match Juan's work on the horse. The crowd wanted livelier action, and there were cries of 'Torellas! Torellas!' The bugle sounded, and Torellas came. 'Ah-h,' sighed they—you could hear them—'now we shall see something.' Torellas, holding the red cape before him, lured the bull, turned him skilfully, and, spinning on his heel, tempted the bull to wheel and charge again, and when the bull did so, and yet again and again, Torellas, holding him always at arm's length, swung him back and forth, himself retreating a step at a time, and with every step the bull plunging on after him. It was just as if he were snapping the bull on the end of the cape, snapping him back and forth across his path, as he made his way backward. Torellas was never so far away but what the bull, with one unexpected lunge, would get him. But Torellas kept the bull too well in hand for any accidental lunge. At short range he kept him going, drawing him half way across the ring at one time, until at last the bull himself, seeming to understand that he was being fooled, stopped short, and Torellas pulled up, too, and let his cape hang loosely by his side; but as he did so, instantly and at full tilt at Torellas went the bull again; but that seeming carelessness on the part of Torellas was part of his play. With a light upward bound, as the bull lowered his head to gore him, Torellas stepped between the horns, and when the great head came up, with the spring of his leap to the toss of the bull's head, away he went sailing, twenty feet beyond the bull and landing like a breath of air on his feet.

"While the people were still making the air explode with their applause, Cogan saw Torellas look wistfully up to where Valera and her people sat. Cogan looked too. She, leaning back between her mother and Senor Guavera, with her face cloaked, was almost hidden. Her mother and Guavera were talking across her as if all this bull-fighting was of all in the world the thing least interesting to them. Cogan looked back to the matador. He was bowing, even smiling, to the audience, but Cogan, who was close enough to mark every line of his face, saw that he was getting no great joy of his triumph.

"Torellas left the ring, and the banderilleros took possession. These were the men with the wooden stakes of the length of a man's arm and the thickness of a thumb, and wrapped around in gay colored paper ribbon streamers, and at one end a thin iron spike about as long as a man's little finger. The banderilleros had to stand in front of the bull, with a stake in each hand, and, as he charged, to step in between his horns and reach over and plant a stake on each side of his neck. 'It is most simple,' explained Ferrero, as he left Cogan to do his part—'only—surely—we must not make mistake.' And Cogan could not help thinking that bull-fighting was like a thousand other games, a man mustn't make mistakes.

"Ferrero, who was rated the best banderillero in Peru, first faced the bull. He held his stakes up near the end furthest from the bull, to get as much distance at the start as possible, though it wasn't that alone which saved him from the bull's rush. That helped, but the bull stopping up short when he felt the spikes going into his neck, was what Ferrero reckoned on, when it wasn't done too late. An instant after the stakes were planted in his neck, the bull continued his charge, but by then Ferrero was out of the way.

"Cogan, watching Ferrero and his companions from his

retreat, began to get the bull-fighting fever. He thought he would like to try the banderillero's game—that is, after he'd had a few weeks' training at it. These were fine athletes—and something more. They were risking their lives every minute.

"They leaped like panthers. The jabbing in of the stakes and the wiggling aside to escape the bull's plunge, it was like one movement. Soon the bull was going round the ring, with five or six pairs of banderillas decorating his neck. Of these Ferrero had planted the first and last pair. When he came back to his place in the refuge beside Cogan, the air was quivering with buenos. 'Buenos!' said Cogan also to him. 'Not bad—no.' said Ferrero very well pleased.

"But the great thing was to come. 'El matador, el matador! Torellas, Torellas,' they were shouting. And again Torellas came. He crossed the ring, with his even, unhurried walk to Cogan's place of refuge, and asked for his cape—'You will allow me—please—yes? Gracias, senor,' and, with the one word 'Americano,' and a nod of his head toward Cogan, Torellas held the cape to the nearest section of American blue-jackets who had been wondering, ever since the word had been passed, which was the American among the bull-fighters. Cogan, of course, was dressed like any other bull-fighter, and being dark-haired and pretty well tanned wasn't to be picked out easily, especially as he buried himself to the eyes in his place of refuge. He didn't want to be recognized—not then, and so he stayed hid away, and so it was Ferrero, in the same refuge with Cogan, but looming above him, who was cheered by the many blue-jackets for their countryman. And Ferrero gleefully bowed and bowed again to their applause.

"Torellas wrapped the cape around his left forearm. He then took from an attendant and gripped in his right hand the espada, the short sword, with which he was to give the bull

James Brendan Connolly

the finishing stroke.

"Now, to Cogan's way of thinking, Ferrero and the other banderilleros took a chance when they placed their beribboned stakes, but they had the length of their stakes the start of the bull, and they did not have to linger over doing it. A light touch, the stakes were in, and they were off. But to drive a knife through twelve or fourteen inches of bull gristle! Cogan pictured himself walking into a butcher's shop, picking out twelve or fourteen inches of tough gristle and driving a knife through it. He could do it, of course he could, or any man, but he would have to brace legs and back to get enough power in the stroke. But to stop to brace for that stroke and a rampant seventeen-hundred-pound bull piling down on top of you, and to pick out a spot on his neck no bigger than a fifty-cent piece! And if you missed your spot! Or were a little bit slow! Even in being too soon there was danger, if you could imagine a man being too quick.

"That was how Cogan looked at it, and he felt himself worrying for Torellas. He looked toward the Rocas. The mother and Guavera were no longer talking, and Valera was again drawn back between them, but her father was leaning well forward with eyes fixed on Torellas.

"There was great shouting when Torellas faced the bull—and then a great silence. Torellas moved his cape-draped forearm—up, down, coaxingly. The bull headed for him. Torellas stepped aside. The bull passed on and wheeled. Torellas took half a dozen dancing steps. The bull followed. Torellas waved his arm, the bull charged. Torellas leaped easily to one side. The bull passed on. More light play, a charge, another charge, yet another, all beautiful athletic play, and Torellas had worked his way across the ring to near the place of refuge where Cogan and Ferrero were. This also brought the bull under the seats of the Rocas. Cogan, studying the matador's face, had a feeling that he had drawn the bull there purposely. It was as if he had said to her up there on the seats: 'Here—here is the product of my highest skill. To do this well I have dedicated my abounding youth. I offer them a sacrifice to you.' So Cogan viewed it. Cogan, to be sure, had a sympathy for Torellas, had liked him from the first. Torellas—he was one who adventured to give the spirit play as now; and Cogan would have liked just then to be in the shoes of Torellas.

"The bull was at last properly worked up. Torellas took his final stand. His feet were well apart, but not too far apart, body and legs set so that he could have leaped instantly forward, backward, sideways. Cogan, watching, thought what a painting, or better, what a bit of sculpture could have been made of him so. He was standing on the balls of his feet, with his torso canted slightly forward from the waist. His head was forward, too, but inclining a little to one side, toward his right shoulder. His eyes were so narrowed that they could hardly be seen, but the glitter of them was plain enough. The sword up to this time he held loose in his right hand, palm up and shoulder-high, with the blade horizontal, the point toward the bull. His left arm held forward, well clear of the body, was the final effect in the miracle of his balance. Standing like that, he was planted solidly enough on the earth, but he gave out, too, such an impression of energy, force, power bottled up, that he made you feel that he could fly if he tried.

"Standing so, he didn't seem to breathe. But the crowd were breathing for him. From the seats behind him Cogan could hear, almost feel, their hot breaths."

"The bull now stopped and studied this last enemy. The others had come at him in groups, but here was one all alone."

James Brendan Connolly

"The bull stood with half-lowered head, weaving it from side to side, like when from behind the barrier he first appeared to the crowd. He eyed the red cape. It must have flamed like blood in the sun to him. His nostrils, his eyes, were flaming like blood, too. He ceased his weaving, raised, lowered his head, and bounded toward Torellas. And everybody there knew that it was the bull or the matador this time. The red cape of the matador seemed to leap forward, no loose ends now for a flying horn to catch, but a tight roll around the matador's left forearm. Standing now four feet away Torellas, to blind the charging bull as the capeadors had done, had to step close in. And now he was close in and his forearm was across the bull's forehead. It was hard to follow, the action was so fast, but Cogan saw that Torellas was already between his horns. Cogan looked for the flash of the heavy blade, but already Torellas' right arm had gone forward, that eye of his had marked the little vital spot, and, as the bull lowered his head and lunged to gore him, the blade was driven forward, and onto the point of it rushed the bull. The blade went home—clear to the hilt—eighteen inches or so. Before the people could clear their choked-up throats to applaud, before many could realize what had happened, the bull was stumbling to his knees and Torellas was unwrapping the cape from his left forearm. One long, thundering in-and-out breath and they were mobbing Torellas with applause.

"The bull rolled from side to side on his knees, tried to balance himself there for four, five, six seconds, and then rolled over. He half lifted his head from the sand, he kicked, once, twice, again, and then the head fell back, a quiver, and he lay limp. It was sad in a way.

"A bugle rang out. Two Peruvian boys came galloping in on horses. The bugle sounded again, they took a bridle hitch on the bull and went galloping out of the ring, bugles going and the bull dragging behind. The noise and whirl of it made Cogan think of a fire-engine coming down the middle of a street up home.

"As the bull was hauled out, Cogan felt a new sorrow for him. Up to that last stroke there was a chance that he would hurt somebody, but he hadn't killed or hurt anybody, and now, when he was dragged out dead, Cogan felt half sad. And he said as much to Ferrero.

"Ferrero looked at him puzzled. 'Such ideas you have in your country? Why? Leesen now, my friend, I also have a sadness, but consider if you was a bull, or I was a bull. Would you prefair to go to your death in a bull-ring or to be led to a man who demolished you on the temple with an axe, or cut your throat with a long knife—a man in a white garment? Which?'"

"Cogan said that if he was a bull, no doubt he'd prefer the bull-ring, but would the bull?"

"'Of a certainty, yes—if he was a blooded bull—yes,' said Ferrero. 'A high class bull always. He should be keeled no other way. No. And in the ring there was always a hope to make man pay—but in a slaughter-house—p-ff-f. And some day, my friend, the bull will obtain his revenge. Have no doubt of it. Bull-fighters die one way—all matadors surely. Let them attend to it long enough and no fear—some day the bull shall get heem. View Torellas now. He is strong, brave, agile, superb, triumphant as he stands there, let him continue and some day a slip shall come and he shall go.'"

"Cogan said no doubt, at the same time wishing he were in the place of Torellas. The matador—he had had his supreme moment."

"Cogan looked up to the Roca's party. Her father was still wildly cheering Torellas. Her mother and Guavera were applauding, too, but their applause did not have the quality of Senor Roca's. Valera's face was still hidden by her fan. Cogan looked to the matador. He seemed to be limp, apathetic. 'The reaction,' Cogan thought, and Torellas, being so young and such a high-strung fellow, maybe it was only natural, and yet, thinking a moment later, it had come rather soon for an athlete in his fine condition.

"In the sand lay the sword with which he had killed the bull, and while the people were cheering, stamping, hurling words of applause, endearment, love, at Torellas, he picked it up. Already the President of the Republic was standing up in his box with the cloak and hat of the master, to hand them back to him with words of appreciation, and to him and the crowd Torellas was bowing."

"Cogan, with eyes only for Torellas and the Rocas, did not see the beginning of what happened next. He first heard a cry, then a loud voice or two, then a hundred, a thousand voices. He turned. The gate which held the next bull in confinement had been opened or else it had burst out. The gateman was there, but with despairing hands on high, and across the ring the fresh bull was coming. Torellas was standing with his back to the gate, and not twenty feet from it, almost in the spot where he had killed his bull, and wiping the sword blade in a fold of Cogan's cape, which he was now holding loosely. He was looking up at the Rocas and seemed at first not to hear the cries. He turned—slowly, with horrible slowness, Cogan thought, when he recalled how fast he could move when he wanted to.

"He turned too slowly. The bull caught him sideways, and when he came down, it was astraddle of the bull's back, from which he fell to the sand beside the bull, who had wheeled and was waiting. He must have been stunned when he landed, for the sword and cape had fallen from him, and he lay motionless. The bull lunged like lightning. The horn went into the left thigh, just above the knee, and, not done then, the bull ripped on upward with that same horn until it came out under the matador's left breast.

"The white tights turned red. The bull was lowering his head to gore him again, but Ferrero had leaped from his place of refuge. Cogan was with him. Ferrero picked up the cape and flouted it in the bull's eyes. The bull lifted his head from Torellas, looked at the cape, and charged. And as he did, Cogan snatched up the matador's sword and waited. The bull charged past Ferrero, then, wheeling quickly, made again for Torellas, and his head was lowered to gore again. Ferrero got desperate and threw the cape from him, and it caught on the horns, and while the bull was entangled and enraged afresh, Cogan stepped close, picked out the little spot the size of a fifty-cent piece at the head of the spine, stood on his toes and came down with all his force. It wasn't any approved matador's stroke, for Cogan, standing behind instead of in front of the bull's horns, drove home in just the reverse fashion, but it wasn't a bad stroke at that. The knife went home. The bull rolled over, and Cogan stood there and looked and looked. Nobody was more surprised than he. Not once in ten times he was saying to himself could he have done it in cold blood. Only when Ferrero pulled him by the arm did he think to turn and bow with the banderillero to the cheering audience, especially to some blue-jackets who had now recognized him as an old shipmate and were calling him by name—hundreds of them.

"In the middle of the excitement he looked up to see how Valera was taking it. She and her father were both leaning far over the rail toward him—he with both arms extended and yelling, she with her handkerchief pressed to her lips.

Her eyes met Cogan's, and Cogan was satisfied. His little Valera of the beach was on deck again. No matter about the rest. That must have been a full minute after it happened and after the surgeon had called out 'It is well. Torellas will live!'"

"But the bull-fighters in the ring did not believe that all was well. 'Torellas! Oh, Torellas!' they were saying, and some were shedding tears, as they carried him to the dressing-room. Torellas was now conscious. He smiled at Ferrero, and he was smiling while they were undressing him, and he took Cogan's hand and held it while the others were telling him how it was. Not until the surgeon said, 'You will live, but your bull-fighting days are done,' did he lose his nerve. He had been pale, but he went paler then. The globes of sweat collected on his forehead. 'Oh, no, no, doctor!' he cried and fainted."

"That night Cogan slipped away from a party of American blue-jackets who wanted to paint Lima in high colors for him, and went down to see Torellas, who had been taken to his home, a fine, large house on a wide street. A crowd was in the street, waiting for word of his condition."

"Ferrero met him at the door. 'They wait for you, good friend.'"

"'They? Who?'"

"'Oh, you shall see.' And he led Cogan to the second floor, to where a fine suite of rooms opened from the wide hall. Her father and Juan were in the outer room."

"These two clasped him to their bosoms. 'You brave one,' said her father—and 'Bueno Americano!'—said Uncle Juan, and patted him on the head as if he were a son. 'He will live—Oh, be sure of that. But never will he fight bulls again. Never, never. And that is sad. But we have him. Let us not mourn. And you'—Juan raised both hands high—'you and Torellas—I love you both.'"

"Cogan thought he heard her voice, the voice which never in his life he had heard, and hesitated. 'Proceed,' said her father, and pushed him toward the door of the middle room. 'She is there. And Tina—you remember Tina—that night in Colon? She is also there. The senora'—he looked at Juan and Juan smiled back at him—'she is too fatigued to come, but Tina came.'"

"Cogan softly crossed the second room, but paused on the threshold of the inner room. He saw a great, stout woman back to. He knew her—Tina. He looked further, and under the half light saw the face of the matador. She was beside the bed. He could not see her face, but he heard her voice, and it was over her shoulder that he saw the matador's face.

"There were murmured words in Spanish which he did not understand, and then a phrase at which he could guess, then words which there was no mistaking, and which were not for him or any other man to hear. He backed out.

"Juan, Ferrero, and her father were still at the outer door of the outer room. They were not looking. He saw that from this middle room a window led on to a balcony. He stepped through the window, found a post, dropped to the ground, made his way through the garden in the rear, and so on to a back street. He ran on—one street, another, a dozen, and then uphill to a wall which he seemed to know. He looked about, and saw that near by was the monastery where he had been given his first breakfast in Lima. It was the same old wall.

James Brendan Connolly

"He climbed the wall and sat there. He had been sitting so that morning when the pretty flower girl had tossed him the blue flower—blue as the sky. Only now it was night and no one to see and smile. He looked up to the sky, the night sky of the tropics. The twisted Southern Cross shone on him. He turned and faced the north.

"Somewhere he could hear a band playing. In one of the parks probably, and there would be leaves rustling there, and the scent of flowers, and the senoritas walking with their mothers, while the young men hung around the edges, striving to get a word, a look. And there would be the arched jets of a fountain playing under colored lights, and back in Portland, Oregon, by this time was perhaps Tommie Jones married to his plump waitress.

"It was a good band—playing something he had never heard before, but something very soothing. He looked toward the Pacific. He knew where the harbor of Callao should lie, and in the middle of the harbor he could see them, one great cluster of lights, the lights of the battle fleet. And there were the fleet's search-lights playing on the great stone pier.

"The band was playing again—something fine."

"And then the monastery bell tolled. And presently he heard a chanting—a slow sad chanting! And then the chanting also died away."

"He had been lying on the wall with his hat in his hand and staring up at the sky. Now he sat up, put on his hat, took another look to the lights in the harbor, and hummed softly the Philippine service song—"

"It's home, boy, home, it's home you ought to be."

"And you've no kick coming. Dreams dreams, always dreams, but you've had your hour, too.' He took another look at the lights of the fleet—another to the lights of the city below him—'Good night, Lima,' he whispered, and dropped off the wall."

The pump-man had begun his story this evening while sitting with back to the rail and feet stretched out on the deck before him. He finished while lying on his back, hands clasped under the back of his head, and wide eyes on the sky.

The passenger leaned on the rail, studied the stem of the ship, and listened to the surge of back wash against the ship's bow as she drove on. Abeam, the young moon drooped.

Kieran said nothing more. The passenger nothing for a long time. Then it was:

"And they were married?"

"I don't know—Cogan didn't wait to see—but of course."

"Of course," echoed the passenger, and in silence resumed his study of the ship's bow cutting through the little seas.

The passenger turned inboard. "But Cogan—where is he?"

"There was no Cogan."

"No Cogan."

"No, no Cogan."

"And no bull-fight, and no Valera, and no Torellas, nor Juan, and it never happened?"

"Why, of course it happened, and just as I've told it. But not to anybody named Cogan. There was no Cogan, or rather"— Kieran rolled over on his side and rested his head on his elbow—"I'm Cogan."

"Oh-h-h. Oh-h-h. And you're Campbell, the old champion athlete?"

"Yes, I'm Campbell. And I'm Cogan. And I'm Kieran, pump-man on this wall-sided oil-tanker at fifty-five per month."

"But why?"

"Why, why?" He sat up. The passenger could see the thick, dark eyebrows draw together. "Why? Why anything? What would you do?"

"Forget it."

"Forget it. But can you?—everything? No—you betcher you can't. And it's every man to his own cure. Some I know get drunk and fight. And some I know who get drunk and cry. Some worry their friends to death, and some others beat their wives. Every man to his way. I have no wife"—he laughed softly—"and I want to keep my friends. So I run my heart out in races and beat up bully bosons, and fight bulls—when I can."

"But when you can't?"

"When I can't? Why, when I can't, I lay out on the fo'c's'le head and bay up at a two-horned moon."

The passenger turned and looked down. "Thank your God, Kieran," he said, "you can laugh when you say that."

The pump-man's smile died away. "Maybe I'm thanking God," he said softly, "for more than that."

James Brendan Connolly

# ABOUT THE AUTHOR

 **James Brendan Bennet Connolly** (October 28, 1868 – January 20, 1957) was an American athlete and author. In 1896, he became the first modern Olympic champion.

Connolly was born to poor Irish American parents, fisherman John Connolly and Ann O'Donnell, as one of twelve children, in South Boston, Massachusetts. Growing up at a time when the parks and playground movement in Boston was slowly developing, Connolly joined other boys in the streets and vacant lots to run, jump, and play ball.

He was educated at Notre Dame Academy and then at the Mather and Lawrence grammar school, but never went to high school. Instead, Connolly worked as a clerk with an insurance company in Boston and later with the United States Army Corps of Engineers in Savannah, Georgia.

Connolly became an authority on maritime writing, after spending years on many different vessels, fishing boats, military ships all over the world. In all, he published more than 200 short stories, and 25 novels. Furthermore, he twice ran for Congress of the United States on the ticket of the Progressive Party, but never was elected.

He never returned to Harvard, but received an honorary athletic sweater in 1948.

# Choose from Thousands of 1stWorldLibrary Classics By

A. M. Barnard
Ada Leverson
Adolphus William Ward
Aesop
Agatha Christie
Alexander Aaronsohn
Alexander Kielland
Alexandre Dumas
Alfred Gatty
Alfred Ollivant
Alice Duer Miller
Alice Turner Curtis
Alice Dunbar
Allen Chapman
Alleyne Ireland
Ambrose Bierce
Amelia E. Barr
Amory H. Bradford
Andrew Lang
Andrew McFarland Davis
Andy Adams
Angela Brazil
Anna Alice Chapin
Anna Sewell
Annie Besant
Annie Hamilton Donnell
Annie Payson Call
Annie Roe Carr
Annonaymous
Anton Chekhov
Archibald Lee Fletcher
Arnold Bennett
Arthur C. Benson
Arthur Conan Doyle
Arthur M. Winfield
Arthur Ransome
Arthur Schnitzler
Arthur Train
Atticus
B.H. Baden-Powell
B. M. Bower
B. C. Chatterjee
Baroness Emmuska Orczy
Baroness Orczy
Basil King
Bayard Taylor
Ben Macomber
Bertha Muzzy Bower
Bjornstjerne Bjornson

Booth Tarkington
Boyd Cable
Bram Stoker
C. Collodi
C. E. Orr
C. M. Ingleby
Carolyn Wells
Catherine Parr Traill
Charles A. Eastman
Charles Amory Beach
Charles Dickens
Charles Dudley Warner
Charles Farrar Browne
Charles Ives
Charles Kingsley
Charles Klein
Charles Hanson Towne
Charles Lathrop Pack
Charles Romyn Dake
Charles Whibley
Charles Willing Beale
Charlotte M. Braeme
Charlotte M. Yonge
Charlotte Perkins Stetson
Clair W. Hayes
Clarence Day Jr.
Clarence E. Mulford
Clemence Housman
Confucius
Coningsby Dawson
Cornelis DeWitt Wilcox
Cyril Burleigh
D. H. Lawrence
Daniel Defoe
David Garnett
Dinah Craik
Don Carlos Janes
Donald Keyhoe
Dorothy Kilner
Dougan Clark
Douglas Fairbanks
E. Nesbit
E. P. Roe
E. Phillips Oppenheim
E. S. Brooks
Earl Barnes
Edgar Rice Burroughs
Edith Van Dyne
Edith Wharton

Edward Everett Hale
Edward J. O'Biren
Edward S. Ellis
Edwin L. Arnold
Eleanor Atkins
Eleanor Hallowell Abbott
Eliot Gregory
Elizabeth Gaskell
Elizabeth McCracken
Elizabeth Von Arnim
Ellem Key
Emerson Hough
Emilie F. Carlen
Emily Bronte
Emily Dickinson
Enid Bagnold
Enilor Macartney Lane
Erasmus W. Jones
Ernie Howard Pie
Ethel May Dell
Ethel Turner
Ethel Watts Mumford
Eugene Sue
Eugenie Foa
Eugene Wood
Eustace Hale Ball
Evelyn Everett-green
Everard Cotes
F. H. Cheley
F. J. Cross
F. Marion Crawford
Fannie E. Newberry
Federick Austin Ogg
Ferdinand Ossendowski
Fergus Hume
Florence A. Kilpatrick
Fremont B. Deering
Francis Bacon
Francis Darwin
Frances Hodgson Burnett
Frances Parkinson Keyes
Frank Gee Patchin
Frank Harris
Frank Jewett Mather
Frank L. Packard
Frank V. Webster
Frederic Stewart Isham
Frederick Trevor Hill
Frederick Winslow Taylor

Friedrich Kerst
Friedrich Nietzsche
Fyodor Dostoyevsky
G.A. Henty
G.K. Chesterton
Gabrielle E. Jackson
Garrett P. Serviss
Gaston Leroux
George A. Warren
George Ade
Geroge Bernard Shaw
George Cary Eggleston
George Durston
George Ebers
George Eliot
George Gissing
George MacDonald
George Meredith
George Orwell
George Sylvester Viereck
George Tucker
George W. Cable
George Wharton James
Gertrude Atherton
Gordon Casserly
Grace E. King
Grace Gallatin
Grace Greenwood
Grant Allen
Guillermo A. Sherwell
Gulielma Zollinger
Gustav Flaubert
H. A. Cody
H. B. Irving
H. C. Bailey
H. G. Wells
H. H. Munro
H. Irving Hancock
H. R. Naylor
H. Rider Haggard
H. W. C. Davis
Haldeman Julius
Hall Caine
Hamilton Wright Mabie
Hans Christian Andersen
Harold Avery
Harold McGrath
Harriet Beecher Stowe
Harry Castlemon
Harry Coghill
Harry Houidini

Hayden Carruth
Helent Hunt Jackson
Helen Nicolay
Hendrik Conscience
Hendy David Thoreau
Henri Barbusse
Henrik Ibsen
Henry Adams
Henry Ford
Henry Frost
Henry James
Henry Jones Ford
Henry Seton Merriman
Henry W Longfellow
Herbert A. Giles
Herbert Carter
Herbert N. Casson
Herman Hesse
Hildegard G. Frey
Homer
Honore De Balzac
Horace B. Day
Horace Walpole
Horatio Alger Jr.
Howard Pyle
Howard R. Garis
Hugh Lofting
Hugh Walpole
Humphry Ward
Ian Maclaren
Inez Haynes Gillmore
Irving Bacheller
Isabel Cecilia Williams
Isabel Hornibrook
Israel Abrahams
Ivan Turgenev
J. G.Austin
J. Henri Fabre
J. M. Barrie
J. M. Walsh
J. Macdonald Oxley
J. R. Miller
J. S. Fletcher
J. S. Knowles
J. Storer Clouston
J. W. Duffield
Jack London
Jacob Abbott
James Allen
James Andrews
James Baldwin

James Branch Cabell
James DeMille
James Joyce
James Lane Allen
James Lane Allen
James Oliver Curwood
James Oppenheim
James Otis
James R. Driscoll
Jane Abbott
Jane Austen
Jane L. Stewart
Janet Aldridge
Jens Peter Jacobsen
Jerome K. Jerome
Jessie Graham Flower
John Buchan
John Burroughs
John Cournos
John F. Kennedy
John Gay
John Glasworthy
John Habberton
John Joy Bell
John Kendrick Bangs
John Milton
John Philip Sousa
John Taintor Foote
Jonas Lauritz Idemil Lie
Jonathan Swift
Joseph A. Altsheler
Joseph Carey
Joseph Conrad
Joseph E. Badger Jr
Joseph Hergesheimer
Joseph Jacobs
Jules Vernes
Julian Hawthrone
Julie A Lippmann
Justin Huntly McCarthy
Kakuzo Okakura
Karle Wilson Baker
Kate Chopin
Kenneth Grahame
Kenneth McGaffey
Kate Langley Bosher
Kate Langley Bosher
Katherine Cecil Thurston
Katherine Stokes
L. A. Abbot
L. T. Meade

L. Frank Baum
Latta Griswold
Laura Dent Crane
Laura Lee Hope
Laurence Housman
Lawrence Beasley
Leo Tolstoy
Leonid Andreyev
Lewis Carroll
Lewis Sperry Chafer
Lilian Bell
Lloyd Osbourne
Louis Hughes
Louis Joseph Vance
Louis Tracy
Louisa May Alcott
Lucy Fitch Perkins
Lucy Maud Montgomery
Luther Benson
Lydia Miller Middleton
Lyndon Orr
M. Corvus
M. H. Adams
Margaret E. Sangster
Margret Howth
Margaret Vandercook
Margaret W. Hungerford
Margret Penrose
Maria Edgeworth
Maria Thompson Daviess
Mariano Azuela
Marion Polk Angellotti
Mark Overton
Mark Twain
Mary Austin
Mary Catherine Crowley
Mary Cole
Mary Hastings Bradley
Mary Roberts Rinehart
Mary Rowlandson
M. Wollstonecraft Shelley
Maud Lindsay
Max Beerbohm
Myra Kelly
Nathaniel Hawthrone
Nicolo Machiavelli
O. F. Walton
Oscar Wilde

Owen Johnson
P.G. Wodehouse
Paul and Mabel Thorne
Paul G. Tomlinson
Paul Severing
Percy Brebner
Percy Keese Fitzhugh
Peter B. Kyne
Plato
Quincy Allen
R. Derby Holmes
R. L. Stevenson
R. S. Ball
Rabindranath Tagore
Rahul Alvares
Ralph Bonehill
Ralph Henry Barbour
Ralph Victor
Ralph Waldo Emmerson
Rene Descartes
Ray Cummings
Rex Beach
Rex E. Beach
Richard Harding Davis
Richard Jefferies
Richard Le Gallienne
Robert Barr
Robert Frost
Robert Gordon Anderson
Robert L. Drake
Robert Lansing
Robert Lynd
Robert Michael Ballantyne
Robert W. Chambers
Rosa Nouchette Carey
Rudyard Kipling
Saint Augustine
Samuel B. Allison
Samuel Hopkins Adams
Sarah Bernhardt
Sarah C. Hallowell
Selma Lagerlof
Sherwood Anderson
Sigmund Freud
Standish O'Grady
Stanley Weyman
Stella Benson
Stella M. Francis

Stephen Crane
Stewart Edward White
Stijn Streuvels
Swami Abhedananda
Swami Parmananda
T. S. Ackland
T. S. Arthur
The Princess Der Ling
Thomas A. Janvier
Thomas A Kempis
Thomas Anderton
Thomas Bailey Aldrich
Thomas Bulfinch
Thomas De Quincey
Thomas Dixon
Thomas H. Huxley
Thomas Hardy
Thomas More
Thornton W. Burgess
U. S. Grant
Upton Sinclair
Valentine Williams
Various Authors
Vaughan Kester
Victor Appleton
Victor G. Durham
Victoria Cross
Virginia Woolf
Wadsworth Camp
Walter Camp
Walter Scott
Washington Irving
Wilbur Lawton
Wilkie Collins
Willa Cather
Willard F. Baker
William Dean Howells
William le Queux
W. Makepeace Thackeray
William W. Walter
William Shakespeare
Winston Churchill
Yei Theodora Ozaki
Yogi Ramacharaka
Young E. Allison
Zane Grey

www.ingramcontent.com/pod-product-compliance
Lightning Source LLC
Chambersburg PA
CBHW020819260626
47169CB00003B/737